THE GOLDEN HOUR

THE GOLDEN HOUR

Maiya Williams

AMULET BOOKS

NEW YORK

Library of Congress Cataloging-in-Publication Data

Williams, Maiya.
The golden hour / Maiya Williams.
p. cm.
Summary: Thirteen-year-old Rowan and his eleven-year-old sister, Nina, still bereft by the
death of their mother the year before, experience an unusual adventure through time when
they come to stay with their two eccentric great-aunts in a small town on the Maine coast.
hardcover ISBN 0-8109-4823-0
paperback ISBN 0-8109-9216-7
[1. Time travel—Fiction. 2. Grief—Fiction. 3.
France—History—Revolution, 1789-1799—Fiction. 4. Great
aunts—Fiction. 5. Brothers and sisters—Fiction.] I. Title.

PZ7.W66687Go 2004
[Fic]—dc22
2003016281

10 9 8 7 6 5 4 3 2 1

Design: Interrobang Design Studio

AMULET
Published in 2006 by
Amulet Books, a division of
Harry N. Abrams, Inc.
115 West 18th Street
New York, NY 10011
www.abramsbooks.com

Printed and bound in U.S.A.

Abrams is a subsidary of

LA MARTINIÈRE

For PMV, *with love*

CONTENTS

THE GOLDEN HOUR

CHAPTER ONE

TWO STRANGE AUNTS

> ## WELCOME TO
> ## ROCKRIDGE, MAINE
> *Home of the "famous" Rockridge Shell Museum*

Rowan READ THE SIGN POSTED ON THE TRAIN platform for the fourteenth time. For the fourteenth time he wondered why there were quotation marks around the word "famous." For the fourteenth time he turned and ambled over to the Visitor's Center, ten yards from the sign. His sister sat in front of it, facing a faded poster of the "famous" museum that was taped to the window, though she wasn't really looking at it. The poster showed a family inside the museum, gazing at cases of shells. The family looked positively ecstatic. "Exciting!" "Wonderful!" "Captivating!" read the poster. Rowan rolled his eyes. This was the best thing the town had to offer. Great. Just great.

Rowan had spent half the day traveling up the coast with his eleven-year-old sister, Nina. Now here they were, literally at the end of the line, in a small town in the farthest reaches of the United States, and it was the last place on earth that he wanted to be.

He wanted to be home playing video games, specifically Phantastic Journey II, the most awesome game ever. Rowan had already risen to the level of Supreme Overlord of Phantom World after spending hundreds of hours studying and mastering the challenges of Phantastic Journey I. When he'd heard a new version of the game was coming out in June, he'd known his summer was set. He would camp in front of his television with a variety of salty snacks, and he would not move until he'd conquered the new and improved evils of Phantom World.

His father didn't think much of these plans. Maurice was struggling with his bakery. He wanted Rowan to take Nina and get out of the apartment while he sorted through his financial papers, met with tax lawyers, and tried to save his business from bankruptcy. So when Aunt Agatha invited Rowan and Nina to stay with her and Aunt Gertrude in Owatannauk, Maine, a small town about an hour from Rockridge, Rowan wasn't given a choice. He didn't even get a chance to buy the game.

Rowan scanned the parking lot, looking for his two aunts—great-aunts actually—Agatha Drake and Gertrude Pembroke. He'd met them only once, very briefly, at a family reunion. The only thing he could remember about them was that one was incredibly tall and gaunt, the other round and squat, and when they stood side by side they resembled a stalk of celery and a pumpkin.

He thought about taking a fifteenth trip over to the welcome sign, but couldn't muster up enough enthusiasm. Instead, he reached into his backpack and brought out a small spiral notebook. It was sort of a diary, but he didn't like to call it that. It seemed very lame for a thirteen-year-old boy to keep a diary. His psychiatrist, Dr. Reynolds, suggested he write his thoughts down as a "therapeutic exercise," so he bought it and filled the first few pages with cartoon doodles. Now, however, he was finally inspired to write something. He turned to the first page and wrote at the top:

Top Ten Reasons My Life Stinks
by Rowan Popplewell

#10.

He paused. He could come up with a hundred things, maybe even a thousand if he had a few minutes. After a few seconds he wrote:

#10. I have no friends.

Actually that hadn't always been true. He'd had friends before he moved. He'd also had his own bedroom with a double bed, not a creaky cot stuffed in the corner of a living room the size of a shoe box. He'd also had a sister who smiled and joked around with him, not this silent lump sitting on the steamer trunk. He'd had a father who didn't collapse on the couch every night smelling of wine. And he'd had a mother.

The death of his mother was clearly number one on the top-ten list. Before her death, there was no need for a list. There wasn't even a psychiatrist or a notebook. He didn't want to think about number one right now. He tried to think of something else, but that only made him think of her more. Her death had become the background noise of his life, like a radio you couldn't turn off. It never stopped.

Aunt Agatha and Aunt Gertrude were still nowhere to be seen, so he continued the list.

#9. *I'm not good looking.*

#8. *I have no personality.*

Number nine he blamed on his father, who looked like a troll. Maurice had what people politely called a "prominent" (big) nose. He had pointy ears, and a barrel chest to match. He had hands like a boxer's, thick and hard from years of pounding dough. Rowan was a smaller, but almost identical, version of that. He didn't look forward to the next few years when he was supposed to "fill out."

On the other hand, Rowan took complete responsibility for his dull personality. He spent most of his time reading books, watching movies, and playing video and computer games. Fantasy worlds made so much more sense than his own. He'd packed every computer program and video game he owned for this trip, as well as twelve videotapes and twenty paperback books. It was his arsenal to battle the long, empty days that loomed ahead.

He went back to his top ten list.

#7. I have no sister.

This would seem a strange thing to write since she was sitting right next to him. But the silent creature on the steamer trunk was not Nina. The Nina he knew was a firecracker, always jumping with ideas. She had wild, black hair that had a life of its own. She would try to control it with what she called "hair toys," but by the end of the day it would be tumbling back around her shoulders and face. Everything about her was a little wild, and she brought this same energy to the piano.

Nina was a musical prodigy. Her gift became apparent to everyone when at age three she began picking out tunes by ear that she'd heard on the radio. Once she started formal lessons she progressed rapidly, and by age eight she'd won the International Chopin contest. The finest piano teachers in the country clamored to teach her. Her life was a series of recitals, interviews, lessons, recordings . . . and she loved it. She thrived on challenge.

But after their mother died, Nina shut down. She stopped speaking. Her whirlwind schedule was replaced by grief counseling and psychiatrists. Nothing worked, though. And now Rowan was stuck taking care of her.

As he sat huddled over the notebook, he was so preoccupied with how unfair life could be that he didn't notice the plump woman, dressed entirely in purple, who was quickly approaching, arms outstretched. When Rowan finally saw her he jumped. He thought he was being attacked by a giant blueberry.

"I'm so sorry we're late, Rowan dear. My goodness, how you've grown!" Aunt Agatha tweaked his cheeks, smoothed his hair, and straightened his collar. Rowan thought she should pay more attention to her own appearance. Her light brown hair was coming out of the bun she'd arranged with what looked like a couple of chopsticks. She wore a purple cotton jumper that had been misbuttoned, a lavender shirt, which was inside out, and shoes that looked suspiciously like bedroom slippers.

"Of course he's grown," rumbled a deep, melodic voice. "The last time we saw him he was eight. If he'd stayed the same size after five years, he'd need a specialist."

Rowan turned to see Aunt Gertrude towering over him. She had somehow slipped behind him and taken hold of Nina's hand without him noticing, an amazing feat since she was at least seven feet tall. She had a perpetually severe expression, a thick braid extending down her back, a pointy nose, and a way of cocking her head and staring into the distance as though she were picking up signals from outer space. Her breath smelled of medicine. Her striped, dark gray poncho billowed around her shoulders, giving her the appearance of some great, terrifying bird.

"Well, of course I knew he'd be bigger," Agatha clucked, "but I barely recognize him."

"That's absurd. Maurice sent us his school picture last Christmas."

"Well, maybe . . ." Agatha mused. "Perhaps I remember seeing a picture somewhere . . ."

"It's right on our mantelpiece, Aggie, we see it every day."

"Those are our trunks . . ." Rowan interrupted, starting toward them.

"Gertrude will take care of it, dear." Agatha knelt in front of Nina. "Nina, I'm your aunt Agatha. I'm so happy you came."

Nina stared at her, unimpressed.

"It takes a while for her to warm up to strangers," Rowan said, placing his arm around Nina's shoulders. "She's a little shy."

"Oh, we know all about Nina," Agatha said simply. "Well! I think it's time you saw the house! Gertrude!"

Gertrude had loaded the trunks onto a hand truck. "I'm all set," she said. In a matter of seconds she was far ahead of them, charging toward the parking lot.

"I wish she wouldn't do that," Agatha sighed. "She forgets we're not all built like giraffes." They hurried after her, arriving finally at an old-fashioned, blue pickup truck that looked like it was in remarkable shape.

"Wow, you don't see trucks like this anymore," Rowan said. He had seen one like it once in a car museum. This one looked fifty or sixty years old. He ran his hands along the chrome. It was shiny and clean. In fact, the entire truck was shiny and clean, not a nick or scratch. The upholstery in the cab was a butter yellow leather, and the wheels had white walls, not like the dark, heavy-duty wheels he was used to seeing on trucks. "Did you have the whole truck redone?"

"Oh, heavens no," Agatha giggled. "This is brand new." Gertrude gave her a stern look. Agatha seemed to shrink slightly. "That is to say, uh, it's new to *us*. We got it this way. Whoever had it first did a nice job putting it together, though."

Gertrude loaded the trunks in the rear while Rowan and Nina climbed into the backseat of the cab. After a few failed attempts, Agatha finally hoisted herself in and shut the door. Gertrude folded herself into the driver's seat.

"Hold on," she said, her knees straddling the steering wheel. "This baby's got a bit of a kick when she starts." She turned the key, the motor rumbled, and after an initial jolt forward, they were on the road.

Rowan sat back, enjoying the scenery. They were following the main highway that hugged the coastline, and he caught glimpses of the Atlantic Ocean as they whizzed through one town after another. Nina had fallen asleep and was leaning awkwardly against the window. Rowan shifted her body to a more comfortable position. He was just about to relax himself when he was seized by a sudden realization. He was going to be spending *an entire month* with these two very strange women. What were they thinking? They didn't know him. Not really. For all they knew, he could be a closet psychopath.

Then another thought seized him. Maybe *they* were the psychopaths. They had to be. What old women in their right minds would want to spend any time at all with a teenage boy or a catatonic girl? For the hundredth time that day, he questioned the wisdom of this trip.

"Horehound drop?" Gertrude asked, handing him a tin of hard candy. Rowan took one of the brown, egg-shaped candies, popped it into his mouth, and immediately gagged. It tasted bitter and nasty. He spat the offending nugget into his hand and sucked on his sleeve to get the taste off his tongue. That explained Gertrude's medicinal smell. He handed the tin back to her.

"Thanks," he said. *She should switch to peppermints*, he thought. *Then maybe she'd smile once in a while.*

Agatha burst out laughing. Rowan looked at her suspiciously. "What?" he said. "What's so funny?"

"Oh, nothing, nothing. You're awfully quiet," Agatha chirped. "Are you enjoying your trip so far?"

Rowan plastered on a smile. "Yes. It's very . . ." He tried to think of a nice word for "boring." Finally his mental thesaurus came through. " . . . quiet. Peaceful. Serene."

"'Boring' is the word I believe you were looking for." Agatha laughed. Rowan wondered if she had ESP, on top of being a psychopath. "Of course I don't," she said, waving her hand. "I don't believe in that mumbo jumbo." Rowan started to say something else, then stopped. This Aunt Agatha was a tricky one.

"Don't worry though," Agatha continued. "There's plenty of things to do. And you may find that you like being out of the city. Fresh air, nature, countryside . . . it rejuvenates the spirit. And we all need that once in a while, don't we?"

Rowan nodded. For the time being, there was nothing more to be said.

Owatannauk, Maine, was a small, quaint community with a main street that consisted of one short block of shops and civic buildings. A small sign read, "You are now entering Owatannauk, Maine. Population 104. Discover and Enjoy."

"One hundred and four?" Agatha remarked, peering at the sign. "Mrs. Jessup must've finally had those twins." Gertrude nodded and pulled up to a coffee shop with a gas pump in front of it.

"I just want to fill up while we're here," Gertrude said.

"Are you children hungry?" asked Agatha, already climbing out of the cab. She didn't wait for a response, but headed toward the shop. "This place is very good," she continued as Rowan and Nina caught up with her. "It's the coffee shop–grocery store–gas station. You know, a lot of businesses out here double as something else . . . it increases revenue."

They went inside. The space was split between a small grocery store and restaurant. Eight tables sat at the far end. Each table had a blue-checked tablecloth and a small vase of cheerful, white daisies.

"Yoo-hoo! Hello, Hilda!" Agatha called out.

A stocky woman wearing a gingham apron emerged from the back room. "Well now!" she said. "These must be the nephew and niece I've heard so much about!"

Agatha made the introductions and chatted with Hilda for a few minutes about her large, extended family. After covering the health of Hilda's second cousin's parakeet, Agatha finally sat down. They each ordered a piece of pie, which Agatha explained was the house specialty. Hilda served them after only a few minutes.

"Now, I know your father's a wonderful baker," Agatha said, "but just taste these and tell me what you think."

Rowan hesitantly took a bite of the lemon meringue pie. It was amazing. His tastebuds tingled as the sweetness and tartness slid over his tongue, the flaky crust dissolving like spun sugar. He quickly popped another forkful in his mouth, and another, until in no time the pie had disappeared. He looked over at Nina. She had polished off her cherry pie before he'd even finished.

"That lemon pie is a recipe that's been served to kings!" Agatha laughed. "Gabriella loved this place. Her favorite, of course, was the strawberry pie. She couldn't get enough of it."

Rowan's face flushed.

"Oh, I am sorry," Agatha gasped. "I didn't mean . . . sometimes I get so excited I forget other people's feelings. More lemonade?" Rowan shook his head.

"So, I guess you knew my mom pretty well," he mumbled into his shirt.

"Yes, yes, she spent quite a lot of time up here. She loved Owatannauk." Agatha glanced around and raised a finger to get Hilda's attention. Hilda walked over with a cup of sassafras tea, anticipating Agatha's order.

"I don't remember her ever coming up here," Rowan said, playing with the crumbs on his plate. He started eating them with his fingers. He wanted to lick the plate, but thought better of it.

"That's because she came up here before she got married. Once she married your father and had children I guess she didn't feel she had a need for Owatannauk anymore. You filled her life with immeasurable pleasure. She told me so herself. We'd try to coax her up—we missed her, you know—but she wouldn't come. Having too much fun, she said. We told her to bring the family, but it was never the right time. I'm glad you two are here now, though," Agatha added gently. "We were afraid you'd turn down our offer."

"So . . . how exactly are you related to my mom?" Rowan asked. "Are you her mother's sisters or her father's?"

"Oh, we're not related at all," Agatha replied. "At least not by blood. We were Gabriella's godmothers. She called us 'Aunt Agatha' and 'Aunt Gertrude' as a sign of affection, not family."

Rowan frowned. Somehow this changed everything.

"We were very close friends of her parents and didn't have any children of our own," she continued, "so they gave us the very important responsibility of giving her guidance. Spiritual guidance, that is. When your grandparents moved away from Maine down to New York, they started sending Gabriella to visit us for the summers. It was a nice way for her to get out to the country, it gave her parents a break, and we loved it of course. Such a delightful, bright little penny she was! And we introduced her to all the secrets of Owatannauk . . ."

"Agatha!" Gertrude, back from pumping gas, and Hilda simultaneously barked her name from opposite sides of the room, startling her in stereo.

Agatha dropped her teacup into the saucer at an awkward angle, splashing tea onto the tablecloth. Hilda scurried over and wiped up the spill with a checkered towel.

"Oh, how you do go on with your stories," she said, pointedly placing the check onto the table. "These youngsters must be bored out of their skulls!" She turned to Rowan. "I'm afraid your aunt can be something of a chatterbox. We love her imagination, though. Such a character. She keeps us in stitches!"

Rowan nodded.

"Mom?" A thin girl with wavy, dark hair appeared at the door to the back room. "Could you please help me? I can't figure out how to put on the . . ."

"I'll be right there, Margaret," Hilda called back to her. She turned to Agatha. "I'm helping my daughter prepare for a long trip. So if you'll excuse me . . ."

"Oh, go right ahead. We were just leaving, weren't we, children? Now if I could just find my billfold . . ." Hilda headed for the back room as Agatha fumbled around in her purse. A flurry of crumpled tissues flew from the bag. "Gertrude, you wouldn't happen to have a twenty, would you? I must have left my billfold in my other bag ... Gertrude?"

Gertrude glared from the doorway. After a moment, her expression softened to a mere grimace. She took a money clip from her pocket and removed a bill.

"I'm going to the shop," she said, tossing the twenty onto the table. She flicked her poncho over her back like a cape and left the restaurant. Agatha visibly exhaled.

"That's an excellent idea," she said, pushing the mounds of tissue back into her purse. You should come and see our shop."

"What shop?" Rowan asked.

"Gertrude and I run a little curio shop out of our house," Agatha answered. "It's filled with all sorts of stuff, odds and ends, bric-a-brac, this and that. It keeps us busy. Now let's go, we've warmed these seats enough."

The curio shop was within a few blocks of the coffee shop so they walked, giving them a chance to digest the pie and take in the town. Red-leaf maples lined Main Street, and though the ocean wasn't visible, the air was tinged with salt and the faint smell of crab. After buying chocolates at Munson's Candies and making a quick stop to check the aunts' post-office box, they walked up to a three-story Victorian mansion with a wide front porch and a round turret. A large sign on the lawn read, "Curios, Notary, Homemade Preserves."

"I'm the notary," Agatha said. "I also make the preserves."

"What does Aunt Gertrude do?" Rowan asked, staring up at the house.

"She runs the shop with me, of course, and she also . . . well, it's a little complicated to go into right now. Let's just say she's good at tracking things down."

"This is where you live?" Rowan asked, getting excited. He'd never been in a private mansion, let alone slept in one.

"Well, yes and no. We used to live in 'the big house,' as we like to call it, but the business kept growing and it kind of pushed us out. So now we live in the side house." She gestured toward the backyard.

Rowan craned his neck. All he could see was a garage on top of which somebody had had the poor judgment to build two extra stories. The addition was haphazard in design; the top portion spread out over the bottom portion, odd chimneys and lanterns poked out in surprising places, and an outdoor staircase spiraled down from one floor to the next. It looked as if a strong breeze or a woodpecker could knock it down.

"You mean . . . that?" Rowan asked, pointing. Agatha nodded cheerfully. Even Nina's eyes widened.

"Is it safe?" he asked doubtfully.

"Of course it's safe! A friend of ours designed it. He's the local architect. He also runs a puppet theater for children on the weekend." Agatha opened the door to the big house and they followed her in.

Rowan could see why the sisters had had to move out. Every corner of every room was crammed with junk. He was so overwhelmed by the sheer volume of knickknacks and baubles, furniture and artwork, decorative pieces and crockery, that he felt a little dizzy. Gertrude came down the staircase carrying a large box.

"Rowan asked to see the shop. I didn't think there would be any harm . . ."

Gertrude shrugged. "Of course not. Go ahead and look around . . . but be careful. Most of these items are irreplaceable. And please, don't go into the attic. Or the basement." She continued down the stairs and into what appeared to be the former dining room.

"What's in the attic and the basement?" Rowan asked.

"That's where we keep all our records," Agatha replied, "and the basement is where we print up the catalog. We do a very nice mail-order business."

"You mean you actually know where everything is? This is in order?"

"Oh my, yes. This isn't just a business, my dear, this is our hobby. We know everything about every piece we have. We collected them personally. Now go on, you'll never be able to see everything before dinner."

Rowan and Nina wandered through the rooms. There were cabinets of china, teapots, vases, oddly shaped cookie jars, crystal, old-fashioned dolls, rocking horses, and tin windup toys. They found wheelbarrows, spinning wheels, a butter churn, a loom, and strange musical instruments. There were cases of jewelry, intricately decorated knives, swords, ancient guns, suits of armor—one of them from a samurai.

Stashed in the corners were paintings, statues, figurines, clocks, needlepoint pillows, quilts, old-fashioned cameras, apothecary materials, early radios, televisions, phonographs, telephones, lamps, coat racks, plaques, vintage clothing, and on and on through the house. Rowan didn't know how long they'd been there, but he was starving, and they had barely finished exploring the first floor. He had just found Nina look-ing through a box of old postcards when Agatha appeared from behind a totem pole.

"Hungry?" she asked. "I believe Gertrude has prepared pumpkin soup and beef stew. She's an excellent cook, you know. Grows her own vegetables."

When they finally entered the odd house in the back, Rowan had forgotten his misgivings, his head now swimming with questions. Over dinner he shot them out, in between bites of stew and hot, home-baked bread.

"Where did you get all of that stuff? That had to take you years to collect so much."

"Oh, we do some trading, but mainly we like to travel," Gertrude said. "You find the most interesting pieces when you travel."

"Do people actually buy any of that junk?"

"I wouldn't exactly call it 'junk,'" Gertrude growled.

"Oh, you'd be surprised," Agatha jumped in. "I told you we have a brisk mail-order business. We have customers all over the world."

"It's a rather small, select group that receives our catalog," Gertrude explained. "We don't really want to be too well known. We'd rather be a sort of secret among serious buyers. That 'junk' is treasured by our customers. You can't find these things anywhere else, you know. You have to come to us."

"Of course we get the tourist trade," Agatha added. "They're always around in the late spring and summer. Owatannauk is a little out of the way, but some people seem to find us."

Rowan ate silently for a while. Nina had already finished and seemed to be in her own world again. He watched Gertrude as she started to clear the dishes. He was more than a little frightened of her.

"Let me help you," he said bravely, starting to pick up the dishes around him. "I do the dishes at home all the time."

Gertrude regarded him for a moment, then nodded. "Thank you," she said. "If you just clear the table and pile everything in the sink, I'll get dessert ready."

After he cleared the table, Rowan started to wash the dishes. The kitchen was equipped with old appliances that, like the blue truck, were in pristine condition, their white metal clean and smooth, their chrome gleaming by the light of the gas lamps.

Rowan stopped. Gas lamps? He looked around. Sure enough, there wasn't a lightbulb to be seen. He examined the stove more closely. It was a gas stove, and apparently the burners were lit with the kitchen matches in the box on the counter. Surely the refrigerator used electricity . . . but there was no refrigerator. At least not one he recognized. Eventually he realized that the cabinet with metal clamps on the doors was where the few perishable items in the house were stored, along with a huge block of ice that kept the unit cold.

Rowan opened the basement door and peeked into the cellar. Baskets of vegetables lay in the dark, next to shelves containing jars of jam. He heard somebody come into the kitchen and quickly closed the door, then turned to see Gertrude looking down at him.

"I was just poking around," Rowan muttered guiltily.

"What are you looking for?" Gertrude asked.

"I . . . I don't know. Answers, I guess."

Gertrude barked a laugh. It was so unexpected that Rowan jumped. Agatha appeared in the doorway.

"Come, come!" she said, grabbing his hand and pulling him toward the door. "We're all going up to the terrace. Hurry, before you miss it!"

"Miss what?"

"It's the golden hour!" Agatha ran out the door.

"The what?" Rowan asked, following her.

Agatha herded Rowan and Nina up the outside staircase, finally reaching the terrace on the top level. From there they could see above the trees, toward the ocean. The sky was a shade darker in that direction, a sign of the coming night. Toward the west the sun hung low and fat, like a ripe peach poised to fall at any moment. A trio of birds warbled as the wind played among the leaves. In the distance a dog barked. They stood there, catching their breath.

"It's the golden hour," Agatha spoke in a hushed voice. "That short period of time between day and night . . . right before sunset. Look, everything takes on a golden quality. Mud holes, garbage cans, buildings, even the most wretched individuals seem to glow."

Rowan looked again and saw that she was right. Gertrude, who normally looked like a scary crow, took on a remarkable, queenlike quality. Agatha seemed enormously loveable. Even thin, sad Nina seemed infused with the power of the sun, but only for a moment. Then the sky turned purple, orange, red, and yellow, and the sun dipped behind the trees, returning the world to its former state.

"Come," Gertrude said. "Dessert is ready."

After a delicious cherry cobbler, Gertrude went back to the big house to work on the catalog. Agatha, Rowan, and Nina relaxed in the living room with glasses of iced mint tea. Rowan settled himself on the large, velvet sofa as Agatha lit the tinder in the fireplace. Nina wandered around the room, looking at the artwork, photographs, and books in the many cases along the wall.

"So," Agatha said, nestling in what was obviously her favorite chair. "What would you like to do now?"

"I brought some videotapes," said Rowan. "I've got a whole bunch to choose from."

"I'm sorry, we don't have a television set." Agatha took a sip from her glass.

How could she be so calm? Rowan wondered. No television set? Well, what could he expect, they didn't seem to have any electricity at all!

"I suppose I won't be able to play my computer games either. Or my video games."

"No, I'm afraid not," she said, shrugging as if to suggest that his disappointment should be slight, rather than immense, which it was. Now he knew he was trapped.

"Well, what do you do for fun around here?" Rowan sighed.

"Oh, we talk, play card games, chess, Scrabble . . . all kinds of things."

"Let's play chess," Rowan suggested. Anything to keep them from talking. He was afraid he'd have to explain Nina's behavior, and he really didn't feel like going into it. Besides, he'd gotten pretty good playing chess against the computer. Playing a person instead of a machine could be interesting.

Agatha brought out a beautiful board made of green and white marble with gold inlay. The pieces were Asian in design: the pawns were samurai; the knights were dragons; the king wore an emperor's robe; the queen wore an impressive headdress. Rowan fingered them apprehensively.

"They're more durable than they look," Agatha assured him. "I picked it up in Japan. They're made of ivory and jade. I'll be white."

As they started to play, Rowan quickly realized that Agatha was no novice. She moved her pieces confidently, taking only a few seconds to study the board and make a move. In no time, Rowan's queen fell to her bishop, and soon after that, his king was trapped by two knights and stood in a firm checkmate.

"Let's play again," Rowan said. "I didn't realize you were going to be so good."

"Actually, chess is Gertrude's game," Agatha said, setting up the pieces again. "I'm better at Scrabble. I'm a word person, she's the logician."

"I've gotta say, it's hard to believe you two are sisters," Rowan said.

"Oh yes, a lot of people say that," Agatha said, studying the board. She moved a pawn.

"I mean, you don't look at all alike. Not even a little bit. And you don't sound alike, or act the same . . . you're about as different as two people could be."

"That's because we're not related!" Agatha chuckled. "We're not birth sisters, we're church Sisters. We're both nuns."

Rowan's jaw dropped. "*Nuns?* Well . . . what are you doing here? Why aren't you living in a . . . nunnery or something?"

"Well, it's a little involved. Gertrude and I are from different orders: she's a Dominican, I'm a Franciscan. We met through a mutual friend and found that we both had a passion for travel. We both love seeing new things and meeting new people and having interesting experiences. We started taking vacations together, one thing led to another and eventually . . . well . . . it no longer made sense for us to continue to lead our lives the way we had been, and so we . . . we left."

"You left the Church?" Rowan was intrigued. He'd never had a conversation with a nun before. He'd always thought they were supposed to be either somber and stern or meek and gentle. Yet Agatha made it sound like she and Gertrude were thundering around the countryside like a couple of rogue elephants.

"Oh my, no! We still dedicate ourselves to doing God's work. No, that hasn't changed. We just found a different way to do it, that's all. Now it's your move."

Rowan looked at the board. He could tell she was trying to do something tricky the way she'd innocently exposed her bishop. He glanced at her. She smiled pleasantly. He knew she wanted him to take it, so he let it stand exposed and took her pawn instead.

As he gloated over his move, music wafted in from the parlor. It was a classical piece, which started very simply—a sad little theme in a minor chord—but grew robust and hopeful through a series of variations on the theme.

"I like that music," Rowan said, watching Agatha like a hawk.

She nodded, her concentration unwavering. "Yes. Beethoven, I believe." She moved her knight.

Rowan couldn't see where she was going with that move. She seemed to be thinking five or six moves ahead and he was having trouble keeping up. "Nina loves Beethoven. She must've found your CD player." Rowan sat up. He knew that couldn't be right as soon as it left his mouth.

"We don't own a compact disc player. She probably found our piano."

"That's impossible. Nina doesn't play piano ... I mean, anymore. She hasn't played for a whole year. Ever since ...". But Rowan could tell the music was pure, each note filled with energy and life. He ran into the parlor and saw Nina seated at the piano, her eyes focused on the sheet music, her fingers racing along the keyboard. She finished with a final, solemn chord, then turned suddenly, grabbing the music from the piano stand. She walked up to Agatha, who had joined Rowan in the room, and held the music out.

"Where did you get this?" she whispered.

CHAPTER TWO

XANTHE AND XAVIER

The sound of Nina's voice shocked Rowan. All he could think to do was grab her and squeeze her tightly, to keep her from slipping away. She was back. She was back!

"Let go!" she squeaked. "I can't breathe!" Rowan loosened his grip. Nina staggered backward. "Man, Rowan," she groaned. "I think you cracked my rib cage!"

"You're back!" he said, grinning foolishly at Agatha. "She's back."

"This is quite a surprise," Agatha said.

"Are you kidding?" Rowan cried. "It's a miracle! We've got to call Dad!"

Rowan grabbed Nina's arm. She wrenched away and picked up the music, which had fallen to the floor. "Where did you get this?" She asked Agatha again.

"Nina! Talk to me!" cried Rowan. "You haven't said anything for a whole year! What happened?"

Nina avoided his gaze. After a long pause she murmured, "I had nothing to say."

Rowan couldn't reach their father. The answering machine was full of messages—probably bill collectors—and he knew his father had stopped checking the machine for just that reason. If he was out on one of his long, nightly walks, he wouldn't be in any shape to have a conversation anyway, so Rowan decided to try again tomorrow morning.

The guest room was small, but cozy. It had two single beds, a dresser, a small closet, and a bathroom. When Rowan went in to brush his teeth, he was confused by the toilet until he realized that it was the old-fashioned kind, with a pull chain attached to a box that was mounted on a tall pole. There was no shower, just a small tub that squatted on four gilded claws.

"Weird bathroom," he said to Nina, who was gazing out of the window.

"Weird *bathroom?*" she said, turning to him. "*Everything* about this place is weird."

"I know," Rowan said, climbing into bed. "They are the worst pair of pack rats I've met."

"That's not what I mean," Nina said, joining Rowan on his bed. "Look at this." She handed him the piano music. "I know what sheet music is available for Beethoven, and I've never seen this composition before. I've never *heard* it before! It doesn't even have a cover. And look . . ." Nina pointed to the bottom of the page, at a smudged scrawl in the corner. "That's his signature, isn't it? Beethoven's signature. See how shaky it is? It looks like it was written when he was going blind. It's real ink—I smudged it myself—but the paper looks brand new. No yellowing. It's like those 'curios' in the shop. They're not 'curios,' they're antiques. They just don't look old."

"Maybe they're good at repairing stuff." Rowan really didn't care what they were doing, he was just thrilled that Nina was having a conversation with him. There were so many things he wanted to ask her . . . but he held his tongue. The truth was she wasn't really back, she was merely talking. His Nina, his friend, his buddy who made up secret codes with him, performed in his video movies, and joined him in midnight raids on the ice cream cart—she was still hidden somewhere. He didn't want to scare her away.

"I think it's worse," Nina said. "I think they're counterfeiting. They hide the counterfeit stuff among the worthless junk, claim they have found it in someone's attic, and charge more for it."

"They don't seem like crooks. Aunt Agatha told me they were nuns."

"You believe that?"

"Relax, Nina, they may be strange, but I don't think they're dangerous."

"I don't know what they are," Nina countered. "But one thing's for sure, they aren't what they seem."

The next morning Rowan woke up early. He bathed and dressed quickly, then rushed down the spiral staircase and into the kitchen. Nina sat at the dining room table flipping through a photo album.

"Good morning!" chirped Agatha. "I hope you're hungry, Rowan. Gertrude couldn't be here for breakfast, but she left us a big basket of homemade buns!"

"That sounds great," said Rowan.

"And I also whipped up some scrambled eggs and bacon," Agatha said, serving him from a large platter. "So that should hold you for a while."

Nina shut the photo album as Agatha slapped a whopping spoonful of eggs onto her plate. "Oh, I see you've found my travel pictures," Agatha remarked.

"Yes," said Nina curtly, and she started to eat.

"I'm afraid I also have some business to do this morning," Agatha said, pouring herself a cup of tea. "So this would be an excellent time for you to explore the area. It's almost impossible to get lost. Do you have money?"

"Yeah, my dad gave me a hundred bucks," said Rowan. "I'm sure we'll be fine." The buns were sweet and soft, and made him a little homesick. But this was only day two . . . he had twenty-nine more to go.

After breakfast, Rowan and Nina walked down Main Street. They discovered that not only was it the *main* street, but the only street; the only one that was paved, anyway. All the roads that fed into it were made of a hard, brown sand that was firmly packed, but made a crunchy sound when you walked on it. They went to the theater and saw a double feature, two movies starring an actor named Peter Sellers who played a bumbling,

French detective. Rowan laughed so much he started to hiccup, but Nina didn't even seem to be watching. That took some of the fun out of it. After the movie ended, they revisited Hilda's coffee shop for lunch and another piece of pie.

"What's going on?" asked Rowan after Hilda cleared away the remains of his tuna sandwich and brought dessert. "You're not going to stop talking again, are you?"

"I was just thinking," Nina said. "That photo album I was looking at this morning . . . something was wrong about it. The pictures didn't look right."

"Not everybody is good at taking pictures," Rowan said, finishing his blueberry pie and eyeing the slice of fluffy, coconut cream that his sister was neglecting.

"I mean something about them didn't make sense. And leave my pie alone, you pig."

Rowan thrust the stolen forkful of luscious cream and crunchy coconut into his mouth and gulped it down when another thought occurred to him. Nina noticed and sat up.

"What? What are you thinking?" she asked.

"Well, don't laugh, but . . . do you think they could be, you know . . . witches?"

"You mean like practicing-black-magic, kettle-of-brew, riding-on-broomstick witches?"

"I know it sounds idiotic. It's just that Agatha always seems to know what I'm thinking. And the other one, Gertrude, is just plain scary. And why don't they use electricity? What's up with that?"

"You think electricity is like holy water or a crucifix to a vampire. They can't stand to be around it?"

"It might also explain that nun story. I mean, they don't seem to be connected to a church. Maybe they were kicked out when they were discovered, and they're hiding out here, where nobody will bother them."

"Hmm. There's only one thing wrong with that theory," Nina mused.

"What's that?"

"There's no such thing as magic." She quickly inhaled what was left of her pie before Rowan could get another bite.

They left the restaurant and wandered toward the ocean. The beach was hard to walk on, so Rowan removed his shoes, letting the warm sand sift through his toes. He noticed the colorful shells outlining the tide. He started to scoop them up, using his shoes as buckets once his pockets were full.

"What are you doing?"

"I'm thinking of starting a collection," Rowan said, plucking a particularly large conch shell from the sand. It was smooth and pink and reminded him of the poster of the "famous" Rockridge Shell Museum. Maybe it was worth visiting after all. He put it to his ear and listened for the hollow sound of the sea.

"Hey! Look out!" someone called.

Suddenly the surf exploded close to Rowan and something threw itself against him. He lost his footing and fell backward. He opened his mouth to cry out, but ended up swallowing saltwater. Nina rushed over and grabbed him, but the creature was wrapped around him, pulling him down.

"Get it off me!" Rowan gagged. Suddenly there were many hands peeling off the creature, which turned out to be just a few pounds of seaweed.

"Hey, are you all right?" A girl handed him a towel. She looked about his age, with brown skin and hair plaited into hundreds of beaded braids, all the same length, that hung down to her chin. Her brown eyes were almond shaped. To Rowan, she looked like an ancient Egyptian princess, except for the cutoff overalls.

"I told my brother launching rockets at the beach was too dangerous," she added, shooting an exasperated look at the approaching boy.

"The beach is the safest place to launch them," said the boy, slightly out of breath. "There are fewer windows to break, and usually there's nobody here." He turned to Rowan. "I'm sorry, that last rocket didn't make the trajectory I thought it would." His hair was a brownish red and he was perhaps two inches taller than his sister.

Nina pointed to an object caught in some rocks off the shore. "If you want to save your rocket, it's over there."

"Oh yeah, thanks!" He started to wade toward it, then turned back. "You sure you're okay?"

Rowan nodded, picking seaweed out of his hair. The boy removed his shoes and T-shirt and dove into the water, cutting easily through the waves. He hoisted himself onto the rocks.

"You're not all right," the girl said. "You're soaking wet. Why don't you come to our house and get a change of clothes? We're staying with our grandmother . . . she doesn't live far. We can toss your stuff in the dryer."

Rowan was about to say that his aunts didn't live far either, and he could get his own change of clothes, but he remembered that without electricity they probably didn't own a dryer, and they weren't really his aunts anyway. The girl smiled and picked some of the seaweed off his shoulder.

"You can't see yourself," she giggled, "but you don't want to walk down Main Street looking like the creature from the Black Lagoon." She held out her hand. "I'm Xanthe," she said. "Xanthe Alexander. That's my brother, Xavier. We're twins, but I'm still older—by twenty-one minutes."

"I'm Rowan Popplewell, and this is my sister, Nina." Rowan said. "Maybe we will come over, if it's okay."

"Sure! No problem. Come on, it's about half a mile away." They started walking along the shoreline.

Xavier caught up with them, carrying his rocket. "Hi, I'm Xavier," he said.

"Yeah, your sister told me."

"Did she also tell you about the twenty minutes?"

"Uh-huh . . ."

"That's twenty-*one* minutes," Xanthe corrected. "I'm twenty-*one* minutes older."

"Twenty minutes . . . twenty-one minutes . . . what difference does it make!" Xavier snapped. "It doesn't make you smarter, or stronger, or a better human being."

Xanthe rolled her eyes and walked faster.

"You mention those stupid twenty-one minutes to everybody! Who the heck cares who was born first?"

"Apparently you do," Rowan said.

Xavier looked surprised for a moment, then grinned. "You know what? I guess I do!" He laughed.

"It's the curse of being twins," Xanthe said. "We tend to get a little competitive."

Rowan shrugged. "I don't have that problem," he said. He glanced back at Nina, who had dropped several paces behind the rest of the group. "I know Nina's smarter than I am, and she's only eleven. It sounds pompous to say 'genius,' but she's way beyond anybody else her age."

Xanthe and Xavier exchanged glances. "We can sort of relate," Xanthe said. "We were both taken out of regular school after third grade because we were too far ahead, and they didn't want to skip us into the next grades."

"They thought one of us was too immature to handle the age difference," said Xavier, nodding his head meaningfully in Xanthe's direction.

"Yeah, you," she countered. "The one who liked to eat paste."

"I didn't eat paste. I *tasted* paste. I think they were referring to a certain somebody who couldn't stop shooting rubber bands at people during class."

"Class was boring. I had to keep myself entertained somehow."

"Very entertaining, interfering with somebody else's education."

Rowan remained silent. He had plenty of experience being the target of rubber bands, spit balls, mucus, paper airplanes, dissected frogs, and numerous other small objects at school.

"So, what, do you go to boarding school?" Rowan asked, wondering if Xanthe and Xavier were wealthy. You couldn't tell from what they were wearing. It was considered cool among rich kids to wear old clothes with holes in them. Of course, the rich kids always wore something to set themselves apart, like diamond-stud earrings, or a nice watch. Rowan noticed a ring on Xavier's finger that looked like a tiny silver snake.

"We don't go to school at all," Xavier said. "We're home schooled. Our mom and dad take turns teaching. Dad's a historian, so he takes over history and English . . ."

"But really, Mom does most of it," Xanthe interrupted. "She's the one who has time. She used to be a marine biologist, then decided to go on leave to focus on our education. We have a very motivated mother. She's fantastic."

"Oh, that's great," Rowan said, halfheartedly.

"What do your parents do?" Xanthe asked.

Rowan heaved a sigh. "Well, my dad's a baker . . . he owns a little bakery shop in Brooklyn, New York. And . . . I don't have a mom. She's dead."

"Oh . . . I'm . . . I'm sorry," Xanthe said, embarrassed.

"Nice going," said Xavier, shaking his head.

"How was I supposed to know?"

"It's okay," Rowan said, tiring of their bickering. "It happened over a year ago."

They walked in silence until they reached a small, yellow summer cottage on the beach, festooned with brightly painted birdhouses of all shapes and sizes.

"Our grandmother makes them," Xavier explained. "She's really into birds." As they drew closer, they could hear screeching, twittering, and throaty *chuk-chukking*; a multitude of conversations among the feathered guests. A brown-skinned woman wearing a batik-print dress waved from the porch.

"There she is. That's Nana," Xanthe said, waving back. "Nana! We brought company!"

"And some laundry," Xavier added as soon as they got close enough. "This is Rowan and Nina. Rowan, Nina, this is our grandmother."

"Pleased to meet you, Mrs. . . ." Rowan said, extending his hand.

"Oh no, no need for formalities. You call me 'Nana,'" she said in a warm Jamaican accent that made Rowan feel immediately at ease. "Everybody calls me 'Nana.' That, or 'Crazy Bird Lady,' but 'Nana' is gentler on the ear."

After Rowan got cleaned up they toured Nana's house, lingering in her workshop, where she designed and built her birdhouses. They called Agatha to let her know where they were, then sat down to a delicious supper of chicken and mushroom soup in a coconut broth. Afterward, Rowan, Nina, Xanthe, and Xavier sat on the porch and ate fresh blueberries with sugar and drank tall glasses of ice-cold milk.

Once he relaxed, Rowan realized that he was actually having a good time. The air was warm with a slight western breeze, he had a pocketful of some truly beautiful shells, and Xanthe and Xavier seemed friendly and interesting, more so than any of the kids at school.

Xavier left to get another bowl of blueberries and Nina wandered among the birdhouses, leaving Rowan alone with Xanthe, something he had secretly wished for since they'd met.

"So, what's up with your sister?" Xanthe asked, popping a blueberry into her mouth with her fingers.

"What do you mean?" Rowan responded dully, knowing perfectly well what she meant.

"I guess she must be kind of shy," Xanthe said, nodding in Nina's direction.

Rowan sat there for a moment, letting the warm breeze waft over his forehead as the sun continued its slow descent toward the woods. "Well," he said, "she used to be a lot more friendly, but she took our mom's death pretty hard."

"How did she die, if you don't mind my asking?"

"She was hit by a car," Rowan answered. "She'd gone out to get some ice cream. While she was crossing the street she was hit by a drunk driver. Nina was staying with a family friend in Boston, visiting a music conservatory she was thinking of applying to, when she found out. She tried to get back in time, but her flight got delayed because the airport was snowed in. By the time she got back, Mom had passed away."

"That's awful," Xanthe said.

Rowan nodded. Predictably, his stomach hurt. Even after

months with Dr. Reynolds, it still hurt to talk about it. He'd gotten to the point at which he could sound like he was okay with it, and Dr. Reynolds said he was making progress, but there were things he'd never talked about, not even to Dr. Reynolds. Like the door. The olive brown door to his mother's hospital room. Rowan had waited outside that door with a nurse who had cold fingers, staring at it, while behind it his father consulted with the doctor. Rowan had studied every dent and scratch in that door for the longest half hour of his life. When it finally opened, he rushed into the room . . . but he stopped at the sight of his mother.

Half of her face was covered by a thick bandage. The other half of her face was bruised. Fresh sutures along her swollen lip twisted it into a scowl. She looked like she been sewn together like Frankenstein's monster.

"Mom?" Rowan had whispered. She stared at him, her lips so dry they were white.

"Mom? It's me, Rowan."

Gabriella's expression remained blank.

"Mom! It's me, Rowan!" he'd cried. He'd repeated his name until his father took him, shaking, out of the room.

"She needs to rest," his father had said. That night she'd died.

"Hey look, the golden hour," Xavier said, returning with his refilled bowl topped with an enormous scoop of ice cream and settling back in his Adirondack chair.

"What did you say?" Rowan perked up.

"I said, it's the golden hour. That weird time at the end of the day, right before sunset, when it's not quite night . . ."

"I know what it is," said Rowan, "it's just that the first time I heard of it was yesterday when my aunt Agatha said it. I thought it was something she made up."

"I thought my grandmother made it up," Xavier said.

"Actually, I've heard a couple of people say it around here," added Xanthe, sipping her milk thoughtfully. "It's one of those local things I guess. Like the fact that half the people in this town don't use electricity."

"What!" Rowan sputtered, "I thought it was just the two nutty old women I was with!"

"No, it's really almost everybody. Some people use it more than others," Xanthe said, "but Owatannauk seems to be set up for basic living. There's an ice man who delivers ice. They barter and trade for fresh food—eggs, vegetables, milk—so there's no need for refrigeration."

"The ice-cream parlor has a real freezer," Xavier interrupted. "I've seen it. Seen the electrical cord and everything. And the movie theater must use it."

"Yeah, well, they would need it, I guess." Xanthe swung one of her legs over the arm of her chair. Rowan found himself staring at them, they were so lean, long, and muscular. He looked away but found his gaze wandering back, so he turned his chair toward the water.

"I kind of like it," Xanthe said. "I think it's cool."

"You would." Xavier laughed. "Xanthe likes to think she's a child of the wilderness. Living off the land, communing with animals and trees . . . isn't that right, nature girl?"

Xanthe shrugged. "Nothing wrong with being in tune with nature."

"Speaking of local customs," Rowan ventured, "have you guys noticed anything else kind of strange about this place?"

"What do you mean?" Xavier asked, sitting up.

Rowan was so eager to unload everything that he talked for an hour straight. He described his "aunts" and their business, their relationship to his mother, and their claim to be nuns. He described their house and all the brand-new antiques, including the Beethoven sheet music. Nina, who had returned from the birdhouses, stayed silent and watchful.

"So," Rowan finished, gulping his milk. "What do you think?"

"I don't know your aunts very well," Xanthe said, "but Nana does. She visits them all the time. I think they belong to a book club, or a social circle . . . something that meets every Wednesday night. I'd ask her about it, but to tell you the truth, she can be kind of cagey about certain things."

Xavier nodded enthusiastically, finally agreeing with something his sister said.

"It's funny," Xanthe continued. "When our grandfather passed away, Nana fell apart. She was crying all the time, never wanted to go out, she was driving Mom crazy with her phone calls. My parents started talking about putting her in a rest home. Then all of a sudden, she just picked up and moved up here. We couldn't believe it. The next time we saw her she looked great. She had a bunch of new friends, she had a new hobby . . . but she'd also gotten really secretive."

"Xanthe and I thought she'd joined a cult," Xavier added, "but she doesn't seem to be brainwashed. If this is a cult, they're doing something right." He stuffed a huge spoonful of ice cream in his mouth and washed it down with milk.

Rowan was envious that a kid who ate like that could be so thin. He made a note to start doing push-ups in the morning. He looked down and noticed to his horror that the shirt he'd borrowed from Xavier had crept up his midsection, exposing his flabby belly. He quickly tugged it down, glancing at Xanthe, hoping she hadn't noticed. Of course she hadn't. Why would she have any interest in him? He mentally filled in the next line on the top-ten list he'd started in Rockridge:

#6. *Girls don't notice me.*

"No, it's not a cult. There's no leader," Xanthe said.

"Well, cult or no cult, I just get the idea that something funny is going on around here, but I just can't figure out what it is," Rowan said.

Xavier tugged on Xanthe's elbow. "Let's take him to, you know . . . the place."

Xanthe looked at her twin questioningly, then her eyes widened. "Ohhh, that's a good idea." She checked her watch and frowned. "It's too late. It'll be dark by the time we get there."

"Come on, we can take our bikes. If we leave now there should be enough light."

"Xave, I don't want to be there when it's dark. It's too dangerous."

"What's 'the place'?" Rowan was intrigued. "What place?"

"There's something else weird in this town," Xavier said, his eyes bright. "It's an old resort hotel, the Owatannauk. It's abandoned. And I think it's haunted."

"Bad idea, Xave," Xanthe said.

"Rowan wants to go, don't you Rowan?" Xavier looked at him pleadingly.

"Sure," Rowan said. "I don't believe in ghosts. And a big, abandoned hotel sounds cool. I don't know about Nina . . ."

"Don't worry about me," Nina said crossly. "Why do you think it's haunted?"

"It's not haunted," Xanthe said. "It's all just a bunch of stupid rumors."

"That's not true," Xavier said. "I *have* seen something."

Xanthe rolled her eyes. "Xavier 'thinks' he saw some people walking around the place . . ."

"I *did* see people. A lot of people. It was late in the day. Xanthe and I were out poking around the woods. We had seen the hotel and thought about exploring it, but we didn't feel like trying to get past the barbed-wire fence."

"There's a fence? You didn't mention a fence," Rowan said, deflated. He imagined trying to heave himself over a fence. A faster way to embarrass himself in front of Xanthe, he couldn't think of.

"There's a clearing in the woods where you can get a good view of the Owatannauk," Xavier continued. "The hotel overlooks an inlet . . . a sort of bay. It's got an old broken-down pier for sailboats or rowboats maybe, and a patio with a big, empty, swimming pool. I got to the clearing first, and when I looked over at the hotel, it looked like it had just been painted. There were a bunch of boats all along the pier and in the water, and people wearing old-timey bathing suits . . ."

"Tell him about the party," Xanthe said sarcastically.

"I'm getting to that. People were all over the place, but they all wore old clothes. And there was music. That 'oom-pah-pah' merry-go-round kind of band music, with tubas and stuff. And then a waiter wheeled out this gargantuan cake . . ."

"Maybe someone was filming something," Rowan suggested.

"The whole story is bogus," Xanthe said. "Xave comes tearing down the trail, grabs me, and drags me to the clearing. There was nothing there. No music, no party, no people, just an old, broken-down hotel."

"I know what I saw! My guess is that something horrible happened a long time ago that killed everyone in the hotel, and ever since, these ghosts have been roaming the grounds, unable to rest because of their unnatural and untimely demise . . ."

"I don't believe in ghosts," Nina said. "The dead are dead. They don't come back."

"Look, as the oldest I'm pulling rank," said Xanthe. "We're not going. It's just too late."

"She's probably right," Rowan said, somewhat relieved. "Agatha and Gertrude are expecting us soon. We did say we'd come home after dinner."

"Then let's go tomorrow," Xavier suggested. "You guys free?"

Rowan shrugged. "As far as I know, we're free for the whole month."

"All right then," Xanthe said, taking charge. "We have to go into Rockridge with Nana in the morning, but why don't we all meet here around four?"

"We'll be here," said Rowan. "And if my clothes are dry now, we should get going."

That evening, Rowan couldn't get tomorrow's plan out of his head. Gertrude had left to do her "other job," whatever that was, and Agatha was beating him easily at chess.

"What's on your mind, dear?" she asked, taking his queen with her pawn.

"I don't know," Rowan said mischievously. "You tell me."

Agatha smiled. "Perhaps you had such a good time today, you can't wait for tomorrow."

Rowan watched her carefully. At times she seemed so befuddled, but then she would say something incredibly savvy, and perhaps a little bit sly. Just as that thought crossed his mind, her eyes twinkled. Suddenly, he knew.

"You're cheating!" Rowan cried out triumphantly.

"Whatever do you mean?" Agatha said calmly.

"You're reading my mind! You know all my moves before I make them!"

"Oh, posh," Agatha said, pinning a stray lock of hair back into her unkempt bun. "What do you think I am, a fortune teller? I'm just good at reading faces, and your thoughts are written all over yours."

"I don't think my chess moves are written on my face," Rowan said, satisfied that his losses were no reflection of his chess skills.

Agatha shrugged and took a sip of tea. "You're awfully superstitious, believing in ESP and ghosts. Don't they teach real science at your school?"

Rowan's head snapped around. Ghosts? He'd never mentioned it to Agatha, but he'd been thinking about ghosts since leaving Xanthe and Xavier. The truth was, he did believe in them. And he was extremely superstitious. Omens, spirits, karma; he believed it all. How else do you explain why life is so unfair to some people, while others have all the luck?

Why had he agreed to go to the hotel? He knew why. He was showing off for Xanthe. But no matter how much he wanted to impress a girl, it would never change number five on his "Why My Life Stinks" top-ten list:

#5. I am a huge coward.

While Agatha continued to easily capture his pieces, he puzzled over how he could get out of the whole thing. He could fake being sick, but then he'd have to stay in the house the whole day. He could get Agatha or Gertrude to insist he do something for them, but that would require some clever manipulation on his part, and they were too smart for that. He could blame it on Nina, and say she was the one who was scared, but she would never forgive him.

Of course, there was always the truth. If he told Xanthe and Xavier the truth, they wouldn't force him to go, but they'd laugh at him behind his back. Rowan sighed. It was just as well. Xanthe and Xavier . . . they were your typical cool kids. Good looking, confident, independent; it was only a matter of time before they figured out he was just a big, fat nothing.

Agatha snagged his rook with her knight, then laid Rowan's king across the board. "Checkmate," she said kindly. "I'm afraid you've got no place to go."

"No, I guess I don't," Rowan said sadly. Piano music drifted in from the parlor as Nina played a familiar Chopin prelude. "I guess I'm not much of a challenge."

"On the contrary, I think you are quite challenging," Agatha said as she gathered up the pieces. "But you should take more care with your first move. Your first move sets your direction and from that a strategy develops. And another thing. You seem to keep yourself boxed in."

"You mean my king?" Rowan scratched his head, his attention back to the game. "I guess I'm trying to create a fortress around him, to keep the other pieces from breaking in."

"That fortress becomes a prison. You can move, you know. You don't have to stay on the same space." Rowan mulled that over. He never moved his king. Never. Maybe it wasn't such a bad idea to bring him out.

"I understand you met Xavier and Xanthe today," Agatha said brightly as she carefully slid the board back into the cloth bag.

"Yeah, they were pretty nice."

"I know their grandmother," Agatha continued. "They're very sweet children. I'm glad you found some friends. I only caution you about one thing," she said, suddenly serious. "There is an old hotel called the Owatannauk. It's about five miles from here. A lot of kids get it into their heads that it's a neat place to explore . . . but I wouldn't go there if I were you."

"Why?" Rowan asked innocently. "What's wrong with it?"

"Well, for one thing, it's against the law. There are 'No Trespassing' signs posted all over it. I think that some people injured themselves poking around."

"Is it . . . haunted? Not that I believe in that stuff," Rowan added quickly.

"Oh my, no." Agatha laughed. "No ghosts, or monsters, or whatever else the locals say to keep their kids away. And yet . . ." She frowned.

"What?"

"Well . . . strange things do seem to happen around there." She opened her mouth as if to say something, then closed it quickly, shaking her head. She started into the kitchen.

"What were you going to say?" asked Rowan, following on her heels.

"What do you mean?" Agatha said innocently. "Would you like some rice pudding?"

"You were going to say something. What was it?"

"Well, I . . ." Agatha glanced around nervously, then lowered her voice to a whisper. "I really shouldn't tell you. Only a few people know about it, and Gertrude and I promised each other to keep it to ourselves."

"Don't worry, I won't tell anybody," Rowan whispered back. "I promise."

Agatha glanced around again, then opened the door to the cellar and motioned for Rowan to follow her. They descended into the cool, dank-smelling room. Agatha lit a gas lamp, which cast a warm, orange glow, then she turned an empty pail over and sat on it. Rowan found an old half-barrel to sit on and waited, hoping he looked trustworthy.

"The Owatannauk," she began, "has a rather unusual history. It actually precedes the town; the town was named after the hotel. It was built in eighteen-ninety by a wealthy inventor—Archibald Weber was his name—brilliant man. A genius, really. He started out as a toy maker who specialized in puzzles. Anyway, to make a long story short, he made an enormous amount of money from a handful of patents.

"Mr. Weber lived in New York, but enjoyed bear hunting and fishing in Maine. He wanted to build a lodge that reflected his sense of adventure and fun, but that still maintained an air of refinement. He didn't want anything to do with the rustic buildings that the local architects proposed, so he designed the entire resort himself.

"The plans he drew were clearly inspired, but also bizarre. They called for an abundance of courtyards and secret gardens; meandering, convoluted walkways; and other hidden delights. The central building was an odd blend of architectural styles, from Queen Anne Victorian to Japanese pagoda, with an inexplicable lighthouse on the top ... well, the whole thing was considered outrageous among professional builders. They called it confusing, fanciful, silly. But Weber didn't give up. He found somebody to build it, a robust, self-taught man named Jack Everett, who had a similar sense of fun.

"Once it was built, everyone assumed it would be a financial disaster. But instead it attracted a loyal following of adventurous spirits. It quickly became the most popular resort in New England. People traveled from all over to stay there. Artists from the theater and the opera, world leaders and other politicians ... Teddy Roosevelt was a regular guest, drawn, no doubt, by the hunting. It was enormously successful. For thirty years they were always full. And then, suddenly, it closed."

"Why? What happened?"

"It began with a disappearance. An elderly woman vanished. Her secretary was accused of foul play, but nothing was ever proven, and anybody who knew the secretary had no doubt of his innocence. But as others started to disappear, the police insisted that the place be closed until they could conduct a formal investigation. They suspected a serial killer was on the loose, except they weren't sure that anyone was actually dead; there were no bodies, no signs of struggle or violence—they just vanished without a trace. They never did find any real suspects, and they released the hotel back to Mr. Weber. But when they did, they discovered that Mr. Weber had disappeared as well, leaving the hotel in a trust that pays the property taxes in perpetuity. Nobody knows where he went. He had no family. Local superstition has turned the whole thing into an elaborate haunted house, but like I said, it was never proven that there were any murders. Others of us believe that there is something else at work, not supernatural, but completely scientific. We believe the Owatannauk is a door. A portal, if you will."

Rowan licked his lips. "A portal to what?"

"I'm not sure. That's the funny thing about doors, you don't always know what's on the other side until you go through them." She stood up suddenly. "But that's not really our concern, is it? I believe your sister has finished playing. You should go upstairs before she thinks *you've* disappeared. It's time for bed anyway."

Rowan rose from the barrel. He felt giddy with excitement. Agatha pulled a stack of labels and a pen from the drawer of an old wooden writing table that had been wedged between two baskets of potatoes.

"I'm going to finish labeling these preserves," she said. "Rowan—" Rowan had started up the narrow staircase, but turned back. "You'd do well to forget what I've said. That hotel is no place for children."

Rowan nodded, and quickly ran up the remainder of the flight.

After Rowan left, Agatha sat at the small desk and started to write out the labels: boysenberry, blueberry, blackberry, raspberry.

"Sister, I believe that young man is going to do exactly the opposite of what you suggested." Gertrude, who had been sitting under the staircase, emerged from the darkness. "Your overcautioning and mystified gobbledygook has only emboldened him to explore that rundown resort with his friends."

"Yes," said Agatha. "I was worried that his fear of ghosts would keep them from going there. I had to give him a push."

"And brilliantly so, Sister. It is time."

CHAPTER THREE

THE OWATANNAUK

ROWAN HAD BLABBED TO NINA ABOUT HIS SECRET conversation with Agatha as soon as he got upstairs. Nina had listened with great interest and Rowan had felt the tug of their old bond. In an effort to reel her in, he'd talked until she fell asleep.

Now, as they walked to the twins' house, they continued their conversation. Nina knew quite a bit about the theories of time and relativity. That, coupled with information Rowan had picked up from science fiction movies and books, kept them debating the possibilities. Once they got to Nana's house, Rowan immediately told the story to the twins, down to the last detail. In no time they were all tramping along the trail that led through the woods to the Owatannauk Resort Hotel.

"A door?" Xavier mused, pushing a low-slung branch out of his way. "A door to what?"

"Agatha didn't say," Rowan answered, trying to avoid a patch of mud. "And that's kind of where the conversation ended."

"She probably realized she'd said too much," Xavier said.

"Maybe it's a doorway to another dimension," Xanthe said mysteriously. "You know, like a black hole on earth that only opens for a moment, and even then just a little crack . . . just enough to swallow one person and send them hurtling through time and space."

"It can't be a black hole," Nina said. "It would be sucking everything into it. And it wouldn't send you through time, it would just crush you in the center of it."

"It does bring up an interesting question," Rowan said. "Why would it occur on this site? Why here?"

"Why not here?" Xanthe answered with a shrug. "The Bermuda Triangle is in the middle of the ocean, off of Bermuda. Why there?"

"You actually believe in the Bermuda Triangle?" Nina said wryly.

"I don't know enough about it," Xanthe answered. "But I do believe that some things are unexplainable, and that it is always good to keep an open mind."

The grounds to the Owatannauk Hotel were surrounded by a chain-link fence topped with barbed wire. Rowan read the metal sign affixed to it. "No trespassing by order of the Sheriff's Department. Violators will be fined $1,000." He tried to imagine even having a thousand dollars and what he would do with it.

"How are we going to get over it?" Nina asked.

"Not over it, *under* it." Xavier walked along the fence, testing the earth beneath it with his feet. "I doubt we're the only ones who've wanted to explore this place ... ah, here's a good spot!" He dropped to his knees and started to dig. "Come on, the more hands the faster it'll go and the sooner we'll get inside."

Forty minutes later, clothes stained and faces streaked with dirt, they stood on what appeared to be an old golf course, now hopelessly overgrown with weeds. The only signs of its former use were the sand traps dotting the rolling meadow. In the distance, the Owatannauk stretched out in all directions. A labyrinth of trellis-covered walkways radiated from the Victorian behemoth, which sat like a spider in the center of the web.

Rowan also noticed the profound silence of the place: no breeze, no birds, no buzzing insects. The only sound came from their tentative footfalls as they approached the main building. When they finally stood in front of it, they looked up at the five stories of peeling paint, broken windows, rotting wood, and tattered awnings.

"How sad," Xanthe said, breaking the silence. "It's like a queen who's been reduced to a homeless person."

"Yeah," Rowan added, "it's too bad it never went up for sale. Somebody might've tried to fix it up."

Xavier started up the steps.

"Careful," Xanthe cautioned, "these porches are falling apart."

"I know, I know. Hey, look!" Xavier peered through one of the windows. "All the furniture is still there!" Rowan, Nina, and Xanthe rushed up to join him. A shaft of sunlight illuminated the reception area. A long, mahogany desk commanded the center of the room, while two staircases at either end curved up to the second story. Though the exterior of the hotel was falling apart, the interior had been better preserved. The violet carpets and drapes, thick with dust, spoke of the luxury that once was. A crystal chandelier hung over the center hall, blankets of cobwebs obscuring its former brilliance. A grand piano sat in a rotunda with windows that faced the bay.

"Wow. It looks like it hasn't been disturbed since the place closed," Xanthe said.

Xavier was trying to force the door. "Yeah, like a tomb." He gave the door a shove with his shoulder, but it was unmoveable.

"You don't really think it's unlocked, do you?" Xanthe asked.

"Maybe we should go," Rowan said.

"You know what?" said Xavier, after inspecting the door more closely. "I don't think this is the front door. In fact, I don't think this is a door at all!"

"Of course it's a door," Xanthe said. "What else could it be?"

"A wall," Xavier answered. He pointed at the edge of the door. "Look. It's a solid piece of wood, carved to look like a double door. And the knob doesn't move either, because the turning mechanism isn't there. It's just attached."

Rowan looked where Xavier was pointing. Sure enough, it wasn't a real door.

"Well, if this isn't the front door, where is it?" Nina asked.

Xavier looked through the windows. "I can see it . . . but I don't see how to get to it."

"It must be just around the corner," Xanthe said. "Let's go see."

What was supposed to be a trip around the corner turned into a two-hour hunt. Agatha's description of the Owatannauk did not even begin to convey the perplexity of the convoluted paths, which led through so many gardens, and past so many patios, porches, and porticoes, that the group found themselves doubling back and passing the same places more than once. The path they had currently chosen had led them far from the main building.

"I wish there was a map," Rowan moaned after seeing the same dried-up pond for the third time.

"I wish I had a jacket," added Xavier. "It's getting cold. It's almost sunset."

Suddenly Nina clutched Rowan's arm. "You guys! It's the police!"

They all looked where she pointed. Sure enough, a squad car slowly rolled along the road that circled the property.

"Oh man, someone must've seen us and called them!" Xavier cried.

"No, they'd be going faster," Xanthe said. "This is probably just on their patrol route."

"Let's hide," said Rowan. "Quick, over here!"

He scrambled to an old utility shed and pried open the door. They just managed to squeeze inside before the squad car rolled by.

"Man, that was close," Rowan exhaled. He was suddenly aware that he was squashing Xanthe, and that her arms were wrapped around his waist. His face turned bright red as he stumbled out the door. "Sorry," he mumbled. "I didn't mean to back into you."

Xanthe staggered forward. Rowan realized she'd only had her arms around him to keep from falling over.

"I . . . I don't feel so well," Xanthe said, sitting on the ground.

"Me either," said Nina, clutching her chest. "My heart is pumping really fast. Feel!"

Rowan was breathing heavily as well. A strange tingling sensation coursed through him, and soon his entire body went numb. He tried to speak, but his lips wouldn't move. And yet he still felt something . . . something like electricity. He closed his eyes and imagined billions of electrons swirling around him. He felt incredibly cold, so searingly cold that it burned . . . then suddenly it was over. He opened his eyes, rubbing his arms and fingers. The others were doing the same.

"What was that?" Xavier said.

"I don't know," said Rowan, "but there's something creepy about this place. I don't know if I want to find out what it is."

"Yeah." Xanthe nodded. "Let's get out of here."

They brushed themselves off and started toward the old golf course, which was off to the right. Rowan noticed that there was a brand-new stream rushing past them toward the pond, which didn't seem so dried-up anymore. In fact, it was brimming with water. Water lilies and lily pads floated on the top and two ducks paddled among some tall reeds. He was about to tell the others when Nina screamed.

Rowan rushed to her side. She was staring straight ahead. A clean, white golf ball had just bounced over the crest of the hill and was rolling toward her.

A man appeared at the top of the hill, dressed in tweed knickers. "Sorry about that," he said jovially, scooping up his ball. "That should cost me a stroke, but I think I'm going to fudge it. I'm hopelessly over par." He tipped his hat, put his fingers to his lips, and jogged back over the hill.

The foursome followed him slowly, and though they could not believe it, their ears told them what they would find. They heard laughing and conversation, doors opening and closing, water splashing and tennis balls bouncing, birds singing and insects humming, and when they reached the crest of the hill and gazed at the hotel it was confirmed: the Owatannauk had come to life.

Rowan had never seen so many different kinds of hats. The men wore derbies and "newsboy caps," gray and brown mostly, though a few sported straw hats with colorful bands around the brim. But the ladies! Wide brims and neat little caps with feathers, bows, stripes, swirls, flowers, in all varieties of colors, hues, and patterns adorned their heads, perfectly matching their dresses, which lightly brushed the ground as they swept past. A boy ran by in short pants and suspenders. He noticed Rowan staring at him and smiled pleasantly.

"You want to come to the boathouse?" he said. He seemed to take it in stride that Rowan was wearing jeans and a T-shirt with a Batman logo on it.

"There's a boathouse?" Rowan asked.

"Of course there's a boathouse! It's right next to the maze. And the swan pond."

"I've been all over these paths. I didn't see any of those things," Rowan said.

The boy gave Rowan a funny look, something between pity and amusement. "Well, sometimes if you want to see the really interesting stuff, you have to get *off* the path." He shook his head and ran over the hill.

"This place *is* haunted!" said Xavier, his voice squeaking badly. "I knew it! I knew it!"

"I don't think these are ghosts," Rowan said thoughtfully. "They're solid and alive. You saw that boy, and the golfer. They're real people!"

"I know what was strange about those photographs in Aunt Agatha's album," Nina said suddenly. "They were in color. They were pictures of people just like this, in old clothes from another time, surrounded by old cars and old furniture . . . but all in color. But they were taken before color film was even invented."

"Don't you see?" Xanthe cried, grabbing Xavier gleefully. "Agatha said this was a portal. It's a *time* portal! These aren't ghosts! Look at the hotel. Just look at it!"

They all looked. The awnings were crisp and bright. The wood was pristine, the paint gleaming. This was no dilapidated, abandoned structure. It was new and glossy and magnificent.

"Somehow we stumbled into something, and we went back in time. *We're* the ones who don't belong here!" she cried.

"You think the utility shed was the portal?" Xavier shook her head. "That doesn't make sense. If we actually went back in time, these people would notice how different we look. They aren't paying attention to us at all."

"Maybe we should go back into the town and see if it's still there," Rowan said nervously. "Has it occurred to anyone that we might not be able to get back?"

"Well, wait a minute," Xanthe said thoughtfully. "We know we can get back because when Xave first saw this place change, we were in the present. Maybe we haven't gone anywhere after all."

"Thank you for finally admitting I was right," Xavier said. Xanthe rolled her eyes. Xavier pretended not to notice. "I think the only thing that has changed is this property. It brought the past *forward*. We haven't gone anywhere. And I for one am not leaving. This is totally awesome!"

"I've got an idea," Nina said suddenly. "The hotel is unlocked. Let's see if we can find the front door!"

Nina started to follow a group of people tramping along the grass toward the hotel. Sure enough, as they turned the corner, a wide staircase led directly from a small patio up to a pair of doors very similar in design to the false doors they had first found. Rowan noted that the only way to find this entrance was to ignore the paths altogether. From this angle of the building, they were nowhere in sight.

The cleaned-up interior of the hotel shone with jewel-like brilliance, beyond what the children imagined it could be. The chandelier sparkled like icicles in the sun. The vibrant raspberry and gold upholstery on the furniture created a festive atmosphere in the lobby, and this extended into the sitting area, where a young man in black tie played the highly polished grand piano.

"Wow," Rowan murmured. "It's just like being in a dream!"

Nina frowned. "I don't know what's going on," she said. "But if you were going to guess what period of time this hotel was in right now, what would you guess?"

"Nineteen twenties?" Rowan said.

"No, earlier than that," corrected Xavier. "It's got to be, like, turn of the century. Nineteen hundred."

Xanthe rolled her eyes. "I hate to fulfill the gender stereotype," she said, "but you guys clearly don't know anything about style and clothes. Look at these ladies," she said, gesturing to a nearby group. "See how proper and stiff they are? Their hair is pulled back so tightly it raises their eyebrows, and those ridiculous bustles they're wearing make their butts look enormous. Do they look like they could suddenly start dancing the Charleston? And at the turn of the century, men didn't wear so many beards, Xave. Look around, there's a lot of facial hair happening here. No, these people are definitely Victorians. Eighteen eighty, eighteen ninety, tops."

"Hey, that was pretty good," Rowan said.

Xanthe shrugged. "Like I said, my dad teaches history. I've got it in my blood."

"Didn't your aunt say this place was built around eighteen ninety?" Xavier said eagerly. "These could be people from back then!"

"The point I'm trying to make," Nina interrupted, "is that the guy over there at the piano is playing a piece by Satie. It's one of his nocturnes and it wasn't written until about nineteen twenty. So how did he get hold of it?"

They all stood in silence, pondering Nina's question, when Rowan noticed someone standing behind the check-in counter. He hadn't noticed him before, perhaps because the counter itself was so ornate that the balding, slightly built man didn't stand out. He was wearing a rose-colored jacket and black pants, and had a wide silver mustache that connected to his sideburns and seemed to curl up, as though it were an enormous smile. He looked directly at them, so Rowan gave him a polite wave, which the man returned.

"I'm going to go over and talk to that guy behind the counter," Rowan said to the others. It sounded like a good idea, so they all walked over.

"Hello," the man said with a country accent that conjured up images of dirt roads and maple-sugar candy. "I'm Otto. How may I help you?"

"Well, I'm Rowan Popplewell, this is my sister, Nina, and these are my friends, Xanthe and Xavier Alexander . . ." He intended to continue, but Otto was smiling so widely that his mustache seemed to grow even longer.

"Ah, yes. Popplewell. Welcome to the Owatannauk," he said, placing a large golden key on the counter. "We've been expecting you."

"What?" Rowan nearly fell over. "I've got a room?"

"This isn't a room key," Otto explained patiently. "First time here?"

"Well . . . yes! But what *is* here? Who made reservations, anyway? And what year is this?" Rowan hadn't meant to spew all of his questions at once, but now that he'd gotten started it was hard to stop.

"Today?" Otto opened a leather-bound book on the counter. He carefully removed a pair of wire spectacles from his pocket and placed them delicately on his long and pointy nose. "Why, it's the year two thousand and four."

"Why did you have to look in that book to tell me what year it is?" Rowan asked. "Don't you know without it?"

"Usually. But I prefer not to rely on my memory. You see, the book has everything in it, it's quite complete." He turned the heavy volume around so that Rowan could see it. There seemed to be thousands of entries, written in the tiniest handwriting by a leaky fountain pen. The page was covered with black smudges and blotches.

"That's a mess!" Rowan blurted.

"Well, it's not necessary for you to be able to read it," Otto sniffed. "It's my book."

"What did you mean when you said you were expecting

us?" Xanthe asked. "We didn't even know we were coming here until yesterday, and we didn't tell anybody."

Otto ran his finger down the page of the book and adjusted his glasses. "Here you are, Popplewell. Arriving Thursday, July eleventh, two thousand and four, the golden hour." Otto glanced out the window. "You're actually a little late. The golden hour is almost over."

"The golden hour!" Xavier exclaimed. "How do you know about the golden hour?"

"Young man," Otto said patiently. "We have only two hours here. The golden hour and the silver hour. Most people prefer the golden hour: it's prettier. But the silver hour comes just before daybreak, when the sun is about to rise and the darkness starts to dissipate. It is not so flamboyant, but perhaps more mysterious. Personally, I prefer the silver hour. It's quieter. More subtle. But it's not for everybody."

"Excuse me for being rude," Rowan said, "but who exactly are you?"

"I'm the concierge of the hotel. If you need anything, particularly in utilizing the many features of the hotel, just call on me. It's my job to make sure you have a pleasurable stay."

"We're staying here?" Rowan asked.

"No, not here." Otto didn't elaborate. Rowan was getting a little fed up with him.

Nina stepped up to the desk. "We want to see the time portal," she said.

Otto brightened. "Certainly. Come right this way, please." He picked up the key and placed it carefully in his vest pocket.

The foursome stood there for a moment, stunned, until Xavier smacked his palms together with a gleeful whoop. Otto turned and looked at him quizzically. "I beg your pardon, young man?"

"Nothing, nothing," Xavier giggled. "We're right behind you!"

As they followed Otto down a long hallway, Rowan rubbed his knuckles nervously. *What are we getting into?* he thought. Standing in the hotel surrounded by Victorians was weird enough, but at least it seemed safe. But going back in time? He shuddered. Two days ago Owatannauk was the last place on earth he wanted to be; now he was desperate to stay.

"This is definitely the coolest thing that has ever happened to me!" Xavier said, practically skipping.

Rowan nodded, trying to appear enthusiastic. *Look on the bright side,* he thought, *at least Nina's excited.* Her eyes shone and her hair bounced as she jogged after Otto, practically treading on his heels. This was the wrong time to be a party pooper.

"Maybe it *is* all just a dream," Rowan said, noticing the large collection of oil paintings on the wall. It was a world-class collection: Rembrandt, Michelangelo, Vermeer, Rousseau, and Monet.

"Well, do me a favor and don't wake me up." Xavier laughed. Xanthe nudged Rowan and pointed out a small sketch that he had missed, a harlequin by Picasso, drawn well after Victorian times. It was yet another anachronism.

At the end of the hall they turned left and found themselves facing a bank of ornate elevator doors. Otto stopped in front of them. "These will take you where you want to go."

"Elevators?" asked Nina, a little disappointed.

"Not elevators," Otto replied, "alleviators. For, you see, that is ultimately their purpose."

Indeed, these were no ordinary elevators. They appeared to be made of brass, yet on closer inspection the metal shimmered and pulsed, as though the doors had a life of their own. They also emitted a faint, harmonic hum, like the strum of a harp or a breeze through tall grass.

"Alleviators? What do they alleviate?" Xanthe asked.

"Curiosity," answered Otto.

"Cool!" said Xavier. "Can we take them for a spin?"

"My dear sir," Otto retorted, "time travel is no simple feat. It can be quite dangerous. This is not an amusement-park ride. It takes a certain type of person to accept such risk."

"What's that supposed to mean?" Xavier asked.

Otto peered at him over the top of his glasses. "We often admire people who are passionate about something," he explained. "Their interest and dedication can be admirable. But sometimes passion is like a sickness. It can be very painful to be so absorbed in something, to the exclusion of all else. It can cause headaches, heartache . . . mania. Such people are often so consumed by their questions that they simply can't bear to be without answers. So they go back. When they find their answers . . . *if* they find their answers, they are relieved of this passion, and return stronger, wiser, and satisfied."

"You mean we just get in and go? That's it?" Rowan asked.

"Oh my, no." Otto chuckled. "You have to sign a waiver. There are a few rules we need to go over." Otto produced a contract, apparently from thin air. "You might want to sit down," he said. "It takes a while to read."

Rowan sat on the bench, which faced the alleviators, as Nina, Xavier, and Xanthe gathered around him. He held the document out so that everyone could see it.

OWATANNAUK TWILIGHT TOURISTS PROGRAM
RULES, REGULATIONS, INSTRUCTIONS

Welcome to the Owatannauk Twilight Tourists Program! For over a century we have sent satisfied travelers back in time, all around the globe, to exciting and wondrous explorations of our world's history. To ensure your safe passage, please read the following contract and sign at the bottom of each page to indicate your understanding of the regulations outlined herein:

1. The alleviators are for guests of the Owatannauk Hotel. Those without reservations are not allowed to use the facility.

2. You must be in good health to use the facility. (a) Pregnant women and people with heart problems, back injuries, or severe physical or mental disabilities are discouraged from riding as there is no guarantee of quality medical care at your destination. (b) If you are carrying a disease, virus, or bacteria of any kind, no matter how mild, you MAY NOT use the facility. Please do not spread your sickness to people in the past! They are not protected by our modern-day immunizations!

3. Only six people may travel to a destination at the same time.

4. Please choose only one destination per day. Do not push multiple buttons or other patrons will have to wait for the machine to return from all of those destinations before they can ride.

5. No food or drinks are allowed on the alleviators.

6. As a traveler on the alleviator, you may be visiting eras and countries whose customs are unfamiliar to you. It is therefore STRONGLY SUGGESTED that you research your destination before you depart so as to prepare yourself for any situations you may encounter. It is our motto that "when in Rome, do as the Romans do."

7. Please do not try to change the events of history. It will affect your ability to return.

8. UNDER NO CIRCUMSTANCES MAY YOU CONTACT YOURSELF AS A YOUNGER PERSON.

9. No sexual relations with people of the past.

10. Keep track of anything you bring with you, especially your key.* The Owatannauk is not responsible for any articles left behind, or the fact that if found they may be attributed to aliens.

WARNING: Time travel is only made possible by the reconfiguration of the electrons in your body as you pass through the fourth dimension of space-time. Though you will return to your natural state, there are side effects, which may include some or all of the following: dizziness, nausea, sensitivity to electricity, tingling sensations in the fingers and toes, sudden bouts of static electricity, ringing in the ears, synesthesia, mental acuity, the urge to create. Though these side effects wear off, repeated use of the alleviators may cause some to become permanent.

At the bottom of the page was the standard statement, "I have read and fully agree with all of the aforementioned policies stated here. I waive all claims against the Owatannauk Hotel and its employees for injury, accident, illness, or death occurring by reason of participation. Participation may include, and is not limited to, usage of the alleviators, living in the past, eating and drinking food that is unregulated, meeting violent people, living in wilderness, being exposed to unfamiliar viruses and bacteria from the past, being subject to unfamiliar, unfair, and entirely corrupt legal practices and/or societal mores. In case of emergency, I authorize the Owatannauk to send one of its agents to render whatever actions are deemed necessary to rectify the situation."

Under the statement was a line for signatures. Xavier took out his pen.

"What do you think you're doing?" Rowan asked.

"I'm signing!" Xavier said gleefully.

"Well hold on," Rowan said. "I have a couple of questions. What's this one in all capital letters? Rule number seven. What happens if you contact yourself?"

"Are you familiar with particle physics and the laws of matter and antimatter?"

"No . . ." Rowan shifted uncomfortably.

"Here's a brochure if you'd like to read about it." Otto handed Rowan a thick brochure. It began with a history of particle physics along with a glossary of terms and led into a series of complicated equations using the Greek alphabet. Rowan shut the brochure.

"Can't you explain it in simple terms?"

"Certainly. The universe is balanced by matter and antimatter. When the alleviators take you back through time, they reverse the polarity of your protons and electrons, thus rendering you into an antimatter version of yourself. The result is that once you arrive at your destination you've created an instability: there is now an extra amount of antimatter without the matter to balance it. That is why we limit the number of people traveling together, to control that level of instability. Moreover, if you, in your antimatter state, find yourself in the past, you will be irresistibly attracted to yourself, like a magnet. The inevitable physical contact would cancel you both out, producing a marvelous burst of gamma rays."

"Even simpler, please?" Rowan asked.

"You explode."

"Well, that's pretty simple, Rowan." Xavier laughed. "Can't get simpler than that."

"I've got a question, too," Xanthe piped in. "Why can't you change history?"

"Are you familiar with the multi-universe interpretation of quantum mechanics?" Otto asked.

"Not really."

"Here's a brochure if you'd like to read about it," Otto said, handing Xanthe a thick brochure, which she took reluctantly.

"Could I have the simple explanation, too?" she asked.

"Imagine that the universe is a branch," Otto began. "Suppose you are faced with a decision that has only two possibilities. You make a decision. Now suddenly the branch divides in two, one for each possibility; the branch of the possibility you chose and the branch of the possibility you didn't. Both branches represent actual dual universes, even though you are personally only aware of one. Each decision you make causes more branching until you have millions of parallel universes all moving through time. Do you follow?" The children looked at one another blankly.

"Good," Otto continued, oblivious. "Now, if you go back in time and change something, for instance if you stop President Lincoln from being assassinated, it places you on a branch different from the one we are all now on. It changes nothing for us here, but you are now in a whole different universe, the one where President Lincoln was not assassinated. Unfortunately, it is nearly impossible to return to your original branch. Instead, when you try to come back to the present, you will find yourself in a world that may be totally unrecognizable to you. Our agents can only help people who are still on our universe's branch. Once you hop to a different branch, you're on your own."

"But what if you do something by accident?" Rowan asked.

"Don't," Otto said simply. Rowan waited for him to continue. He didn't.

"I thought all of this stuff about identical matter and antimatter forms and multiple universes was just science fiction," Nina said. Rowan noticed a strange, faraway look in her eyes.

"Of course, if you don't believe my explanation, you don't have to go," Otto said kindly.

"No, no, we definitely want to go," Xavier said, raising his pen again.

"Just hold on a second, will you? One last question." Rowan turned to Otto. "What's this about a key? There's an asterisk next to it."

"That asterisk refers to the small print at the bottom of the page."

Rowan looked at the contract. "What small print?"

Otto leaned over and pointed. Beneath the signature line there appeared to be something that Rowan had assumed was decoration, but on closer inspection, was a statement written in very small italics.

"It's quite small," Otto said. "Perhaps this will help."

Otto handed Rowan a magnifying glass. Rowan held it over the page and read the statement aloud. "You will be issued one key for the purposes of travel only. The key is the sole property of the Owatannauk Hotel and may not be copied. Do not lose your key or you will be unable to find the alleviator for your return."

"How does that work?" Xanthe asked, peering over Rowan's shoulder.

"When you are ready to return to the present, you must go to the area where you originally disembarked. The alleviator will be there. The only way you can see it, however, is if you have your key. And the only way you can board is if you have your key. This keeps patrons from unwisely bringing back stowaways from the past."

Rowan looked up. "There's another asterisk."

"Yes, that refers to the smaller print at the bottom of the page."

Rowan looked again. "You mean this series of dots? It's unreadable."

Otto offered Rowan a microscope, apparently pulling it from the same hiding place in which he'd kept the magnifying glass and the contract. Rowan took it warily and placed the bottom of the contract on the glass slide. He looked through the eyepiece and adjusted the focus.

"I got it," Rowan said finally. He started to read. "Patrons must return within seven days of their departure or the key will disintegrate." He looked up, shocked. "Well that's kind of an important thing to put in such small writing!"

Otto shrugged.

"You mean if you stay longer than a week, you're stranded there for life?" Xanthe asked.

"It's a flaw, I grant you that," Otto said simply. "But as I've said before, time travel is an unstable business. I should point out that the golden hour is almost over. If you'd like to go somewhere today, you need to decide now."

"Let's go!" Xavier urged. "Come on, before he disappears!"

"Don't be stupid, Xave!" Xanthe snapped. "We have to be careful about where we decide to go. It could be dangerous. Didn't you hear him? This isn't like going to Disneyland."

"She's right," Rowan agreed. He looked over at Otto, who seemed to be slowly fading.

"We'll come back tomorrow!" Rowan called to him.

Otto nodded.

"Where are you going?" Nina asked Otto.

"We're always here," Otto said, his voice becoming tinny as he grew less distinct. "You just can't see us." With that, he was gone. The children glanced around at the hotel, which had returned to its rundown state. The elevators no longer gleamed and the contract was gone. Otto had taken the key with him.

"Listen," Xanthe started as they walked back through the darkening woods, "this is a chance for us to do something really important! We can discover the answers to questions that historians have fought over for years! We can fill in gaps of knowledge, uncover details that may have been lost or forgotten . . ."

"Oh, quit making speeches," Xavier interrupted. "The important thing is, we can meet some really cool people. Think about it. King Tut and Cleopatra."

"They weren't contemporaries," Xanthe sighed.

"So? We can meet them both anyway. Abraham Lincoln. Henry the Eighth. Joan of Arc. Nina, you can take piano lessons from Mozart himself."

That got her attention. She caught up with the rest of the group.

"You really think so?" she asked.

"I can't guarantee it, but you have seven days to try. We just have to make sure we choose a time and place that was good to brown-skinned people," he added. "I don't want to be stuck picking cotton."

"Wait you guys," Rowan interrupted. "Let's not get so excited about this. Think about what we're actually talking about doing. Now maybe I am a big chicken, or maybe I just value my miserable life enough to want to keep living it, but we are American kids from the twenty-first century. Our lives have been pretty easy. We've never had to face horrible sickness, like the plague. We've never had to live without electricity, cars, grocery stores, bug spray . . ."

"Yeah, Xanthe," Xavier said, suddenly serious, "what are you going to do without strawberry lip gloss?"

Xanthe shot him a withering look.

"You know what I mean," Rowan said. "It's way too dangerous."

"Now you listen, Rowan," Xanthe began. "We're not stupid you know, we know there is some risk involved. But isn't that what life is about? You just said your life was miserable . . ."

"No, I didn't . . ."

"Yes, you did. You said you value your miserable life. Why?"

"That's really none of your business." Rowan's neck started to get hot.

"You've made it my business. I think maybe your life is miserable because you don't *do* anything. In the two days I've known you, all you talk about is stuff you've gotten from books, movies, and TV, or your computer, like you just sit around on your butt all day absorbing information. Well, I've got a surprise for you. Experience is *fun*. Experience is *exciting*. Life *is* experience. What good is all that information going to do if you don't apply it to anything?"

Rowan said nothing.

"I think we should take a vote on whether we go or not," Xavier continued. "Majority wins. Anyone who wants to go back to the Owatannauk tomorrow and try the alleviators, raise your hand."

Xanthe and Xavier shot their arms up into the air.

"All opposed?"

Rowan raised his hand.

"Oh well, it's a tie," Rowan said, trying to hide his relief.

"No it isn't," Xanthe said, nodding at Nina. "Your sister didn't vote. It's two to one. We're going."

"She agrees with me, don't you, Nina?"

Nina looked at him, then lowered her eyes. "Yeah," she said quietly. "It's too risky."

"You guys are a couple of wimps!" Xavier shouted. "Xanthe and I will go by ourselves!"

"No, forget it Xave," Xanthe muttered bitterly. "Rowan had the reservation. Otto offered Rowan the only key. We were just Rowan's guests. If we go back alone, we may not be allowed to use anything. Remember rule number one, 'alleviators for the use of guests of the hotel only.'"

Xavier kicked a flurry of pebbles into the street.

"We can talk about it tomorrow," Rowan said. "I just don't want to rush into it. Besides, we would all have to agree on where to go, and you know we'd never reach a decision," he joked.

"I'm going to work on you, Rowan," Xavier said angrily. They reached the intersection where Rowan and Nina had to branch off to get back to the Sisters' house.

"We'll talk about it tomorrow. I promise," Rowan called after the twins. They didn't turn back. Rowan and Nina started down Main Street.

"Do you think we're making a mistake?" asked Nina sadly.

"No, I don't," Rowan replied. "That contract was filled with holes. And when something goes wrong, do you think it's a contract that would hold up in court? Of course not! What would we say, that we went to an abandoned hotel that's plastered with 'No Trespassing' signs and signed a contract with a man who only exists two hours out of the day?"

"What makes you think something would go wrong?"

"Because I read the small print. And the smaller print. And I could've sworn I saw another asterisk. I don't trust asterisks."

That evening Rowan and Nina saw the Sisters' house with new eyes. Suddenly everything made sense. Agatha and Gertrude were clearly the most active tourists since time began. The curios sold in their shop were souvenirs that they'd picked up on their travels through time. They couldn't call them "antiques" because they weren't old; they were as new as if they'd been made yesterday. And the aunts' frequent use of the alleviators had made them sensitive to electricity.

It also dawned on Rowan and Nina that the entire town was probably in on the secret of the Owatannauk Resort and that many of the things they had seen in the Main Street shop windows—the intricately carved marionettes, the blown-glass figurines, the exquisite embroidery on the bridal gown—were the results of skills learned in different eras altogether.

That night Rowan couldn't sleep. He heard Nina tossing under the covers and glanced over at her. She was sitting up, watching him.

"Rowan, can I ask you something?"

"Sure, of course." He sat up. "What's up?"

Nina crossed over to his bed and sat at the foot. She folded her knees up to her chin and clasped her arms around them.

"Did you mean it when you said your life was miserable?"

"Well, yeah. I don't think my life is so great. I'm . . . not happy much."

"Is it because of me?" Her mouth quivered.

"No, no, no!" he said, touching her shoulder. "Don't think that. Don't ever think that! I've just had a tough time fitting in at school . . . and everything going on with Dad . . . and I guess it's been lonely having no one to talk to about it."

"Then it is partly my fault. I'm sorry I haven't been there for you to talk to. But my life has been miserable, too!"

She closed her eyes, clenching her jaw. Rowan wondered if she was going to cry, but she didn't. She just pressed her head with her fingers as though it were splitting apart. Rowan put his arm around her and gazed out of the window at the moon, which was round and full, illuminating the room and the rooftops beyond. Nina looked up suddenly, her eyes bright.

"I wonder if there was ever a time when everything was good, when people were surrounded by beauty, music, art . . . when style and manners still meant something and people had high standards . . . you know what I mean? So that no matter what happened, they could look out at the world around them and say, 'I don't care, life is still great!'"

"That would be nice," Rowan mused. "You know last year I took a class in world history. The teacher was boring, but there was one period of time he talked about that sounded like what you're talking about. The Enlightenment."

"The Enlightenment? When was that?"

"You know, I'd have to check my notes . . . I forget a lot of what he said, but it was centered in France, under Louis the Fourteenth . . . in the late seventeen hundreds, I think, right near the turn of the century. There was a lot happening in philosophy, science, and art, and it all centered on the idea that it was possible to have a better world. It was just a very optimistic time. Galileo, Kepler, Copernicus, and Isaac New-ton were making major discoveries, people were starting to use their intelligence and reason instead of superstition, and artists were inspired by reality and nature. Everyone was excited about life and learning. Pretty cool, huh?"

Nina's eyes sparkled intensely. Rowan knew she'd like the Enlightenment. Anything intellectual and artistic was right up her alley.

"I wish we were in a time like that, it sounds so . . . so . . . big and important. And beautiful."

"Forget about it," Rowan said. "Things really stink now. People don't like each other, everyone's polluted the planet, everything's about money." He shrugged. "Ah well, that's the world we live in."

"We don't have to, though," Nina said, facing him. "You know we don't. We could escape this world and go anywhere we want. And I know you want to do it."

"What are you, a mind reader, too?"

"I can see it in your eyes."

"Well, you're wrong. I don't want to go. It's too risky . . ."

"Yeah, I heard you say that this afternoon, but you're not afraid of getting injured or catching a disease. You're afraid that once you're there, you won't want to come back."

Rowan was silent. He hadn't known it until then, but Nina was right. Somehow she'd cut through his protests and hit the heart of the matter, which was his desire to run away, leave everything behind.

"I don't want to leave Dad," Rowan said.

"We'll come back for him. We'll find a time we like, come back for him, and . . ."

"No, Nina! It's not right. You can't run away from your problems, you have to face them and deal with them. Otherwise you're nothing but a quitter."

"You don't really believe that . . ."

"Yes I do. You talk about a time when people had high standards? Well here's a standard for you: courage. Courage to deal with your problems instead of ducking them with . . . with magic."

Nina folded her arms.

Rowan didn't care that she was angry. He was angry, too.

"We can talk about it later with Xavier and Xanthe, and maybe, *maybe* we'll try out the alleviators. But shut up about running away and staying back in time. All right? That's ridiculous. You're never going to get me to agree to that, so don't even try."

"Fine. Forget it then. Forget I ever said anything." She hopped back into her own bed and pulled the covers up to her chin, her lip poked out petulantly.

After half an hour Rowan heard the soft whisper of Nina's breathing as she slept. But he was too agitated to sleep. He had worked so hard battling his way back to a normal life, beating down his emotions until they no longer tortured him . . . and here she was stirring things up. He stared at the ceiling for a full hour more before he finally fell asleep, dreaming of diving into black holes and being crushed in the center.

The next morning Rowan woke up with sunlight on his face. He stretched drowsily and looked over at Nina's bed, where she was still curled up under the covers. He went into the bathroom, relieved himself, washed his face, and brushed his teeth. When he came out, Nina hadn't moved. It was already nine o'clock. They would have to hurry if they were going to eat and meet Xanthe and Xavier by ten. He hoped she would wake up in a better mood than she was in last night. The probably both owed each other an apology.

"Hey, sleepyhead," Rowan said, "it's time to get up." Nina didn't answer. Rowan started tickling her, expecting a squeal and a windmill of slaps. But as soon as he touched her he knew something was wrong. She was too soft. He threw back the blankets and saw a pillow folded up to look like a body. Attached to the pillow was a note.

"Dear Rowan," it began. "I'm sorry, but it's something I have to do. Love, Nina."

Rowan stood holding the note, a lead weight descending into his stomach. "Nina? Nina?" he croaked. But of course he knew she was gone.

CHAPTER FOUR

THE TWILIGHT TOURISTS

ROWAN RACED OVER TO THE TWINS' HOUSE AS fast as he could. At breakfast he'd greeted Agatha with as much cheerfulness as he could muster, grabbed a muffin, and then bolted out the door, hoping against hope that she was not interested in his thoughts that particular morning. What she would've found whirling through his mind was sheer panic; images of Nina hurtling through time, in search of . . . what? He had no idea. All he knew was that he'd lost her once before, and he wouldn't let it happen again.

Xanthe opened the door and gave him a funny look. "You're about half an hour early," she said. "Is something wrong?"

Rowan swallowed the gob of spit that had developed in his mouth. "Nina's gone," he sputtered, then lowering his voice, "She's run off. I think . . . I think she's gone to you-know-where to use the you-know-whats."

"What?" Xanthe joined him on the porch, closing the door behind her. "Why? Yesterday she voted not to use them."

"I don't know for sure, but she got upset last night, and I only made it worse . . . I just didn't see it coming. Look at this." He handed her the note as Xavier came out on the porch, munching an apple.

"Hey . . . what's up?" he said, then pointed at Rowan's feet. "Did you know that your shoes don't match?" Rowan looked down. Sure enough, in his haste he'd put on one white deck shoe and a blue running shoe. "I think this is a job for the fashion police." Xavier laughed.

"Quiet, Xave, this an emergency," Xanthe said. "Nina's in trouble." She studied the letter again, then looked up. "Wait a minute, Rowan, are you sure she went back there? The letter says, 'It's something I have to do.' Maybe she went back to see your dad."

"No, she's at the Owatannauk. We were talking last night about where we would want to go in time, daydreaming about how nice it would be to find a place where everything was wonderful . . ."

"I don't mean to burst your bubble, but you'll never find paradise on earth, no matter where you go in history."

"Well, yeah, I know that. But still, I knew of a time that would appeal to Nina, so I told her about the Enlightenment, you know, in France? About the optimism, the philosophy, the science . . . the beauty and style under Louis the Fourteenth."

"Technically, the Enlightenment didn't start till the death of Louis the Fourteeth," Xanthe said.

"Well, technically, it doesn't really matter," Rowan continued. "The point is, I convinced her to travel back to France in the late seventeen hundreds."

Xanthe's head jerked up. "What did you say?"

"I said, I think that after talking to me she decided to go back to France in the late seventeen hundreds."

"Wrong!" Xanthe cried suddenly, jumping to her feet. "Wrong, wrong, wrong!"

"Well, thanks for trying to make me feel better," Rowan said, "but if I hadn't told her about the Enlightenment, she probably wouldn't have thought of a place to run away to."

"I'm not trying to make you feel better!" Xanthe yelled. "In fact, I'm about to make you feel a whole lot worse! Louis the Fourteenth's rule and the discoveries that led to the Enlightenment didn't take place in the late seventeen hundreds. They happened in the late seventeeth *century*. That's the *sixteen hundreds*."

"So . . ." Rowan started hesitantly. "So if the Enlightenment wasn't at the end of the seventeen hundreds . . . what was?"

Xanthe sighed. "Rowan. If Nina followed your advice and traveled to France at the end of the eighteenth century, that is, from seventeen eighty-eight or so up to the mid–seventeen nineties . . . she's right smack in the middle of the French Revolution!"

Rowan, Xanthe, and Xavier lost no time in reaching the Owatannauk, but of course, it was deserted. It would be eight hours before its next transformation. When they clambered up the rotten porch to check the front door they found it locked, but they were sure Nina had been there; Xavier found her headband caught in the fence where she must have crawled under.

"Maybe we're making it out to be worse than it is," Xavier said, with unconvincing optimism. Rowan was sitting on the steps, his head cradled in his hands, while Xanthe gazed into the distant forest, chewing her lip to the point of bleeding. "We don't even know how these . . . these 'alleviators' work. Maybe Otto figured out where she really wanted to go and sent her there. Then our problem is just finding her."

"Just finding her? *Just* finding her?" Xanthe rolled her eyes. "Xave, she's in a foreign country in a period of time she knows nothing about. She could be anywhere! What do you think this is, a mall? Like all we have to do is call security?"

"Hey, I'm just trying to be positive," Xavier said. "We're not getting anywhere just sitting here waiting for the stupid place to open up, making Rowan feel like a murderer."

Rowan jerked his head up. "What do you mean, 'murderer'? You think she's dead? You think my sister's dead?"

"Oh, very smooth, Xave," Xanthe muttered. "You've made him feel much better."

"I didn't mean that, Rowan. I don't think she's . . . well, I have no idea."

Rowan had never felt so alone. What had his mother always said? That whenever he was in trouble he could count

on his family for help? Well, where were they now? He had
nobody. And it was all his fault. The top-ten list had its next
two entries.

#4. I'm an IDIOT. A STUPID, STUPID IDIOT.

#3. I am alone.

He wiped his eyes with his sleeve. He had to get himself
together. He wasn't a quitter. He might be many things, but
not that.

"Hey, I just thought of something!" Xanthe cried sud-
dently. "I bet she couldn't even use the alleviators. She didn't
have a key! And the rules said 'no guests.'"

"Well then where is she?" Rowan moaned.

"We won't know for sure whether or not she went until we
ask Otto," Xavier said, brushing off his pants. "But we can't just
sit here for eight hours. Let's do something constructive."

"Like what?" Xanthe asked, folding her arms.

"Well, just for the sake of argument, let's assume the worst.
Let's say she's in the middle of the French Revolution. Well,
what does that mean? I don't know much about it. Do you,
Rowan?"

"Obviously I don't if I got the dates all wrong."

"Well, then. Let's do a little research."

"I *do* know about the French Revolution," Xanthe said. "It
wasn't pretty. But it is a good idea to do some research. That
way, if we have to go, we'll know what we're in for."

• • •

The library was the largest building in town. When Rowan first saw it he thought it was City Hall. The collection of books was also impressive; the fiction section was average, but the history and biography sections seemed endless. A pretty woman with strawberry blond hair approached them.

"Hello," she said brightly, "I'm Miss O'Neill, the head librarian. Can I help you find something?"

"Yes, we need to do some research," Rowan said.

"Well, this is the place to come. I have a whole staff of people whose only job is to do research. I even do a little myself. It's my favorite part of the job."

Her eyes twinkled when she said this. Suddenly Rowan realized what she meant by "research" and why the library was so huge. It was probably the first stop for anybody who wanted to time travel, and Miss O'Neill was a frequent flier herself.

"We need to find out as much as we can about the French Revolution," Rowan said.

Mrs. O'Neill nodded, rubbing her chin. "Really? Fascinating, complicated period. But not a nice place to be." She gave Rowan a hard look, which he understood immediately. She was trying to figure out if they were time travelers or just innocent tourists. He looked to Xanthe and Xavier, saw they understood her meaning as well, took a deep breath, and explained to her their predicament. When he finished, Miss O'Neill nodded grimly, expressed her sympathy, then disappeared into the library stacks. In less than forty minutes she returned with twenty-seven books, all on French history, Louis XVI, and Marie Antoinette. There were books about the style, fashion, and etiquette in the Renaissance; popular culture in the Renaissance; political history; art history; and a videotape on ballroom dancing. She then led them to a small study room where they could talk freely.

Their research was not encouraging. It wasn't easy to get a handle on French politics at the end of the Renaissance leading toward the Revolution, and after seven hours of solid reading, Rowan had a splitting headache. He could barely keep anything straight; the gossiping courtiers and their court intrigue, the wealthy businessmen (the "bourgeoisie") vying for more power in the government, the starving peasants suffering from a severe wheat shortage, the weak king, the despised queen . . . it was like one incredibly complicated soap opera. And still he couldn't understand how a society that celebrated culture and refinement could descend so quickly into insanity, culminating in the Reign of Terror, one of the most gruesome bloodbaths in history. One image gripped his thoughts so fiercely it was difficult to think of anything else; two grooved wooden planks, each fifteen feet tall, which were connected by a third from which hung a heavy, angled blade made of steel. It was the guillotine, a machine for cutting off heads.

When they finished reading as much of the books as they could, they brought them back to the front desk, thanked Miss O'Neill for her time, and started to leave.

"Wait!" Miss O'Neill called out. "You can't go anywhere without your clothes!" She whisked them into an arm of the library building that served as an enormous costume storehouse. Room after room held racks of clothing, all authentic, Miss O'Neill assured them, for they had been personally collected by her team of librarians. "You have to look the part, you know," she said as she quickly measured them. "By the way, what part do you want to play, exactly?"

"Well, Nina would never be a peasant," Rowan thought aloud. "She went there for the beauty and the arts, so my guess is she'd be a noblewoman."

"I don't know, Rowan," Xanthe said thoughtfully. "Nina didn't talk much, but I'm a pretty good judge of character . . . I think she'd be turned off by the snooty nobles. And she's creative. I bet she'd hang out with the middle-class writers and artists."

"Remember, you guys," Xavier said, "she probably went back in time without anything—without the right clothes, or any research, nothing. And she's just eleven. The easiest place for her to meld in would be with the poor people. At least until she figured out what she was going to do."

Miss O'Neill thought for a moment, then ran the mechanical clothing rack with a remote control until she'd collected several outfits. "Why don't you each cover different parts of the society," she said, handing Rowan a bag with a costume in it. "Rowan, you dress as a noble. It will give you access to the palace and the courtiers. Xanthe, you be an artist. It's a good occupation for a woman. You will be able to mingle with the business class, and also have some access to the nobles since they respect and cultivate the arts. Your skin color will make you seem exotic and exciting." She handed Xanthe a bag and turned to Xavier. "You will be a freed slave."

"Hey! Why do I have to be the slave!" Xavier protested.

"Well, there weren't that many black people in Revolutionary France," Miss O'Neill explained. "Some of the French had slaves, but, unlike Americans, they didn't keep them in their own country. Slave labor was limited to the Carribean colonies, where they needed the manpower for their crops."

"Oh, man," Xavier groaned. "Oh, well. I guess it's just for a week."

"Hopefully less," Rowan said.

"The sun is starting to go down," Miss O'Neill said. "You'd better be on your way." She led them back to the main room of the library. "Oh, I almost forgot. There are instructions for how to put everything on inside the garment bag."

"How are we going to blend in if we can't speak French?" Rowan asked. Actually, he could speak a little French. He had taken a semester of beginning French in junior high, but he doubted he could get very far on "Here is a pen" and "The pants are green."

"Don't worry," Miss O'Neil said, "Otto will help you with that. Good luck, you guys."

As they walked back to the hotel with their costumes, Rowan realized that he hadn't said good-bye to anyone, to Agatha or Gertrude, or even to his father. He wondered if he'd ever hear his father's voice again, or if he'd even see the twenty-first century again. He watched Xavier and Xanthe as they strode ahead of him. They seemed so sure of themselves—eager, excited, courageous. But Nina was *his* sister, *his* flesh and blood, *his* responsibility, and he didn't feel brave or eager. He felt like throwing up.

When they got to the Owatannauk Resort, the threesome immediately changed into their costumes, each getting dressed in privacy. Rowan chose the boathouse, Xavier the utility shed, and Xanthe the swimming-pool cabana.

After allowing his eyes to adjust to the dim light, Rowan opened his bag, removing the instructions from an inside pocket. Then he pulled out an elegant suit: a rich, dark brown velvet coat decorated with gold embroidery, a waistcoat and breeches of rust orange velvet with a similar embroidery pattern, and a white shirt with a ruffle along the sleeves and neck. He was shocked when he pulled out a girdle, an article of clothing he associated with flabby old women, but once he put it on he actually liked it. It flattened his stomach and forced him out of his usual slouch. There was no mirror around, but Rowan thought he looked pretty good. He was not happy about the shoes, however. He put on the black leather shoes with large silver buckles and tried to walk. The heels rose one-and-a-half inches from the ground. They made his legs hurt, and he couldn't get across the boathouse without losing his balance.

Even worse was the wig. It had two rows of tight curls and

a small ponytail in the back, tied by a velvet ribbon. The whole thing was thickly dusted with white powder.

"Hey Rowan, what's taking you so long?" Xanthe called from around the corner. Rowan sighed and put the wig on his head. A flurry of powder fell to his shoulders. Now he knew what the whisk brush was for. He cleaned himself up, stuffed his own clothes into the plastic bag, and went outside. When he saw Xanthe, he stopped in his tracks.

Gone were the overalls and the high-top sneakers. Xanthe wore a gown of embroidered light green silk. From the elbow-length sleeves flowed a frothy fountain of lace, and a floor-length skirt billowed out from her waist. She also wore a wig: dark, bouncy ringlets with a purple velvet ribbon.

"You look . . . you're beautiful," Rowan stuttered.

"Oh, please," Xanthe answered, slightly embarrassed. "I feel like I'm walking around in a puffy green marshmallow."

Xavier walked over, wearing a plain gray wool coat and long brown pants. He also wore black shoes, but the heels were lower and the buckles were much smaller than Rowan's.

"You thought the Victorians had butts that looked big . . . take a good look at yours, sister! Yow!" Xavier smacked Xanthe on the backside with his black tricorn hat.

"Ha, ha, very funny." Xanthe swatted Xavier with her fan and winced. "Ouch! I'm in sheer agony here. I can barely breathe in this stupid corset."

"That's the Renaissance for you," Rowan said, thinking the corset made her look pretty good. "We're stuck with the fashion."

"Just one more way to keep women under control," Xanthe muttered to herself. She wrinkled her nose thoughtfully. "Hey, speaking of fashion, Rowan, aren't you supposed to be wearing makeup? The nobles all powdered their faces."

Rowan took a small cannister of powder from his costume bag, along with a powder puff. "I was afraid that was what this was for," he sighed.

"I'll do it for you," Xanthe said.

"Don't forget to give him a beauty mark over his lip," Xavier teased. "It's all the rage!"

"Don't listen to him. He's just an uncultured peasant," Xanthe said, tapping Rowan's face with the puff. She gently blew away the excess powder. "There. I think you look quite dashing," she said, pleased with her handiwork.

Rowan blushed, but Xanthe didn't notice; it was hidden under the fine, white dust.

Before Xavier could make another joke, the hotel started its transformation. Rowan felt the tingling sensation, just as before. His body went numb, he felt the hot and cold flashes, and then suddenly the colors, the noises, the vitality rushed at them like a tidal wave.

Rowan was the first into the lobby. Otto stood calmly behind the front desk.

"Otto!" Rowan called, stumbling across the room in his high heels. "Has my sister Nina been here?"

"Yes, she was here."

Rowan held his breath. "Did she use the alleviators? Did she go back in time?"

"Yes."

"Where did she go?"

"I'm really not at liberty to say."

Rowan was stunned. He felt the hair on his neck rise.

"Wait . . . what's that supposed to mean? She's gone! We have to find her!"

"I understand your disappointment," Otto replied, "but we have a policy of absolute privacy."

"She's just a kid! Don't you have any policies about child endangerment?"

"I thought your first rule was that you had to be a guest of the hotel to use those machines," Xanthe said, holding Rowan back. "Why did you let her use Rowan's key without him being with her?"

"I beg your pardon," Otto said, "but the key of which you speak was not intended for Mr. Popplewell. It was his sister who had the reservation."

Rowan blinked. "Nina had the reservation? But you said the key was for . . ."

"Popplewell. Yes. Nina Popplewell."

"But why?" Rowan blurted.

"Reservations are based solely on need. She had a need to go somewhere. And now she is there."

"So that key was only for her? We couldn't go anywhere, even if we wanted to? As her guests?" Xavier asked.

"Only hotel guests. That's our policy."

"You know, for a concierge, you are really unhelpful!" Rowan yelled, breaking away from Xanthe's grip. "Anything could happen to her! And you're telling me we can't follow her? That's . . . that's criminal! I'm going to report you to the . . . the manager . . . whoever that is . . ."

Otto tilted his head slightly. "Mr. Popplewell, these histrionics are quite unnecessary. Your sister had to go somewhere. If you'd like to use the alleviators to find her, you only need ask. You see, we've been expecting you." Otto reached under the desk and placed three golden keys on the counter. Xanthe, Xavier, and Rowan stared in disbelief.

"Well, why didn't you say so?" Rowan sputtered.

"Yeah," Xavier joined in, "all this talk about having a need and only one key was just meaningless. You can hand out keys any time you want!"

"No, " Otto replied firmly. "Yesterday only Miss Popplewell had the reservation and subsequently only she could use the key. She was the only one with a true need for travel. Today, however, you three also have a need, and that is why you have reservations. Now, if you are ready, you may follow me to the alleviators."

After collecting their signed contracts, Otto pressed a button next to the first alleviator. The doors slid open, revealing a gate of the same shimmering material. The low hum was louder now. Otto pulled the gate back. When they entered, the sound surrounded them, as though they were standing in the center of a hive swarming with melodic, chiming bees.

Once inside, it was clear that the alleviators were not elevators. They were considerably longer, perhaps twenty feet long, and the walls were lined with buttons, each one the size of a dime, with a year inscribed on them. A panel protruded from the wall. It had a keyboard numbering zero through nine, and a decimal point. It also had a small screen.

"Wow, this is amazing," said Xanthe, running her fingers over the buttons. "Who built these? And why isn't this technology anywhere else?"

"Excuse me, Miss," Otto replied kindly, "but we request that you refrain from playing with the buttons. Accidental trips really do waste a considerable amount of time."

Xanthe crossed her arms.

"The most popular way of operating these machines is manually," Otto began. "Most people have done their research and have a pretty good idea of where they want to go. In that case, we just find the year and press the appropriate button. Each button is inscribed with a year, going back to about 7,000 B.C., the Neolithic Age in southeast Asia. You'll notice the buttons change color at a certain point, at the year 1 B.C. That's merely a convention for finding that date; so many people who use the Christian calendar find that to be a helpful marker. Incidentally, we can set these buttons to the Chinese calendar if you prefer, or any other calendar, but I assume this is the one that will serve your purpose."

"Yes," said Rowan, getting somewhat anxious. He wasn't sure how much time had passed. He felt strange inside the alleviator, as though he were in a timeless state. He placed his hand to his heart and was alarmed when he couldn't feel it beat.

"Now, the year you visit is your choice, however the month, day, and time are predetermined. It's always the day you travel, at the time you travel. For instance, if you were visiting the year 100 B.C. today, you would arrive at your destination on July twelfth, 100 B.C. —or what would be July twelfth if one extrapolates the calendar backward—at the golden hour. Any questions?"

Xanthe raised her hand. "What if you want to go to a specific date, but it isn't the day you're traveling?"

"Then you have to wait," Otto replied, "and come back on that specific date. Is that clear? Good. Now, after you choose the year and punch the button, it will appear on this screen." Otto gestured to the panel, which had "July 12, 2004" at the top. "The next step is determining the coordinates of your destination." Otto opened a cabinet by the panel and produced what appeared to be a globe and a handheld microscope.

"Once you determine the latitude and longitude, you enter it here, and it will appear under the date." He pointed to the keypad next to the screen. Then Otto put the microscope up to the globe and motioned for Rowan to take a look.

Rowan peered through the glass at the globe. The magnification was incredible. He was looking down at New York City. As he adjusted the focus, he could even see Rockefeller Center and the Empire State Building. A thin line below the building had a sequence of numbers and degrees etched above it, which he read aloud.

"Ah. The Empire State Building," Otto remarked, apparently having memorized the coordinates.

"You can see that?" Xanthe said, intrigued. "Let me have a look."

She reached for the microscope, but Rowan held on to it. He'd noticed something odd.

"Hey!" he yelled. "There's something moving down there!" In point of fact, there was quite a bit moving. As he continued to adjust the focus, he could see traffic, people walking, and a purse snatcher running through Central Park.

"What kind of globe is this?" he squealed, nearly dropping the microscope. Xanthe grabbed the eyepiece and peered down at the dark sphere.

"It's merely a globe," Otto answered simply. "A representation of the world. And a very useful device for our purposes."

"It's awfully . . . precise," said Rowan.

"Of course it's precise. Precision is absolutely essential in time travel, as it is in most things," Otto retorted. "Time itself is precise. Things may happen in a single moment. If the moment is lost, then so is the event. I can't stress enough the importance of accuracy. My goodness, if you're a few feet off in your measurements, you could place yourself in the wall of the Empire State building, rather than the lobby! That's why we urge our guests to place themselves in wide-open spaces, where you won't be stumbled over or melded into a solid object. Now, let me show you something else.

"The machine is currently set for today's date," Otto continued. If we were to set it for . . . say, 1600 . . ." Otto pressed the appropriate button on the wall. The globe flickered slightly.

Xanthe's jaw dropped. "What happened? The buildings are all gone. There's just . . . wilderness . . . wait! I can see a hunting party . . . are those the Iroquois?"

Now it was Xavier's turn to wrestle for the instrument. "Woooo! This is fantastic!" he howled, peering through the eyepiece. "Can you set it to nineteen twenty-nine? I want to see New York at the stock market crash . . ."

"We're getting sidetracked," Rowan protested. "Listen, Otto. This is all very fascinating stuff, but I want to find my sister. Now, can you tell us where she went?"

"I'm afraid not," Otto said simply.

"Then we'll never be able to find her!" Rowan cried. "We don't know the coordinates she typed in! It's like looking for a needle in a haystack!" Rowan searched for any sign of sympathy in Otto's face, but saw nothing.

"You're really not going to tell us? Not even a hint? Nothing?"

Otto only tilted his head slightly and continued to smile pleasantly.

Rowan shouted and stomped out. The twins followed. "I can't believe that jerk!" Rowan seethed. "Pretty soon the golden hour will be over, and we'll have to wait another day. What's wrong with him?"

"Wait a minute," Xavier whispered excitedly. "I've got it! It's a puzzle! This whole operation, the hotel, the grounds, and now the alleviators . . . it's one big mental maze!"

"What do you mean?" Rowan said.

Xavier drew them slightly away from Otto, who didn't

seem to mind. "I've been thinking about this place, what it really is and why it's here . . . and I haven't really figured it all out, but one thing is clear; it runs by very specific rules, only these rules are not obvious. The only way to understand the hotel is to understand and follow the rules. It's kind of like hacking into a computer program without having the manual. Remember, Rowan, when Agatha told you about that guy, what's his name? The guy who built the hotel?"

"Archibald Weber."

"Yeah, Archibald Weber. She said he was a genius toy maker who specialized in puzzles. Now, I don't know if you've ever taken any IQ tests . . ."

Rowan shook his head.

"Well, Xanthe and I have. And most of them don't just test how much you know. They test how agile your mind is. How quickly you can twist a situation and see it from another angle. Once you twist it just the right way, the solution jumps out at you."

Xanthe nodded eagerly. "Like that kid we met outside, the first time we were here," she said. "We couldn't find the front door because we were using the paths. And he said 'sometimes you have to get off the path.' We hadn't even thought of that, but once we did, we found the entrance to the hotel."

Xavier continued. "I think that Otto is a puzzle. I actually believe he's a very sophisticated robot. With all these other amazing gadgets, I'd believe someone could create a robot that real. But even if he isn't, he responds to certain rules. He's already told us that precision is very important. When we talk to him, sometimes he responds with the right answer, and sometimes he ignores us altogether."

"So he's just waiting for us to ask the right questions?"

"Exactly. He's not going to tell us where Nina went, but if we ask him the right questions, we'll be able to figure it out for ourselves."

Rowan thought for a moment, then walked back over to Otto. "You said that most people use the alleviators manually. How else can you operate them?"

"The alleviators have a memory," Otto replied. "It's a little bit like instant redial on your telephone. After a patron departs, the machine doesn't reset automatically. The next person to use that machine can call up its last destination by merely hitting the white button to the left of the keypad."

"Which one of these alleviators was used this morning, at the silver hour?"

Otto consulted a log, which he produced out of nowhere. It was written in the same scratchy, inkblot print as his guest book. "Five alleviators were used this morning."

"Which one did Nina use?"

Otto blinked. "I'm sorry, I'm not at liberty to reveal that information."

"Where did the different alleviators go?" Xanthe interrupted. "Can you tell us that?"

"Certainly," Otto replied, again consulting the log. "Number two went to New York City, nineteen ninety. Number three went to Bethlehem, in the year 1 B.C. Number seven went to San Francisco, eighteen forty-nine. Number eight went to the North Pole, nineteen ten. And Number twelve went to Paris, seventeen eighty-nine."

"That's the one," Xavier said grimly. "Paris, seventeen eighty-nine. French Revolution."

"Oh no!" Rowan cried. "She couldn't have picked a worse year!"

"At least we know where she is," Xanthe said. She turned to Otto. "This is the one we want to use."

"Very good. Now, this is an essential piece of equipment," Otto said, handing them each a plastic bag.

"What is it?" Rowan asked, opening his bag. He took out a device that looked like two small, torpedo-shaped microphones held together by a clear filament.

"It's your language interpreter," Otto explained. "You are going to have to speak and understand French perfectly, the way it was spoken in the eighteenth century. That earpiece will automatically translate what you hear into English. The micro-translator muffles whatever you say in English and transmits it in French. There is a very slight delay, so don't worry if it sounds like you are pausing before you say something. Incidentally, when you swallow the microphone, hold on to the filament so that it doesn't go into your stomach. Then attach the other end to one of your molars with that clip so that it stays in your throat."

Xanthe and Xavier followed along with Otto's directions. Xavier cleared his throat. "Excuse me," he said, but it came out "*Excusez-moi.*" He laughed. "*Ecoutez: je peux parle Francais!*" Xavier laughed again.

"*C'est vraiment bizarre*," said Xanthe, nodding. Her eyes widened and she cupped her hands to her mouth, giggling.

Rowan turned the device over in his hands. It felt extremely delicate. When he looked closely at the filament he saw rainbow colors, like a prism. The micro-translator looked very thin and small, and seemed to be made of a soft, flexible material. He was certain he would gag on it.

"If you accidentally swallow it, you'll stop speaking French," Otto continued. "You'll have to come back here for another one or wait for it to 'come out the other end,' so to speak."

Rowan frowned. Otto's voice sounded strange, as though he were walking away from them. When Rowan looked up, he realized that Otto was slowly fading.

"Oh no!" Rowan shouted to Xanthe and Xavier. "Quit cracking up, you guys! We're almost out of time!" Indeed, the sky outside the window was taking on the rosy colors of sunset, and Otto was hardly more than an outline of his former self.

"Quick!" Rowan yelled. "Jump into number twelve!" The three rushed to the last alleviator. Rowan pounded the button, and the doors slid open. Xavier pulled back the inner gate and they clambered inside.

As they shut the gate and pressed the button to close the doors, they heard Otto call out in a voice that sounded like a distant echo, "Enjoy your trip! And don't lose your keys! The only way you can find your way back is to use your key!"

Rowan jabbed the large white button next to the keypad. Suddenly the machine flashed, and the pitch of the hum started to rise. As it got higher, the walls vibrated and shimmered with increasing intensity. Rowan thought he could see the actual atoms moving, the electrons careening past him. He knew he'd lost his balance, but he couldn't tell if he was on the floor or still falling. Now the pitch was so high it was practically inaudible to the human ear, and the flashing had become one great bright whiteness, so white that it hurt his eyes.

As Rowan swooned into unconsciousness, he was seized with sudden dread; in the excitement of the moment he had focused only on their transportation. Now that they'd crossed that hurdle, he remembered just where they were sending themselves, and what horror lay ahead.

CHAPTER FIVE

THE MARQUIS D'ORANGE

Rowan emerged from the great whiteness as though coming up from a deep sleep. He had no idea how long he had been out; it could have been an instant, it could have been years. As he became more alert he felt every neuron is his body crackling, trying to make new connections that his brain could understand. The smells were different, the sounds were different, even the air tasted different. But what confused Rowan most was the eighty-foot-tall hot-air balloon.

It rose before him, a fat, gold-and-blue exclamation point, more oblong than round, decorated with rose-colored swags. A young man stood inside the basket below, burning straw and wool to heat the air that inflated the massive balloon. All around them the crowd shouted and laughed; some people broke into song.

The young man stopped feeding the fire and gestured frantically to a friend, who unwound the ropes that anchored the basket. The balloon lurched upward. The crowd's gasps turned to cheers as it rose higher and higher, now moving across the field at a rapid pace, and they followed this enormous bag of hot air, sometimes east, sometimes north, whichever way the wind blew.

"Rowan! Rowan!"

He turned to see Xanthe waving to him several yards away. As she tottered toward him he noticed that he wasn't the only one who found it hard to walk in high heels.

"Que se passe-t-il?" Xavier said, coming up behind them.

"Je crois que c'est une fête," Xanthe answered.

Rowan frowned, then remembered the translator in his hand. He looked at it, pressed the earpiece into his ear, and swallowed the microphone, clipping the other end to his tooth. It slipped a few times, but he finally felt it click into place as Xanthe finished her thought.

" . . . I think hot-air balloons were just becoming a fad around this time," she said. "Is everyone okay? Rowan?"

"Yeah, yeah," he said. The filament tickled the back of his throat. It would take some getting used to. "We've got to figure out how we're going to find Nina," Rowan answered.

"Well, the sun is setting," Xavier pointed out. "I doubt we'll get much done tonight."

"We should find a place to stay," Xanthe said, rubbing her waist. "I've got to take this corset off. I feel like a squeezed tube of toothpaste."

"I'm hungry," added Xavier.

"Why didn't you eat before we left?" Xanthe chastised.

"Hey, I remembered to go to the bathroom . . ."

"I'm hungry, too," Rowan said, feeling like an umpire. "Let's just get to Paris. We can get settled and come up with a plan."

"Uh, where's Paris?" asked Xavier. "We don't really know where we are. We're at the mercy of that alleviator."

"Otto said the machine was set for Paris, but probably just outside Paris," Xanthe reminded him. "Remember? It's better not to materialize in the middle of a city because it's too crowded. I'm sure this field would've been a great place to land if there hadn't been the balloon-launching festival, or whatever that was."

Rowan scanned the landscape. In the distance, about a hundred yards to the south, he saw a group of horse-drawn carriages.

"Look!" he said. "That's probably how those balloon wor-shipers got here. Let's see if we can grab one of those carriages." Xanthe and Xavier gave no argument, and followed Rowan across the field.

Rowan approached the first carriage. The driver stood with the other drivers enjoying a smoke, but as soon as he saw Rowan he bowed reverentially. Rowan was taken aback at first, but then remembered that he looked like a nobleman and that the driver was only performing a customary gesture.

"We'd like to go to Paris," Rowan stated in his snootiest tone.

"I'm sorry, Monsieur," the driver said. "I'm afraid this carriage is reserved for the Marquis de Marechal. I'd accommodate you, but I dare not offend him by leaving early."

Rowan grimaced and started to move to the next carriage.

"The Marquis de Marechal? What fantastic luck! He's Monsieur's cousin!" blurted Xavier, indicating Rowan, who stared at him in shock.

"I'm sure he wouldn't mind if we borrowed his carriage," Xavier continued, ignoring Rowan. "Just tell him my master, the uh . . . the uh . . . Marquis d'Orange, needed it desperately."

Rowan glanced down at his orange attire and rolled his eyes. Xanthe flicked open her fan and hid behind it, coughing uncontrollably to keep herself from laughing.

"The Marquis d'Orange?" The driver sounded skeptical.

Rowan was convinced this ploy had played itself out when he noticed a heaviness on his waist. He felt the side of his coat and discovered that his pocket contained a money bag . . . a rather heavy money bag. While Xavier continued to lie to the driver, Rowan peeked inside the bag. It was filled with gold coins. He remembered Miss O'Neill saying that she had provided some extra props with their costumes and silently thanked her.

"Perhaps this will sweeten the pot," Rowan said, holding up a coin and trying his best to sound like a nobleman.

The driver's eyes brightened. He snatched the coin and opened the coach door with a flourish. "Thank you, Monsieur!" he said, bowing deeply. "I would be honored to take you to Paris. Please, be careful as you step into the coach . . . it's quite high, Mademoiselle."

As Xanthe took the driver's hand, she got her foot caught in the hem of her dress and fell awkwardly into the coach, exposing her petticoats to anyone who cared to look. Rowan tried to help her up, but couldn't reach her over the mounds of cloth that made up her skirt and underwear. When she finally hoisted herself onto the seat, Rowan pushed in next to her and realized that the dress barely left enough room for either one of them to sit comfortably. Xanthe could only perch on the seat miserably. The driver watched, smirking.

"Mademoiselle seems unused to fine clothing," he sniffed.

"Mademoiselle is a celebrated artist from the United States of America!" Rowan snapped, raising his voice. "She is good friends with Benjamin Franklin! You would do well to hold your tongue in her presence!"

The driver shrank back. "Forgive me, Monsieur, I meant no disrespect. I am a fool. You are most welcome, Mademoiselle. If you are ready, your servant may join me." The driver motioned to his seat at the front of the coach. Xavier hoisted himself up, the driver closed the coach door, and they were off.

As they rolled along the dirt road, across the field, and into the forest, Rowan was pleased with himself. He had taken charge. He'd defended Xanthe's honor. He'd actually made a grown man cringe. Whether it was confidence from the clothes or being light-headed from time travel, he didn't know, but he felt on top of the world. He could get used to this.

"Thanks, that was some quick thinking," Xanthe said. "I almost blew it back there. I really hate this dress."

"You just need practice moving around," Rowan said. "And think of it this way. You are the very first American tourist to make a fool of herself in France. It will become a time-honored tradition."

Xanthe laughed. "So I'm an artist from America, huh? Friends with Ben Franklin? I like it."

"It's the first thing that popped into my mind," Rowan said. "I remembered that after the American Revolutionary War, the French loved anything American. They're totally into scientific stuff, too. What better name to drop than Mr. Electricity himself, Benjamin Franklin?"

"And we were lucky you found that money," Xanthe added. "How much did you give the driver, anyway?"

"I have no idea," Rowan said ruefully. "Probably a million dollars."

They passed a clearing in the forest where the balloon fanatics had gathered. The hot-air balloon had crashed and caught fire. As the pilot sat on a log nursing his wounds, a young man with long brown hair addressed the crowd. He gestured dramatically with his hands. Even without hearing what he was saying, Rowan was struck by his passion. The crowd punctuated his statements with applause and shouts. Part of the group paid him no mind, however. They had broken off to stare at the bonfire, hypnotized by the glittering flame.

By the time the threesome reached Paris, night had fallen. For a city that in the future would be called "The City of Lights," Paris seemed dark and gloomy. Rowan had to remind himself that the Eiffel Tower wouldn't be built for another hundred years, the Arc de Triomphe would have to wait for Napoleon's empire, and the Louvre wasn't an art museum yet, but a royal palace. One building was identifiable however: Notre Dame Cathedral. The enormous Gothic structure, on an island in the center of Paris, stood in silent judgment of the city spread out beneath it.

During the ride, Rowan and Xanthe sketched out their story. Rowan would be the son of a nobleman in search of his sister, who had run away from home for the excitement of the big city. Xanthe would be an artist from America, working under Rowan's father's patronage and studying art in Paris. Xavier would be Rowan's servant, formerly a slave from the Carribean. Rowan had already instructed the carriage driver to take them to a hotel that was reasonable in price and in a central location, so when they pulled in front of the grand, white stone building, Rowan wasn't sure what to expect.

"Well, this isn't the Holiday Inn," he murmured.

"Don't worry," Xanthe assured him, "nobles did so much on credit, we won't have to give very much up front."

They were met at the door by a middle-aged woman with a crisp, businesslike manner. "Good evening, sir. Welcome to the Hôtel Genève. I am Madame Vontighem. How may I help you this evening?"

"We will need a suite, Madame," Rowan replied, using the same snooty tone he had used with the driver. "My friend and I will be staying for . . . no more than a week."

"I believe I can accommodate you and your friend," she replied. "And your servant may sleep in the room next to the kitchen, with the other servants."

Rowan was about to protest, but was stopped by a look from Xavier, who seemed resigned to being a second-class citizen for the next few days. Madame Vontighem consulted her ledger.

"I have two rooms, however they overlook the courtyard of the Palais-Royal. You realize it can be quite noisy at times."

"Noisy?" Rowan asked.

"Yes, always there are women coming and going . . . the cafés . . . the shows . . . they attract all kinds. I hope you are not easily offended." She smiled as though amused by some private joke.

"We'll take it," Rowan said.

"Very good, sir. I'll just call someone to take your bags . . ." Madame Vontighem searched the floor. "Excuse me, sir, but where are your bags?"

Rowan froze. Of course if they were traveling they'd have bags. So where were they? That was a good question.

"Monsieur?" Xavier piped up. "I can relate our unfortunate tale, since I was the one who saw what happened . . ."

"Yes, of course," Rowan said, hoping Xavier knew what he was doing.

"Unfortunately, Madame," Xavier said sorrowfully, "our carriage was attacked in the forest by four men. The driver and I fought them and chased them away before they could rob the Marquis and Mademoiselle Alexander, but they managed to make off with all of the bags."

"Oh! That's a horrible shame," Madame Vontighem clucked. "Especially for Mademoiselle. How frightening! The forest is filled with robbers . . . you're lucky you weren't murdered. People are desperate these days, eh?" She turned to Xanthe. "If you like, tomorrow morning I can direct you to some fine dress shops and tailors, to replace what you've lost . . ."

"Thank you, that would be lovely," Xanthe murmured demurely.

"You have room four, on the second floor. Monsieur, you are in room five. If you are hungry, there is a dining room down the hall. Enjoy your dinner." She gave them a sympathetic smile and handed them their keys.

Rowan and Xanthe ordered their meals and an extra one for Xavier, who had been directed to the kitchen for his dinner. He was supposed to try to sneak into the dining room and join them, but it was twenty minutes before he finally slipped into the room, virtually unnoticed.

"What took you so long?" Xanthe said.

"I got into a conversation," Xavier said. "It's pretty cool in the kitchen, actually. The servants are a lot more easygoing when they're not serving."

"We were just talking about where we should look for Nina," Rowan said. He filled Xavier in on the conversation. He wanted to go to Versailles as soon as possible. He was certain that in his conversation with Nina about the Enlightenment, that was the part that had appealed to her most. Xanthe would hit the boutiques, reasoning that Nina would have to get proper clothes from somewhere.

Xavier nodded thoughtfully, then volunteered to look in the lower-class areas, in case Nina was just living out on the street.

The food arrived. It was a simple meal of chicken, potatoes, and assorted vegetables. The waiter poured them each a glass of wine and left the bottle on the table. They all stared at the glasses, confused.

"Can't he see we're underage?" Rowan whispered.

"I think people our age drink wine here. We're supposed to be melding in . . ." Xavier took a small sip and shrugged.

Rowan tried it and made a face. "Do you think it would be weird for me to ask for a glass of chocolate milk?"

"I think you can get cocoa, " Xanthe reasoned. "That's hot chocolate milk . . ."

"Yeah." Xavier laughed. "But don't ask for a 7-Up."

They ate in silence. Rowan hadn't realized how hungry he was, and the food was fantastic and so fresh. He finished the meal in a matter of minutes. After sopping up the last bit of sauce with some crusty bread and stuffing it into his mouth, he leaned back in his chair.

"Oh man. I ate too fast." Rowan closed his eyes. The girdle was becoming uncomfortable. He massaged his stomach, trying to open up a space for dessert, when Xanthe prodded him.

"Look," she said, pointing out the window that looked onto a courtyard. "That must be the Palais-Royal."

Rowan looked. Though the name suggested that the Palais-Royal was a "royal palace," it seemed to be more like a huge outdoor mall. From the window he could see street performers, cafés, other hotels, and people selling things from carts. And just like at a mall, there were lots of people simply standing around. Nobles with powdered wigs and faces, people in plain clothes of cloth and wool, men in conservative dark suits, soldiers of varying ranks and uniforms, street children, prostitutes; they were all there for an evening of fun, gambling, drinking, and entertainment in what was apparently the hot spot of Paris.

"That's odd," Xavier mused. "I thought there was a class system here. But look at all those different kinds of people hanging out together."

"There is a class system," Xanthe said. "But this place doesn't follow it. One of the books I read at the Owatannauk library said that was part of the attraction. Kind of like going to Atlantic City or Las Vegas."

Xavier's eyes twinkled. "Are you thinking what I'm thinking?"

"Yeah, let's go look around!" Xanthe squealed, jumping from her chair, tripping on the hem of her gown.

"Wait, what about dessert?" Rowan asked, still feeling a bit full.

"There'll be plenty of time for cream puffs," Xavier chided, helping Xanthe to her feet. "But that, my friend, is where it's all happening. Besides, we're in Paris! Let's see some sights!

"I'm not in the mood for sightseeing," Rowan said. "I really think we should focus on finding Nina."

"Rowan," Xanthe began gently, "Nina could be anywhere. But we know one location that she's not. This restaurant. Now, I think we should look around just to get a sense of what this place is. It's not sightseeing, it's investigating. If you have any better ideas, go ahead and suggest something."

Rowan was about to protest when he caught his reflection in the window. The young man staring back at him looked gallant and sophisticated, a man about town. "No, no. You're right. Let's go," Rowan said, standing up. He offered his arm to Xanthe, and felt a small thrill when she took it. Yes, he could get used to this.

Strolling around the Palais-Royal, Rowan was amazed by just how much it contained. There were acrobats, mimes, puppeteers, palm readers, guitar-playing minstrels, and for a little money you could see a four-hundred-pound German sitting on a stool devouring a ham.

Rowan, Xanthe, and Xavier stood in the middle of the avenue, not knowing what direction to take. The ebb and flow of the crowd nudged the three to the side. When they found themselves in front of the Café de Foy, Rowan quickly took a seat at an outdoor gaming table.

"This place rocks!" Xavier said, grinning.

"I don't know," Rowan responded, "it makes me feel kind of . . . creepy. I can't put my finger on it."

"Ugh, maybe it's this," Xanthe muttered. She quickly put down the pamphlet she had been reading.

"What is it?" Rowan asked, reaching for the paper.

"Don't read it," she said. "It's . . . oh, go ahead, if you have to."

Rowan picked up the pamphlet and read it aloud so that it would be translated. It was an essay about the misconduct of the monarchy, focusing on Queen Marie-Antoinette. It said she was an Austrian spy, a spendthrift, a meddler in French politics, and an untrustworthy wife who cheated on her husband. There was a nasty political cartoon of the king stuffing himself with food while the queen reclined on the sofa with a nobleman, naked from the waist down. . . . Rowan put the pamphlet on the table.

"Wow. She's horrible," he said.

"That's a pretty nasty drawing," Xanthe said, wrinkling her nose.

"I guess if you're the queen you can do what you want," Rowan said. "No wonder nobody likes her."

Suddenly a waiter appeared. "Good evening Monsieur, Mademoiselle. The chess table is four cents if you don't order anything," he said. "I have not seen you here before. Are you from out of town?"

"Yes, from outside Normandy," Rowan answered. "We're staying nearby at the Hôtel Genève."

"Very nice place, Monsieur. Very reasonable. What may I get for you and your party this beautiful evening?"

Rowan was about to answer when the waiter suddenly excused himself, and hurried off toward a group of people who were leaving the café. He dashed up to a gentleman wearing a dark green silk coat and bowed deeply. The gentleman had a slight build and small eyes that showed disdain when the waiter took his gloved hand and kissed it.

The waiter returned, his face flushed as though he had just met a rock star. "Forgive me," he said. "You were saying, Monsieur?"

"Who was that gentleman?" Rowan asked.

"Surely you are joking!" The waiter tittered.

Rowan shook his head.

"Oh, I forgot, you're from out of town. He is Philippe Duc d'Orleans, the owner and creator of the Palais-Royal. He is responsible for all of this!" The waiter indicated the Palais-Royal with a sweep of his hand. "The Duc d'Orleans is a man of great talent and power, but truly a man of the people. Now, have you decided on your order, Monsieur?"

"You know, I don't really feel like staying," Rowan said, suddenly very tired.

"I've seen enough, too," said Xanthe. "I can't wait to get out of these clothes. Let's go." The waiter huffed, irritated that his time had been wasted, and rushed to seat another group of people. Rowan and Xanthe started to leave when Xavier stopped them.

"Hey! Did you guys actually read all of this?" He waved the political pamphlet.

"That's practically pornography, Xave," Xanthe said witheringly. "Just leave it there."

"Well, if you two prudes had a little more literary curiosity," Xavier said smugly, "you would've read this part on the last page about the opera."

"What opera?" Rowan asked.

"This says one of the queen's many extravagances is an opera she's commissioning, at some great expense of course, from none other than Wolfgang Amadeus Mozart."

"Mozart!" Rowan cried. "Nina loves Mozart!"

Xavier nodded, scanning the article. "It says she was so impressed by his earlier opera, *The Marriage of Figaro*, that in two days she is sponsoring a recital showcasing the tenor who played Figaro, and it is rumored the music will be provided by none other than the maestro himself, to be followed by a reception where she will be sparing no expense . . ."

Rowan grabbed the pamphlet. "Nina's going to be there. I just know it! She'd never pass up a chance to see Mozart!"

"Do you think she would know about it?" Xanthe asked.

"Well, she's got two days to find out," Xavier pointed out. "If she's at Versailles she definitely knows about it. And if the popularity of this pamphlet is any indication, what's going on at court is what everyone's talking about. There's a good chance she'll hear something."

"Yeah, but that doesn't mean she'll be able to get into Versailles," Xanthe said. "Unless she can fool people into thinking she's a noblewoman. You can't just walk in off the street . . ."

"You guys don't know my sister," Rowan said, excited. "Mozart is like a god to her. And she is a super driven kid. You know, when she was nine she wanted to win this piano contest at a Mozart festival. She practiced night and day, through the weekends. She barely took time to eat or go to the bathroom."

Xavier gave a low whistle. "That's pretty intense."

"She won, of course," Rowan said. "It's amazing how she does it, but she always gets her way. If Mozart is at Versailles, *she will be there.*"

"I guess we should go to Versailles and see if she shows up in two days," Xanthe said.

"Wait a minute . . . I just thought of something." Rowan frowned. "In two days . . . it's going to be July fourteenth . . . Bastille Day!"

"Wow, the queen's actually throwing a big party on Bastille Day?" Xavier said.

"We're the only ones who know it's going to be 'Bastille Day,'" reminded Xanthe. "As far as the queen is concerned, she's just throwing her party on a Tuesday."

"We really don't want to be here for Bastille Day." Xavier shuddered. "We've got to try to find her before that."

Rowan nodded. Xavier was right. According to books in the library, Bastille Day was the beginning of the French Revolution. It was the day that rioters stormed the Bastille, a fortresslike prison in Paris, released its prisoners, and started knocking it down. But the Bastille was more than just a prison. To anyone who wasn't a noble, it was a symbol of evil and oppression. People imprisoned there by order of the king had often been held unjustly, without a fair trial. Underground cells were damp, dark, and infested with rats, worms, and bugs. The food was disgusting. Punishment came in the form of horrific, unspeakable tortures that made prisoners pray for death, and made Rowan ill just thinking about them. When rioters seized the Bastille, they were sending the message that power no longer resided with the king, it resided with the people: the "Republic."

That message, however, came with several days of panic and violence. Nobles became targets, attacked and beaten by mobs, their houses torn apart and their possessions stolen. People raided bakeries for bread and armories for weapons. The palace guard was called out and small battles erupted in the streets of Paris. No one really knew who was in charge.

Even though he knew what was coming, Rowan felt a little better. If they didn't find Nina earlier, there was a good chance they would find her at Versailles in two days. They could leave France quickly then. Suddenly their impossible task had become possible. He folded the pamphlet and put it deep into his pocket, protecting their one and only lead.

CHAPTER SIX

VERSAILLES

A sharp rap on the door woke Rowan the next morning.

"All right sleepyhead," Xanthe called, "let's be on our way. Time's a wastin'." When Rowan opened the door, she looked him over. "You look terrible."

"I know. I fell asleep in my clothes." Rowan checked his pocket watch. "Oh no! It's ten o'clock! Why didn't you get me up sooner?"

Xanthe followed Rowan into his room. She flicked her fan open, practicing her technique in front of his mirror. "I just got up myself. I guess we were a lot more tired than we realized."

"It must be some sort of time-travel jet lag," Rowan said. He opened up a door expecting to find the bathroom. Instead, he found a closet with a low bench that had a hole cut out of it. In the hole was a round, ceramic pot. It took him a moment to realize what the pot was for.

"Have fun," Xanthe said, smirking. "I'll wait for you in the hall."

Rowan couldn't bring himself to go to the bathroom in the pot. All he could think was that some poor servant, who clearly had the worst job in the world, would have to empty it. He opted instead to use the potted plant in the corner, vowing to hold his bowels until he got back to the twenty-first century, with its wonderfully discreet plumbing and soft toilet paper.

"Has Xave come up here?" Xanthe called from the hallway.

"No, I haven't seen him," Rowan responded. "I hope he's not too mad about having to sleep in the servants' quarters." He looked in the mirror and straightened his wig, patting the free-flying strands of hair down as best he could. He reapplied the powder and emerged into the hallway only a little worse for wear.

Xanthe had gotten her fan-flicking technique to an art. When she saw Rowan she shrugged. "Well, it'll have to do. Let's see what Xave's up to."

They found Xavier entertaining the cook. She was doubled over with laughter as he reached what was undoubtedly the climax of his story. Rowan noticed that Xavier had already adopted the flamboyant hand gestures of the French, as well as their lyrical speech pattern; in any language or culture, Xavier was charming. Rowan cleared his throat.

"Ah, Monsieur!" Xavier hopped off the stool and rushed over to Rowan, his hands clutched together deferentially. "Good morning! I hope you slept well! You are looking splendid today! What will you be having for breakfast? What is your will, Monsieur?"

"All right, that's enough," Rowan whispered. "Don't overdo it."

"Is there someplace we can eat something light?" Xanthe asked.

"I ate two hours ago," Xave sniffed. "While you fat, lazy, rich porkers were lolling around in bed, I was helping the servants fire up the oven, chop wood, carry coal, and shine shoes."

"Xave, I'm sorry . . ." Xanthe started.

"Don't be. I wanted to do it. Come on, there's a little café I found around the corner."

Rowan was amazed at how comfortably Xavier blended in with the people of Paris. "If I didn't know any better, I'd swear he'd been born here," Rowan whispered to Xanthe as Xavier greeted merchants they passed in the street.

"Yeah, he's a regular chameleon," Xanthe said.

There was a tinge of something in her voice; Rowan couldn't tell if it was jealousy or concern.

They sat at an outside table at the café and Xavier ordered three hot chocolates, bread, and cheese. "I found out why they don't drink a lot of water," Xavier said when the waiter left to get their order. "Can you smell something in the air?"

Rowan raised his nose and detected the sweet, rank smell of raw sewage. He recalled smelling it on their way into the city, but he'd forgotten about it once they were inside the hotel. "Smells like garbage," said Rowan. "What is it?"

"Garbage," Xavier answered. "Remember those maps of Paris Miss O'Neill showed us in the library? They showed that the city is surrounded by the River Seine. Well, that water is used for just about everything. Washing clothes, dumping garbage, going to the bathroom and—surprise!—cooking and drinking. They may boil it and try to filter out the bad stuff, but this being the eighteenth century, I don't think you're going to get the clean, fresh taste of bottled mountain water."

"Yechhh. Thanks for the tip," Rowan said, feeling slightly queasy. "Look, I want to get to Versailles as soon as possible. Do we all know what we're doing today?"

"Dress shops for me," Xanthe said. "And the art galleries. Supposedly the intellectuals gossiped about everything there. Maybe they'll be talking about a new face in town."

"I've got a full day planned," Xavier said. "There are a lot of back alleys to explore. In fact, since I've already eaten, I'm just going to go now. Let's meet at Rowan's room at, say . . . well, how about the golden hour? We can eat dinner then. Sound good?"

"Xavier, be careful," Xanthe warned. "Don't be reckless. You're a stranger here. And you *do* stand out, no matter how much you think you blend in. Your skin, I mean."

"Don't worry about me." Xavier laughed. "I've gotten some looks, but no one has bothered me. It's not like being black in the South after the Civil War. Honestly, Xanthe, I feel more comfortable here then in a lot of places in modern America." He rose and put a hand on Rowan's shoulder.

"We'll find Nina, Rowan. I can feel it. See you guys at seven!" Xavier turned and rushed down the street.

"He's great, Xanthe," Rowan said. "I thought he'd hate having to be servant, but he's so enthusiastic about it!"

"That's what worries me," Xanthe sighed. "Xavier's impulsive. I just hope he doesn't do something stupid."

None of the pictures Rowan had seen of Versailles could have prepared him for the vast building that rose before him now. As his carriage rolled through the palace grounds it was nearly impossible for him to take it all in: the Swiss Guard executing drills on the parade grounds, the gilded gateway crowned with the arms of France, the brisk traffic of ministers of state and noblemen in the main courtyard, and of course the palace itself.

Rowan had only been to a handful of impressive buildings in his life. There was the Empire State building, the Chrysler building, and the Plaza Hotel in New York, and he had once been on a tour of the White House. Versailles didn't look like any of them. It was covered with ornate carvings, gilded with gold paint, and was shaped like a U, so that as you approached the main door the wings of the building reached out, drawing you in. The palace was not just grand, it was intimidating.

He was relieved to see that there were no guards checking people for passes. Apparently nobody questioned the presence of nobles at the palace. Though he felt like an imposter, his clothing gave him confidence, and he quickly crossed the courtyard and into the palace, the seat of the monarchy.

Two noblemen, or courtiers, whisked up the stairs in heated conversation. Rowan followed in their wake, hoping to blend in.

"My dear Gerard," said the tall, slender one dressed in deep maroon with several rows of curls rolling down his wig. "It should have been *my* honor to hand the king his dressing gown this morning. I believe you have been relegated to *stockings*, with all due respect."

Gerard, a wide-shouldered man dressed in blue and gold with a large, blue bow holding back a four-inch-long powdered ponytail, shook his head vehemently. "No, no, my dear Bertrand, it is *my* honor to hand the king his dressing gown. Your bow yesterday was so awkward the king found it quite offensive. As such, it is *you* who must reacquaint yourself with his stockings, and I will continue as handler of the royal dressing gown."

"But my back has been injured!" cried Bertrand. "I cannot lean forward without causing myself great pain, to the point of near madness. I daresay I nearly swooned with my last attempt!"

"Ah, la la, 'tis a pity indeed," clucked Gerard. "But what can I say? You should make the effort when given the opportunity to hold clothing of such great importance. What is a mere pinch in your back when compared to the glory of the king's dressing gown?"

They continued on with what Rowan thought was probably the dumbest conversation he'd ever heard. Still, he wondered what it would be like if your only problem in life was whether or not it was your turn to hand somebody his pajamas.

He followed them as they glided along the corridor. They

looked so beautiful, waving to the other powdered people dressed in exquisite silks and velvets. *Like a doll's house,* Rowan thought. *Unreal.* Just watching them lifted his spirits. It was *fun* to be a courtier. He tried to imitate them, moving with a fluidity that felt like ballet. He imagined a fanfare of trumpets announcing his arrival. As he puffed his chest out and lifted his nose his eyes were drawn to the domed, painted ceilings where cherubs, Roman gods, and heroes beckoned to him, inviting him into their world.

Suddenly he lost his balance. He had failed to notice that Gerard and Bertrand had stopped walking and were demonstrating to each other what an appropriate bow should look like. Rowan caught his foot on Gerard's cane and fell face-first onto the polished parquet floors.

"Monsieur! Do watch where you're going!" Gerard scolded, as Rowan brushed himself off.

"Are you all right?" Bertrand inquired, offering his hand.

"I'm sorry . . . I was looking at the ceiling," Rowan muttered.

"Why, whatever for?" asked Gerard. "What's on the ceiling?"

"The paintings," Rowan answered. The two fops exchanged glances, clearly of the opinion that Rowan was the biggest bumpkin they'd ever met.

"I'm new here," Rowan explained, "and I was hoping somebody might show me around."

"Young man," Gerard answered with a withering stare. "We are far too busy with important matters to give guided tours."

"Just so, just so," Bertrand added, nodding his head vehemently. "Very important business at hand. You'll have to find
somebody else. Now do show me that bow again, dear Gerard," he said, turning back to his friend.

"I'd be delighted." Gerard bent deeply over his pointed toe,
drawing his arm back with a graceful flourish.

"This is important?" Rowan said aloud. The two men
turned to him, annoyed.

"You certainly aren't going to get very far in this court
with that attitude," Gerard sniffed.

"He says he's 'new.' He's probably bought his title and
doesn't know what to do with it," Bertrand whispered loudly
to his friend. Gerard nodded suspiciously.

"I don't know where you're from, Monsieur," Gerard said.
"But here we pay attention to appearances. I suggest you mind
yours. Every gesture, every expression, every nuance of your
behavior will be noted and interpreted. Take care you don't
misrepresent yourself. That is, if you have any social aspirations at all."

"I'm not here for social aspirations," Rowan answered.

"I suppose you don't have your sights on handing the king
his stockings!" Bertrand spat.

"No, not particularly."

Bertrand eyed him skeptically, then shrugged.

Gerard turned to Rowan. "We have a pressing engage-
ment," he said. "We are on our way to watch his royal highness dine. You're welcome to join us. Anyone who is of any
importance is going to be there."

"You know what? Thanks for the invitation, but I think I'll pass," Rowan said.

"Are you quite sure?" Bertrand asked. "He's having lamb chops."

"Tempting, but no," Rowan answered. "I've got pressing business of my own."

The two courtiers exchanged glances again, silently communicating their agreement that they were in the presence of a hopeless nincompoop, then turned on their heels and disappeared into the next parlor.

Rowan wanted to rest his aching feet. He sat on a velvet stool and wiggled his toes. He saw a number of women being escorted by men, and groups of teenage girls huddling together in secretive conversations, erupting every few minutes in squeals and giggles. The only young girl he saw was with her parents. Rowan tried to figure out where Nina would go in a palace. Perhaps if there was a library or a music room . . .

"Good afternoon, Monsieur, I don't believe I've ever seen you here before."

Rowan turned to see a pleasant-looking man dressed in a brown-and-gold silk jacket and breeches. His simple powdered wig was tied into a ponytail with a bright, gold ribbon. He held a walking stick. He didn't seem to be quite as ridiculous as Gerard and Bertrand, and something about his manner put Rowan at ease.

"No, Monsieur," Rowan answered. "This is my first visit to this magnificent palace. I am a stranger to these parts, but have heard of the culture and style of Versailles. I must say, I am not disappointed." He threw in some hand flourishes for good measure, and ended with a mid-level bow, which seemed to impress the man in brown.

"Welcome, friend, welcome," the man said. "I am Emile Lavois, Comte de Giverney. I, too, was a stranger to the palace only a month ago. But it is not difficult to find your way around here. May I ask what brings you to Versailles?"

"Very sad business, I'm afraid," Rowan answered. "I am Rowan Popplewell, son of the Marquis d'Orange. I have come here in search of my sister. She ran away from home to seek the excitement of court life."

"Ah, well you are in luck then," Emile said, cocking his head. "My wife, Jeanette, is quite the social butterfly. She knows everything about everyone in the palace; nothing escapes her eye. If there is a new young lady at court, I'm sure Jeanette would know about her."

"She's only eleven years old," Rowan said, encouraged. "She has dark wavy hair and green eyes. Her name is Nina."

Emile nodded, and pursed his lips. He seemed to be appraising Rowan.

"I'd appreciate any assistance you can give me, Monsieur. It is very generous of you to offer your help in reuniting my family . . ."

"Actually," Emile interrupted, "I am perhaps not as generous as you believe. There is a favor you could do for me as well. If you agree, then we can call ourselves even."

"What sort of favor, Monsieur?" Rowan asked warily.

"Please. 'Emile.'" He drew Rowan to the side of the room. "Let us speak as friends, Rowan. I have a daughter who needs an escort. It's unseemly for a young woman of quality to be always traipsing about on her own, as is her tendency. I would appreciate it if you spent some time with her. Be her companion at the promenade tonight. I must warn you, she is willful and stubborn, and not particularly beautiful. She needs to be gentled and learn how to behave like a noblewoman. In three years she must be ready for marriage. Who knows? Perhaps you will find you have much in common . . ."

Rowan hesitated. Emile could try to be as diplomatic about it as he wanted, but it was obvious his daughter was a major loser.

"My dear Emile," Rowan began tactfully. "I think you may mistake my years, for I am large for my age. I'm only thirteen . . ."

Emile waved him off. "Perfect! You are the same age. Those are my conditions. As long as you spend time with my daughter, keep her from being so independent and running about like a field rat, I will help you search for your sister. If we are agreed on these terms, I'll introduce you to her."

Rowan mustered a tight smile and nodded. What choice did he have? He would do anything he could to find Nina. The fact that he'd never been set up with a girl before wasn't going to stop him. His hands started to sweat.

He followed Emile back through the series of drawing rooms, downstairs, into a marble courtyard, and through a central vestibule, finally arriving on a terrace that overlooked a lush landscape. Everywhere Rowan looked he saw flowers, hedges, trees, and fountains, and large, geometrically perfect tracts of grass. It reminded him of how much his mother loved gardening. She'd always kept lots of plants on their patio, along with a collection of stone animals that he and Nina had named, pretending that they were pets. His mother spent hours poring over gardening books. When they strolled through Prospect Park on Sunday afternoons, she could name every green thing they saw.

After walking for what seemed like a full mile, Rowan followed Emile into a grove of chestnut trees. There, on a stone bench with her back to them, sat a girl, furiously sketching a fountain.

"Louise!" Emile called out.

She took no notice of them until they were practically on top of her. Suddenly she turned her piercing blue eyes on them, regarding Rowan as one might a garden slug. She stood, unsmiling. "Yes, dear father?"

Rowan understood why Louise's father didn't consider her beautiful. She had broad features, a ruddy complexion, and a stocky, healthy build; nothing at all like the pale, tiny waisted women inside the palace. To Rowan's twenty-first century tastes however, she looked athletic and fantastic. Despite her clear disgust of him, he was captivated.

"This is Monsieur Rowan Popplewell, son of the Marquis d'Orange," began Emile. "Rowan, this is my daughter, Louise." He placed both hands on his daughter's shoulders. "Monsieur Popplewell has generously offered to walk with you at the promenade this evening. It's important that you be there. I hope you will be hospitable, and show him how charming you can be. We're not here for the scenery, my dear."

Louise rolled her eyes.

Emile pulled Rowan aside. "Ignore her bad temper," he said. "She'll be wonderful company . . . once she realizes she has no choice."

"Perhaps this was a mistake," Rowan suggested, but Emile waved him off.

"She has to learn," he said simply. "She's not a child anymore, she's becoming a woman. She has to learn her place." He started off, then turned back. "I'll talk to my wife about your sister," he said, then disappeared from the grove.

Louise immediately resumed sketching. Rowan watched as she deftly moved the charcoal pencil across the paper. She was quite good, he thought, though he really didn't know much about art. He looked at what she was drawing; a statue of an enormous, bearded man, half-buried under a pile of rubble. He knew at this point he should try to make small talk; unfortunately, that was not his best skill, and he proved this by offending her with the very first thing he said.

"Of all the fountains I've seen in this garden," he began, "this has got to be the ugliest." He regretted saying it as soon as it left his mouth, but it was true. All the other statues were graceful, beautiful forms. This one was grotesque.

"To you it is ugly," Louise said, still sketching. "To me, tragic."

"Tragic how? What is it?" Rowan asked.

Louise stopped sketching and gave him a withering look, apparently trying to decide whether to be friendly or not. Finally, she put down her drawing materials. "This is the fountain of Enceladus. Are you familiar with him?" After Rowan shook his head she continued. "Enceladus was one of the ancient Titans in Roman mythology. He attempted, with the other Titans, to climb Mount Olympus to dethrone Jupiter. Jupiter defeated them, however, and buried them under a mass of rocks. Here, Enceladus is struggling for survival. The water shooting from his mouth is his life force gushing out of him."

"And why is that tragic?"

"I'm sure it isn't to everybody. But I sympathize with his pain; he's been destroyed, ruined, and forgotten in the muck while the gods celebrate in the clouds."

Rowan was suddenly aware that Louise was not at all like her father. She couldn't care less about manners and appearances, in fact, she openly rejected them. And it didn't matter how much "training" Emile tried to give her, she would never marry a titled aristocrat. To her, he realized, the Titans were the people of France, Jupiter was the monarchy, and she was revealing her political position as a patriot. Rowan thought of all the wasted hours Emile must have put into trying to tame Louise's spirit and stifled a laugh. Louise raised her eyebrows, confused.

"I'm sure if Monsieur thinks tragedy is funny, it is a joke that escapes me." She started gathering her materials.

"No, please, I wasn't laughing at you," Rowan said,

stopping her with a hand on her arm. "I'm laughing because I understand you, and because you are so different from the people here in Versailles, and because . . . because I know your future," he said, suddenly somber. He *did* know her future. Did she? Could she even imagine? "Please," Rowan said, "walk with me. I admit I only met you as a favor to your father, and I don't expect you to like me. But I hope you'll give me a chance. Not everyone is what they appear to be."

The corners of Louise's mouth threatened a smile. She finished gathering her art materials, and they made their way out of the grove to the long lawn that stretched out along the east-west axis of the garden.

"Your father said you're not just here for the scenery," Rowan said. "What did he mean by that?"

"I'm here to learn how to be a noblewoman," Louise answered. "Father's worried because my two older sisters were both married by the time they were sixteen. He doesn't think I'll attract anyone because of my disposition. I was thrown out of the convent, you know, for speaking my mind too much." She shrugged. "I really don't care. I want to be an artist . . . a painter. Not somebody's wife."

"Can't you be both?" Rowan asked.

"Now how do you think I could manage that?" Louise laughed. "A wife's duty is to please her husband and raise her children. Art is its own master. It is a passion, no?"

Rowan shrugged his agreement, though passion was something he knew little about.

"My father means well," Louise continued. "He wanted so badly to be a nobleman. We're not noble by birth, you know. He's a businessman. He manufactures fabric in Lyon. He's been the primary supplier for the court and it's made him quite wealthy, so he went and bought himself a title. Count. It's really pathetic in my opinion, but it was his big dream. And he's matched my sisters up with noblemen who are so poor and desperate they would do anything for money. They get to lead the lifestyle they think they deserve, and my father gains social legitimacy. Everybody wins, right?"

"It sounds like you disagree with him."

"He only wants to be equal," Louise mused. "It's just that his methods are a bit old-fashioned."

When they got to the end of the lawn, Louise pointed to a fountain with a statue of a man wearing nothing but a cloak, with a wreath encircling his brow. He emerged from the water on a chariot pulled by four powerful stallions, surrounded by leaping dolphins.

"This is the fountain of Apollo," Louise said. "It's supposed to be his birth from the water as he begins his journey across the sky. It was King Louis the Fourteenth's favorite fountain, of course. Apollo, the Sun King. Lord of the sky, center of the universe."

"It's beautiful," murmured Rowan. He didn't bother to point out that the sun was only the center of this solar system. His attention had been captured by the reflection of the water dancing against the bronze, and the whole image was made even more lovely by the fact that the sun was low, and the golden hour was upon them. His eyes were drawn to Louise. As she gazed toward the pool, her hair moved gently in the warm breeze. He knew he was wasting time, and yet he didn't want to leave. He noticed Louise frowning at him.

"What is it?" she asked. Rowan shook off his reverie.

"Forgive me," he said. "But I was distracted by . . . by the beauty of the scenery." Then, with a sudden burst of bravado he blurted, "It's the golden hour, you see, the time of day when everything seems vibrant and beautiful. It's become my favorite time of day. I look forward to it, and I'm never disappointed."

"Oh really?" Louise gave him a hard look. "You should beware of illusions. What seems beautiful by a trick of light is not true beauty. In fact, it's often just the opposite."

"I thought artists were always interested in what is beautiful . . ."

"No, not beauty. Truth. If it's real and natural, then it is beautiful. I hate this fountain. To me, it's ridiculous."

Rowan shook his head, not comprehending.

"Look." Louise pointed. "The chariot is heading from west to east, when everyone knows the sun travels east to west. So why is Apollo going the wrong way? It's no accident. He's heading toward Versailles. The sculptor contradicted nature just to flatter the king. But it's all wrong, you see."

Rowan nodded.

"Your golden hour doesn't last very long," Louise added, heading toward the palace. "No matter how beautiful it is, once it's gone, you're faced with the black of night."

• • •

After Louise left Rowan, agreeing to meet him after dinner for the promenade, he spent the next hour and a half looking for his sister. His exploration took him past almost all of the fountains and through miles of perfectly manicured gardens. He was disappointed but not surprised that he didn't find her. He felt like he was trying to hit a moving target . . . if she was even there at all. He hoped Xanthe or Xavier were having more luck. He was about to search inside the palace again when he realized that he was going to be late meeting Louise and rushed to the grove where the promenade was supposed to take place.

Rowan knew he was dead as soon as he saw the dance floor. He'd thought that by "promenade" Emile had meant that he and Louise would be strolling around a garden with a group of people, perhaps arm in arm, but definitely *walking*. That by itself would be a challenge, given his uncomfortable shoes and the enormous skirts through which he'd have to navigate. But he didn't expect to have to *dance*. Group dancing had been Rowan's nemesis ever since the Hokey Pokey. He was the kid who was always putting his right leg out while everyone else was putting their right leg in.

As he took Louise's hand, he glanced around to see what the other couples were doing. It was a strange hop-skip step that ended with each partner turning to each other and bowing or curtseying. It looked easy enough, but in no time Rowan had kicked Louise in the shins and knocked into the neighboring couple. As he apologized he stepped on the skirt of a woman behind him, ripping her petticoat. Her escort stepped up to him, his eyes blazing.

"You clumsy imbecile," the man hissed. "I should cut your legs off for ruining her gown. I've done worse for less."

Rowan's eyes were drawn to the jeweled handle of a rapier sword hanging at the man's hip. He gulped. "I'm sorry," he stammered. "Please, I feel terrible . . . it was an accident . . ."

The man stared at him coldly. Rowan suddenly realized that it was Philippe, the Duc d'Orleans, the very same man that the waiter had fawned over at the Palais-Royal.

"I don't want to see you again," Philippe said. "Make sure that I don't."

Louise pulled Rowan off the floor and over to the entrance to the grove, then broke out laughing. "You are no dancer," she finally said, composing herself.

"I . . . guess I'm not," Rowan said, starting to laugh as well. "I recognize that man, you know." Rowan gestured to Philippe, who had taken the young woman off the dance floor.

"So?" Louise retorted. "Who wouldn't know the king's cousin?"

"The king's *cousin*?" Rowan said, bewildered. "I thought . . . doesn't he own the Palais-Royal in Paris?"

"You really aren't from around here, are you? You'd better watch out for him. He's something of a snake. And quite dangerous."

Somebody put a hand on Rowan's shoulder, and he jumped, but relaxed when he saw it was Emile.

"Rowan, Louise," Emile said happily. "I hope you two are enjoying yourselves."

"Yes, Monsieur," Rowan answered.

"Yes, Papa," Louise added slyly. "Monsieur Popplewell is quite amusing."

"I have some good news," Emile continued. "My wife says that there is a new handmaiden at the court. She is a young girl, black hair. Perhaps this is the sister you've been seeking."

"What's her name?" Rowan asked breathlessly.

"She couldn't tell me more than that," Emile said. "She did tell me that the girl is employed in the kitchen at the Hamlet. And you are in luck. Jeanette alerted the gracious lady who presides over the Hamlet to your problem. You have been invited to join her for dinner. You can go and see this girl for yourself."

"'The Hamlet?'" Rowan asked. "Where is that?"

"The Hamlet is a small farm at the edge of Versailles," Emile said. "I can direct you there. But you should leave now. The gracious lady of whom I speak is the queen, and it's very poor manners to keep her waiting."

CHAPTER SEVEN

THE QUEEN

Rowan walked quickly through the wooded glade. He had already passed what looked like a large country house, and then a smaller country house, so according to Emile's directions he should be very close to the Hamlet. A horse cart driven by a milkmaid clattered by, which he took to be a good sign.

He twisted his sleeves nervously. Everything he knew about Queen Marie Antoinette was what he'd read in the pamphlet at the Palais-Royal, which cast her as frivolous, greedy, cruel, and sneaky. Unfortunately, he hadn't bothered to read about her in the Owatannauk library; he hadn't expected to ever meet her.

Moreover, he was afraid Emile's wife had told the queen a whole host of lies in order to secure this meeting. Emile told him that he'd been described as charming, amusing, and a remarkable conversationalist. Emile claimed it was the only way to ensure that Rowan would get an audience; Marie

Antoinette was always eager to meet amusing people. He cautioned Rowan not to ask anything from her directly, explaining that she was hounded constantly by people seeking favors. "What she values is friendship and loyalty. She treats her favorites well, but is suspicious of strangers."

Rowan sighed. His mouth was dry and his hands were growing clammy. Then he noticed that the horse cart that had passed him earlier was now barreling at him.

The driver waved frantically for him to get out of the way. As Rowan dove to the side of the road, he noticed the royal emblem, the fleur-de-lis, painted on the wagon. The milkmaid stopped the cart and got out. Rowan was livid; he'd broken a heel.

"I am so sorry, Monsieur," she said when she reached him. "That horse is very spirited . . ." She brushed some of the dust off him then threw up her hands. "Ah! It's useless, you're a mess!"

"You should look where you're going!" Rowan erupted. "I'm supposed to have dinner with the queen! I can't meet her looking like this!" The woman started to laugh. Rowan felt his neck get hot. "You think this is *funny*? You won't think it's so funny when I tell the queen you've been taking joy rides in her horse cart!"

"There is no need to tell her," the woman replied, raising an eyebrow. "You see, I *am* the queen."

Rowan gaped, seeing now what he had missed before: the porcelain skin, the exquisite hands, the commanding gaze, the fine, tapered fingers. She had tucked her strawberry blond hair under a maid's cap, and wore a jumper of brown worsted wool over a loose, cotton blouse, but it was unmistakably Queen Marie Antoinette. He had only seen paintings of her, of course. There was no way he could know that she would be so vibrant.

She laughed, a sound like ringing crystal. Rowan opened his mouth to say something, but nothing came out. Finally he bowed low, practically hitting his knees with his head and squeaked, "Your Highness, I . . . I . . . I'm so sorry . . ." The queen grabbed his shoulders and straightened him up.

"Please, no formalities here. I prefer 'Antoinette' when I am relaxing. Besides, I should apologize to you. I came out here to meet you, and instead almost killed you. Come, let's get you cleaned up. Dinner should be ready." They climbed into the cart. Antoinette raised the whip, cracked it once, and they sped off like bats out of hell.

The queen's Hamlet resembled a quaint country village. It had thatched-roof cottages, a mill, a dairy, and even a fishery. Cows, sheep, goats, ducks, geese, and hens completed the setting.

As they pulled up in front of a particularly large cottage, they were greeted by a group of refined young women, all dressed as country maids. Rowan scanned their faces to see if Nina was among them. She wasn't.

Antoinette stepped out of the cart and gestured to Rowan. "Ladies, I'd like you to meet Monsieur Rowan Popplewell, son of the Marquis d'Orange. He will be our dinner guest tonight."

"Welcome to the Hamlet, Monsieur," said one strikingly beautiful young woman.

She offered her hand to Rowan. He took it gingerly, hoping she wouldn't notice how sweaty his palms were. Now what? Was he supposed to kiss it? He chose to offer her a slight bow instead. She smiled slyly. "You have a wonderful opportunity to view the many pleasures of the queen's sanctuary . . ." she continued, "though perhaps not *all* the pleasures."

The other women giggled at her joke. Rowan had the sudden impulse to bolt. It felt like the junior high cafeteria all over again. Antoinette drew him down from the cart, locked her arm in his, and led him to the main house. She was talking about various features of the Hamlet, but all Rowan could hear was his heart pounding.

The Hamlet's rustic exterior did not extend into the main house, which was as lavish as the palace. A large banquet table, laid with a lace tablecloth, silverware, and silver candelabras, was set in an elegant drawing room.

Rowan quickly excused himself and went into a private washroom. He immediately splashed cold water on his face and took a couple of deep breaths. He wished Xavier was with him; he'd know how to handle a bunch of women. Rowan removed his jacket to brush off the dust and saw that his shirt was damp with sweat. He straightened his wig and reapplied the powder to his face, but there wasn't much he could do about the heel.

As he washed his hands he looked out the window. He saw a fake creek turning the waterwheel at the fake mill, which led to the man-made lake. He figured that the water was pumped back to the top of the creek so that it could flow past the mill all over again. The Hamlet was bizarre. It was like visiting Disneyland as an older kid, seeing beyond the audio-animatronic puppets and the fiberglass rocks, noticing the eyes peering out of Mickey Mouse's mouth and knowing it's all fake, all wrong, not true. He knew what Louise would say—ridiculous.

He also wondered whether the water flowing through this man-made landscape, or the water that gushed from the many fountains at Versailles, came from the smelly River Seine. It didn't seem likely. The air here was perfumed with flowers, not garbage. Versailles felt far removed from Paris and its problems. You could almost forget it even existed.

Rowan was starving. He'd gotten a lot of exercise walking the grounds of Versailles. His hunger was becoming stronger than his discomfort with the queen's circle of friends. Besides, he was here on a mission. He had to find out if Nina was here, or if anyone had seen her. He pounded his chest once for strength, strode purposefully into the dining room, and took his seat next to the queen. Dinner started immediately.

The last time Rowan had eaten this much he was at the "all-you-can-eat shrimp buffet" at the Barnacle Barrel seafood restaurant in Brooklyn. This food was much better. He lost count of all the courses as they made small talk over rich soups, fluffy puddings, and a roasted goose with a savory plum-and-cherry sauce.

Strangely enough, the women did seem to find Rowan amusing. He quickly realized that they laughed at just about everything. They laughed when he told of how he was almost run over by the queen. They howled at his description of the balloon festival. The queen's mood, however, had changed since their meeting. She stared into space, twisting the chain of a small, heart-shaped locket around her fingers.

Because of her despondency, Rowan felt uncomfortable asking about Nina. Now, over dessert, he was wondering if he would ever get a chance. He was also becoming impatient with all the chatter. The women reminded him of Gerard and Bertrand, with their posing and preening and constant babbling about nothing of any real importance. Finally the queen shook off her mood and decided they should all play cards.

"Do you play?" she asked him.

"Yes, quite a bit," he lied. Emile told him that the queen loved gambling. Perhaps it would be a way into her trust.

"We like to play a game called 'Truth,'" Antoinette said brightly. "Whoever has the best hand gets to ask whoever has the worst hand a question, and the loser must be absolutely honest in his . . . or her . . . answer. The winner is the person who asks a question that the other person will not, or cannot, answer truthfully. Are you game?"

Rowan nodded, and she dealt the first hand.

Fortunately, the game was a version of poker, which Rowan had learned years ago from his father. Unfortunately, right from the beginning he was dealt the worst hand twice in a row. First, he was asked if he had a girlfriend, to which he answered no. That sent the women into shrieks and protestations that he must tell the truth. Then, as luck would have it, the next winner asked about his reason for coming to Paris. Rowan eagerly described his search for Nina, and his suspicion that she might present herself as a servant so that no one would question her age. The women all seemed moved, but the queen most of all.

"I am sorry, Rowan," she said. "As a surprise, I had instructed my new handmaiden, the one which Jeanette referred to, to serve us dinner tonight. You have seen her all evening. If she was your sister, you would have noticed her."

Rowan's heart fell. The girl who had been serving them was certainly not Nina.

"I would not know of any new servants at Versailles," Antoinette continued. "And I do not know the people who flock to the main palace very well. Other than Jeannette Lavois, I do not enjoy their company. I choose my friends very carefully," she added with a twinge of sadness. "Especially now. You can't be too careful who you allow into your confidence."

Rowan was afraid he was losing her. "One thing my sister is particularly fond of is Mozart," he blurted out. "I've heard there is going to be a recital . . ."

"Ah yes, yes." Antoinette nodded. "You are very welcome to come. I will put your name on the list. And afterward we are going to have a masquerade ball. They are quite amusing. Bring a costume. We're going to have a contest at midnight."

They continued to play cards. Now that Rowan felt his mission was a bust he wanted to leave. He'd completely forgotten about meeting Xanthe and Xavier for dinner and knew they must be worried or angry or both. But every time he got up to go the queen insisted he stay. As the night wore on, the women started drifting away until the only card players left were Rowan, two other women, and Antoinette.

Rowan finally won a hand. The person with the worst hand that round was Antoinette. Rowan felt slightly woozy from the wine sauce on the goose and the liqueur in the dessert. Whether or not this was to blame for his presumption he couldn't say, but he asked Antoinette the question that had been bothering him all night.

"Antoinette," he said boldly. "Why all this?" Rowan indicated the room and the larger world outside with a sweep of his hand. "What's the point? You're the queen of France, you could have anything you want. What are you doing on a farm?"

Antoinette's eyes widened and Rowan immediately remembered that he was on very thin ice, considering that she was a queen and he was a junior high school student. But before he could apologize, she had started her answer, measuring her words carefully.

"I like it here because it's as far away as I can get from the palace," Antoinette said, her blue-gray eyes hard and piercing. "I'm quite alone there, you see. Queen. Hah! Sometimes I wish I'd never become queen."

Rowan could tell he had hit a nerve. Antoinette settled back in her chair, and stared past Rowan. He felt uncomfortable, as though he were eavesdropping on her.

"I was so carefree as a girl in Vienna," Antoinette continued. "What I would give to go back! Ah well. As I said before, I have few friends, but the few I have are always welcome here. We sing, we hold recitals, we play cards, perform theatricals . . . and I am free. Free of those clothes, free of those . . . people. People with tight smiles, people who judge every little move or gesture. I suppose you could say I use this as an escape from politics. It's funny, Louis never lets me give him political advice, and yet I am embroiled in it."

"I'm sorry," Rowan interrupted, "but I'm not following you." He wanted to leave. *She shouldn't be telling me all this,* he thought.

"Louis is modernizing all of Paris; digging a sewer system, installing street lamps—but the people are hungry, so that is all they care about. And they are angry so they look for a scapegoat, which unfortunately is me. Did I cause the wheat shortage? Of course not. But my reputation is under a warped magnifying glass, where small mistakes become enormous, and generous intentions become twisted. So everything is my fault." Antoinette held up her skirt. "My clothes, for instance. I am accused of spending too much money on my wardrobe. But you can see I prefer simple dress, not the heavy brocade and silk of the court. I've shown the accountants figures that prove I have spent less on clothing than even the old king's mistresses, and what is the result? I am accused of bringing a depression upon the textile industry!

"Here's another example of how blind the people can be," Antoinette said, leaning forward. "It's about a piece of jewelry . . ." One of the women murmured her reservations, but Antoinette waved her off.

"Years ago, the court jeweler, Monsieur Bohmer, created a horribly gaudy riviére style diamond necklace for the old king's mistress, Madame du Barry. This monstrosity had six hundred and forty-seven diamonds, and it cost one million, six hundred thousand livres. Unfortunately, the king died before they could deliver it, and Monsieur Bohmer was stuck with an item that was really suitable for only the most brazen courtesan.

"Now, I admit that in my youth I had a weakness for diamonds. But I was already aware of how closely the public watched my purchases; to add such an extravagant item to my possessions was unwise. When Monsieur Bohmer begged me to buy it from him I told him I could not. I thought that was the end of it.

"Months later, Cardinal de Rohan, a man whom I detest, confronted me with a bill for the riviére diamond necklace. He claimed I'd asked him to purchase it for me. I was shocked! I had no idea what he was talking about. He appealed to Louis, and told him a tale so outrageous that I'd say it was absolutely unbelievable, except that the Cardinal de Rohan is such an idiot, he was the perfect boob for this fiasco."

One of the ladies leaned toward Rowan. "Cardinal de Rohan is somebody Antoinette has avoided since she arrived in France," she whispered. "He was a terrible ambassador to Vienna and alienated Antoinette's mother, the empress of Austria. Antoinette wouldn't even look at the cardinal, let alone speak to him. Subsequently he became a social outcast within the court."

"To think I'd actually ask him to do anything for me is absurd!" Antoinette spat. "Anyway, it turns out the whole thing started when the cardinal had been approached by a young woman named Jeanne de la Motte, who claimed to be one of my intimate friends. She told him he could regain my favor by donating to my favorite charities. For months she tricked the cardinal into giving her huge sums of money. She even went so far as to hire an actress to dress up as me, wearing a veil I suppose, to meet the cardinal at a midnight rendezvous. Eventually Jeanne de la Motte got this poor, stupid man to buy that necklace with the assurance that I'd pay him back. He waited for months for me to wear this thing that I never asked for, nor ever received. Finally, when he asked me for reimbursement, the story came out."

"Surely Jeanne was caught once the cardinal explained what had happened," Rowan said as Antoinette paused to light a cigarette.

"Yes, she was," Antoinette answered, blowing a long stream of smoke before settling back in her chair. "She was caught, and there was a trial. All of the people involved were tried in court. One by one, each was let go."

Rowan blinked, uncomprehending. "But . . ."

Antoinette held up her hand. "The French love what appeals to their emotions, no? The lawyer for the defense knew that and used it. Cardinal de Rohan was depicted as a victim; a trusting, simple soul who only wanted to please the queen. The actress was presented as a poor, vulnerable orphan, tempted by Jeanne's promise of money, which she desperately needed. And the true thief, Jeanne de la Motte? She alone was found guilty and sentenced to Salpêtrière prison. I've recently heard, however, that she's escaped to London. And of course, she must still have the rivière necklace, for it has never been found.

"As for me? I have come out with the worst of it. Poor Antoinette, who had nothing to do with any of it, has been branded a spendthrift, intent on ruining Cardinal de Rohan."

"But why?" Rowan asked. "Why don't people want to see what seems so obvious?"

Antoinette shrugged, and blew out another stream of smoke.

"They take great pleasure in vilifying me. Calling me vicious and depraved. I know what they say in Paris. I know." She paused for a moment, lowering her gaze. "This all happened two years ago. I realized then that my life was doomed, for it is no longer my own; it belongs to the French people. Once it was clear I had little control over my own reputation, I devoted myself to my family . . . to my husband and . . . and children. . . ." Antoinette's voice caught in her throat and she quickly looked away. "But even that has brought me grief. And so, I come here, to my little hamlet, to play milkmaid. Perhaps you think it pathetic, eh?"

Rowan shifted uncomfortably, not sure what to say. Antoinette rose from her seat.

"It doesn't really matter. I don't care what other people think anymore. You win, Monsieur." She pushed the pile of cards toward him. "They are yours. This game has become tedious. Excuse me." Antoinette turned and abruptly left the room. Dinner was over.

Rowan put the deck into his pocket and bade a hasty good-bye to the two women still at the table. He started along the dirt road heading back to the main palace. The moon shone brightly on the mill and the lake in front of it, and the sound of crickets and frogs filled the air. Then Rowan heard another sound, a gasping and snuffling, and as he passed the stable he saw a figure slumped in the hay. It was the queen. Rowan was tempted to keep walking, but his heart went out to her. As he stood there she looked up and saw him. He caught his breath.

"What do you want?" she said weakly.

"Antoinette . . . your majesty . . . I am afraid I have offended you. A thousand pardons, I can't emphasize enough how I am a stranger here. If I said something . . ."

"No, no. It is my own fault really. I have not entertained guests in some time. I was trying to forget, but it is too early. Too early."

Rowan looked at her blankly. "Forget? . . ."

"Do you mock me, Monsieur!" Antoinette's eyes flashed. Rowan shrank back as she rose to her feet and bore down on him. "Oh, you are just like the rest! All you care about is getting your precious favors . . . nobody cares about me. Nobody cares that my heart has been crushed!"

"I'm sorry, I don't know what you mean . . ." Rowan stammered. She was now so close he could see the veins in her forehead.

"How can you stand there denying me my grief? Am I not a mother? Will you not grant me that dignity? My son is dead! Where are you from, that you have not heard that news?" Antoinette turned away from him, pausing for a moment.

Rowan felt slightly sick, but he didn't dare move.

"Only a month has passed since Louis-Joseph, the prince, the future of France, died in my arms, twisted and tortured from sickness," the queen continued bitterly. "He suffered horribly, in constant pain . . . too much for a seven-year-old to bear! Death was a release for him, but not for me. I live in turmoil. I have no comfort. Just the shrieking of Parisians and the bickering of courtiers."

A lump rose in Rowan's throat. "I do understand, Your Majesty. I've lost somebody close to me, too. A year ago . . . I know what it's like. . . ." Rowan fought the hot sting of tears in his eyes. Her words made him feel naked. She had reached inside him to a secret place and tugged on the dark things he kept hidden there, making him ashamed. He looked down at his shoes.

Antoinette regarded him coldly, with regal composure. "Then you have no excuse," she said.

Rowan stumbled out of the stable. He ran all the way to the entrance of the Hamlet without stopping, furious with himself. What had he done? She had poured her heart out, and he just stood there. A carriage waited for him. It didn't occur to him to question this coincidence until he was already inside, and he realized he was not alone.

"I'm going back to Paris with you," Louise stated. Rowan stared at her, then finally found his voice.

"Does your father know?"

"No, but it doesn't matter. I'm old enough to be on my own. I have friends. I can't stand it here. Versailles is old and antiquated. Paris is where everything is happening. How was dinner with the queen?"

She asked the last question snidely, as though Antoinette was ripe for ridicule. Rowan bristled, his emotions still raw, but he told Louise a version of the evening, leaving out the part that happened in the stable. Louise nodded, but it was clear that she was neither interested in nor sympathetic to Antoinette's problems. She wanted to talk about her plans in the city, her goals as an artist, her search for truth. Rowan listened and commented once in a while, but couldn't help feeling that she was fooling herself. The only true thing in the world was death.

His hand wandered to his waistcoat pocket where he had stuffed the playing cards, and felt a small, smooth lump. In her haste, the queen had dropped her locket in the pile of cards. Rowan stared at it, then put it back in his pocket. He rubbed it, knowing that he held the queen's heart in his hand.

After the carriage dropped Louise off at the house of one of her friends, Rowan finally returned to the hotel and found Xanthe pacing in the lobby.

"Where have you been?" she demanded. Rowan was about to answer when she covered her face with her hands and started to cry.

"What happened? Are you okay?" Rowan squeezed her shoulder and Xanthe looked up, sniffling.

"I've been so scared! I didn't know where you were . . ."

"I'm sorry, I had a lead, one thing led to another, and I got stuck eating dinner with the queen . . ."

Xanthe raised her eyebrows. "Stuck with the queen?" Rowan started to explain, but Xanthe interrupted. "Tell me later. I think Xave's in trouble."

"He's not here?"

"No! I don't know where he is! And this whole city's gone crazy . . . there's looting and fighting all over the place! I've been waiting for you, and when you didn't show up I thought I'd look for him by myself, except Madame Vontighem refused to let me leave the building. She said the streets are too dangerous for a lady without an escort. So I've just been sitting here, waiting and waiting . . ."

"I'm sorry, Xanthe, I had no idea. Let's go."

They had just gone out the door when they almost bumped into a thin boy dressed in rags, with skin blackened by dirt. He couldn't have been more than fourteen, but he had the eyes of an old man. When he spoke, he revealed a mouth full of rotten teeth.

"Are you Monsieur Rowan Popplewell?" the boy asked.

Rowan nodded, repulsed.

"I'm Sebastien," he said. "Follow me, sir. Your friend is in the hospital."

CHAPTER EIGHT

THE OTHER SIDE

ROWAN HAD TROUBLE KEEPING UP WITH SEBASTIEN as he led them through the dark, twisted backstreets of Paris. He stumbled over the cobbled roads in his broken heel, twisting his ankles more than once. He'd have taken off his shoes, but the choking smell of rotting meat and urine made him afraid of what he might step in. Several times they had to dodge a shower of filth coming from the upper windows as people emptied their chamber pots right onto the street. Rowan began to wish he was back at Versailles.

Sebastien was a mystery. He claimed he'd met Xavier last night ("when we assumed he was in bed!" Xanthe pointed out) and that they had become friends. He had promised to introduce Xavier to some of the other kids on the street, to help him find a girl he was looking for. They had met this morning and wandered the streets, then gotten caught in the middle of the bread riot. Xavier was pushed to the ground and hit his head on the stones, knocking him out.

Rowan doubted the story from the beginning. Sebastien reminded him of some of the kids who lived on the streets of New York. They were absolutely untrustworthy, living hand-to-mouth, concerned only with survival. And Rowan had lived in the city long enough to recognize a scam when he saw one. Rob somebody, find one of their friends or family members, and tell them the person needs help, then once you have them in a dark alley, rob them, too. It didn't help that Rowan recognized the snake ring on Sebastien's finger as Xavier's.

"Where are all these friends of yours?" Rowan asked. He wished Miss O'Neill had put a pocketknife in his costume. All he had on him was the money pouch, the alleviator key, the locket and cards, and his pocket watch.

"Everywhere and nowhere," Sebastien mumbled.

Every once in a while Sebastien would flick his fingers in the air, and glance down dark alleys. Rowan was sure he was signaling somebody. Was it his imagination or did he see a shadow retreat into a doorway, and a figure duck down on a roof? He wondered if he could use the chain on the queen's locket to strangle somebody. Xanthe seemed not to notice the danger, or was ignoring it out of her concern for Xavier.

"I knew he was taking too many chances," she fretted. "He gets caught up in the excitement and doesn't think about what might happen."

"We should've stayed together," Rowan muttered.

"No, we had to split up," Xanthe sighed. "We couldn't possibly cover as much ground as we needed to in the short

time we have. And every minute counts, right? The farther
Nina gets from her starting point the harder she is to trace."

Rowan suddenly realized that Sebastien had led them to
Notre Dame Cathedral. He hadn't noticed it in the fog, but
when they emerged from the labyrinth of streets onto the
wide courtyard, he found himself gazing up at the famous
flying buttresses, the round, stained-glass windows, twin bell
towers, and graceful spire. As he craned his neck he saw the
silhouettes of the gargoyles against the mist, ever vigilant
guardians against evil. Sebastien continued on around the
cathedral until he got to a door in the back that led into the
basement.

"In here," Sebastien said, leading them down the staircase.
He opened the door.

Rowan hesitated. He heard scuffling sounds . . . and was
that somebody crying? He grabbed Xanthe and pulled her
back from the door. "You go first."

Sebastien narrowed his eyes. "Why? Don't you trust me?"

"C'mon Rowan, it's just a church," Xanthe said, wrestling
her arm away.

"I'd like to know why you're wearing Xavier's ring,"
Rowan said to Sebastien.

"What? Hey . . ." Xanthe's eyes widened as she noticed
the ring, which Sebastien twisted around his finger.

"He gave it to me."

"Really?" Rowan asked. "Why?"

"Ask him yourself. He's in there." Sebastien cocked his
thumb toward the musty hallway beyond the door.

"You go first," Rowan said stubbornly.

Sebastien shrugged and went inside.

Sickness hung on the air like a thick dew. The end of the hallway opened into a white room with two rows of beds. Pale, crooked bodies writhed to a chorus of coughs and moans. Sebastien spoke with a portly man in a brown cassock and skull cap, then brought him over to Rowan and Xanthe.

"Welcome. I'm Brother Michael," the man boomed over the plaintive cries. "You must be Xavier's friends. He's been asking for you."

"Oh, he's really here!" Xanthe cried. "Is he awake? Is he badly hurt?"

"No, just a bad bump on the head. He's lucky Sebastien was with him. He would've been trampled and killed by that crowd. Follow me."

Brother Michael led them past the people in the beds and up a narrow staircase. Rowan heard the crying again.

"What's that?" he asked.

"Our nursery," Brother Michael replied sadly. "Not a day goes by that we don't receive an unfortunate package—a newborn wrapped in rags with a note imploring us to find a home for it. Some of these innocents die here. Others we send out to the countryside with wet nurses, but I don't think they fare much better. It's . . . very bad right now."

"Yes," Xanthe said. "We know."

Brother Michael opened a door and pointed to one of the many beds. Xavier lay in one, asleep. A nun was putting a compress on his forehead. He awoke when Xanthe and Rowan rushed over to him, yelling his name.

"Don't worry, don't worry. I'm all right," he said sheepishly as Xanthe hugged him.

Rowan gently touched the bandage on his head. "What happened to you?" he said, concerned.

"It's a long story," Xavier said, propping himself up. "I'd been with Sebastien most of the day. He's the leader of a gang of kids who live on the streets. It's a huge network of thieves, basically. I thought I might find Nina in it, or at least someone who'd seen her. We were hanging out in this tavern when . . ."

"Xave!" Xanthe chided. "What were you doing in a *tavern*?"

"Relax, it's like hanging out at a burger joint. Anyway, somebody came in, announced that some guy named Necker had been fired by the king, and before I knew it everyone went nuts. They ran toward the bakery and took it apart. Literally! Ripped tiles right off the roof!"

"They're animals," Rowan murmured.

Xavier frowned. "No, they're not animals, Rowan. They're *hungry*."

"Well, I didn't mean they were *really* animals," Rowan said. "I just hate mobs. One person starts something and everyone follows in a free-for-all. They don't even stop to think what their government has actually done for them . . ."

"You mean like making them pay huge amounts in taxes? Ignoring their legal rights? Treating them like 'animals'?"

"No, I mean like putting more lighting on the street. Building a sewer system. Digging wells for clean water . . ."

"What do you know about it?"

"Antoinette told me . . ."

"Antoinette? You mean *Queen Marie Antoinette*? On a first-name basis with the queen, are we? Well la-di-da."

"I'm just saying if these people were a little more patient . . ."

"Listen to you! 'Patient'? Rowan, these people are *starving*! They are filthy and sick! All they eat is bread, and now there isn't any! If they try to get food from the forest, or cut wood for heat, they're thrown in jail or shot. For *firewood*. Just so King Louis can have someplace to hunt with his buddies. What are they supposed to do?"

"I think you're getting carried away in all this, Xave. You're forgetting who you are."

"No, Rowan, you're forgetting who *you* are. Do you really think you're noble? Like you're better than them?"

"Look, I don't want to put people down. Nobody deserves to starve. I just think they could use some self-control . . ."

"You *do* think you're better than them. Unbelievable! Listen. Sometimes people get to the point where they've had enough. You know, Rowan? *They can't take it anymore.* There's a spark, and an explosion. Yeah, it's ugly, but it clears the air."

Rowan rolled his eyes. He didn't want a lecture.

Xavier stood up angrily. "Hey, I *know* what it's like to be judged by what you were born into. To be treated differently because of how you look. I'm like these people. And in many ways, so are you."

"I am not!" Rowan shouted. "Besides, who cares about

any of that anyway? I just want to find my sister, not join ranks with the peasants!"

"Stop it!" Xanthe shouted. "You're both being stupid! There's no point in fighting! Xave, let's get you back to the hotel. Can you walk?"

Xavier answered by stomping out the door. Xanthe ran after him, followed by Rowan. *He's wrong,* Rowan thought sullenly. *I'm not like them. I'm in control of myself.* Someone as impulsive and excitable as Xavier probably couldn't understand how much Rowan prided himself on that fact. This was the second time tonight he felt totally misunderstood.

As the threesome walked back through the room of dying men to the exit, two nuns—one short and round, the other tall and thin—watched them from an alcove.

"Thank goodness Xavier is all right," the round, squat one said. "I said this before and I'll say it again, they shouldn't be here, Sister. It's too dangerous."

"Yes," the tall one replied. "It is dangerous. But one only moves forward by taking risks, Sister. He needs to move forward. Besides, he hasn't found what he's looking for. From that conversation we overheard, I don't think he's even close."

"Oh my, do you think he'll figure it out in time?"

"That remains to be seen. In the meantime, why don't you bring that water to the patients? And stop giving them shiatsu massages. Nurses didn't do that in seventeen eighty-nine."

"Yes, Sister."

• • •

Outside the hospital, Sebastien sauntered up to Xavier.

"You're all right then," he said.

"Yes," Xavier said. "Thanks for bringing me here. I think I owe you my life."

"It's nothing. I'm sure you would have done the same for me." Sebastien turned to Rowan with a self-satisfied smirk and bowed slightly. "I hope you find your sister, Monsieur. I have a sister . . . somewhere. I haven't seen my own family in many years."

Rowan stared at Sebastien's tight, scrawny body, barely covered by dirty rags. His own stomach still held the warm weight of the roast goose and puddings. He felt guilty. He reached into his waistcoat pocket and handed Sebastien a fistful of coins. Sebastien stared, as though he wasn't quite sure what to do with them.

"Thank you for helping us," Rowan said. "And thanks for helping my friend. I really appreciate it." Rowan started to turn away but a thought occurred to him and he turned back, removing his coat. "And here . . . To keep you warm."

Sebastien gaped as Rowan draped the velvet coat around his shoulders. His hands trembled as he gently traced the brocade pattern with his fingers. Suddenly he grabbed Rowan's hand and covered it with kisses.

"That's really unnecessary . . ." Rowan said, embarrassed.

"Thank you, Monsieur, thank you! I will remember you all my life," Sebastien cried. He backed away, bowing again and again until he had disappeared into the shadows.

Rowan hadn't realized how heavy the coat was until he

wasn't wearing it anymore. It suddenly occurred to him that
he hadn't removed any of his costume—the clothes, the wig,
or the powder—since he'd arrived in Paris. Now that the coat
was off he was aware of how itchy his head felt, and he
removed his wig as well. He felt free, though he imagined that
in some respects he had just removed his armor.

As they passed by the front of the cathedral, Xavier
stopped. "Wait a minute," he said. "Why don't we . . . let's go
in here for a second."

"*You* want to go to *church?*" Xanthe exclaimed. "Now I
know we're not in Kansas anymore. The last time you were in
a church you spent the whole time making origami animals
out of the program."

"I just feel like it." Xavier turned to Rowan. "Do you
mind?"

Rowan shrugged his consent. They pushed open the heavy,
wooden doors and entered the cathedral.

Once inside, it seemed even bigger. Arches soared over-
head, crisscrossing like fingers laced together in prayer. Two
rows of stone columns separated by small chandeliers led the
way through the nave, the central part of the church, and
toward the choir. Beyond the pillars were small galleries containing statues of saints and banks of candles, each one flicker-
ing with the hope that a prayer would be answered.

Rowan tried to recall the last time he'd gone to church. He
was Catholic, and his father had always been very insistent on
not only going to mass every Sunday, but being on time and
well dressed. They used to say grace over dinner, and there

was a crucifix that used to hang over his parents' bed and a picture of Jesus with his sacred heart by the front door. But when his mother died, all of those items disappeared and God hadn't been mentioned in his household since.

They sat in the pews, each choosing a different row. Xavier was near the front and he knelt down, clasping his hands together and touching them to his forehead. Xanthe was right behind him. She crossed herself and knelt as well. Rowan just sat there. Their actions were familiar, but he felt nothing. He had prayed when his mother was in the hospital. Did it do any good? No. *Religion is just superstition*, he thought. *You might as well pin your hopes on a rabbit's foot.*

He sighed and looked up at the stained glass. You couldn't see what it really looked like because it was so dark outside. It was dark inside, too; just a few candles illuminated the vast hall. Rowan felt overwhelmed by gloom. The statues lurking in the alcoves seemed like spies. Rowan went to Xanthe. "I'll wait for you guys outside," he said. He left the cathedral.

Rowan sat on the steps and looked out upon the wide, empty courtyard. He could hear the river lapping along the quays not far in the distance, and some shouting, perhaps from a tavern—he couldn't tell. Nearby he heard a slight scratching sound. When he turned his head he nearly jumped; there was a person sitting on the steps, only a few yards away. He looked like a pile of rags, huddled in the doorway. He was flicking cards onto the ground, apparently playing a game of solitaire.

The man lifted his face. Where his left eye should've been there was an empty socket, slightly shriveled in healing, like an old apple. His good eye was not much better; it bulged and listed to the right. It was impossible to tell at any moment where he was looking. He seemed to scrutinize Rowan for several seconds, then went back to his card game.

"Who are you?" the man said, his voice raspy and thick.

Rowan didn't answer him. He didn't see the point of having a conversation with a beggar, but he also wasn't exactly sure what the answer was. Rowan Popplewell? The Marquis d'Orange?

"You look lost." The man deftly tossed the cards in a grid.

Rowan noticed several of his fingers were missing, and that he was grasping the cards with his knuckles.

"No. But I'm looking for someone who's lost," Rowan replied. He wished the twins would hurry up. "A little girl," he added as an afterthought.

"No little girls around here," the beggar said, his wandering eye fixed on Rowan. "You're looking in the wrong place."

"Probably," Rowan answered. "But I'm going to keep looking until I find her. She's all I've got." Rowan didn't know why he told the beggar that. It was how he felt, but he didn't mean to say it aloud. Maybe he was tired.

The beggar's cards were filthy. Most of them were bent or ripped, some looked impossible to read. Rowan took the queen's pack of cards from his waistcoat pocket and handed them to the man, who immediately wrapped his black fingers around them.

"Ah! These are very fine. Very fine indeed. Thank you, Monsieur, thank you. This is who you are, after all. A thoughtful young man, with a good heart. Follow your heart, Monsieur. You'll find her."

Rowan smiled grimly. The click of the doors let him know that Xanthe and Xavier had finally come out. He turned his head and waved to them. When he turned back around, the man was gone.

As they walked back to the hotel, Xanthe filled them in on her day. "The dress shops were a waste of time," she began. "Nobody had seen a girl like Nina. So I started going to some of the art galleries—they're very popular with all kinds of people, so she could easily have been there—but they were so crowded it was hard to tell. I kept hearing bits and pieces of conversations though. Everyone was angry about some financial minister being fired by the king."

"That's Necker, the guy I was talking about," Xavier interjected.

Xanthe nodded. "Apparently the common people love him—they think he's looking out for them—and when the king fired him it was the last straw. Since then it's just gotten crazy. When I went back to the hotel to meet you and Xave and neither one of you showed up, I guess I kind of freaked out."

"Well, I'm really sorry," Rowan said. "I had to find out if Antoinette"—he saw Xavier grimace—"I mean, the queen, knew anything about Nina. I thought I had a lead . . . it just didn't pan out. But I did get us an invitation to the Mozart recital."

"Well, that's something," Xavier said begrudgingly.

"What are you talking about?" Xanthe said excitedly. "That's *great* news. You said yourself she wouldn't miss it for the world! We'll find her there, Rowan, I just know we will!"

Rowan wanted to give Xanthe a hug.

When they reached the hotel, they retired to their respective rooms. Xavier said it would be a good idea to get a lot of rest for the big day ahead, but Rowan suspected that he, like Rowan, still felt bruised from their fight and wanted some distance. Now that he was by himself, Rowan couldn't sleep. He was irritated by Xavier's accusations, and haunted by the image of the beggar with the vacant eye. He also couldn't stop thinking about Marie Antoinette and her inevitable doom. Something about her reminded him of Nina . . . No, he thought, *Antoinette's story is already written. Nina can still be saved.* Rowan rose from his bed. He needed to get out.

The Palais-Royal was not as busy as it had been the last time he'd gone, due to the lateness of the hour. It was also seamier; prostitutes beckoned from doorways and gamblers filled the gaming tables. Rowan wandered around until he finally found a bench off to the side of the arcade, where he could gawk at the nightlife.

Only minutes after he'd sat down he became aware of a conversation taking place just around the corner. One of the voices was high, with a stutter, the other was low and gruff. But the third voice sounded familiar: crisp and cruel.

"S-so? W-what do you think?" said the first voice. Rowan heard some pages rustling.

"I drew the picture," said the second voice.

"It's perfect," the third voice hissed. "You're a magnificent artist. But . . . even so . . . make Louis look more like the fat pig that he is. And draw more jewelry on Antoinette . . ."

"And maybe have her s-sitting on top of a p-peasant, c-c-crushing him," the first voice suggested.

"Yes, yes, very good point," agreed the third voice. "Her disdain for the people of France needs to be absolutely clear."

Rowan got up quietly and peeked around the corner. There were three men. The gruff voice belonged to a broad-shouldered man with a bulbous nose, the stuttering voice to a taller man who kept rubbing his hands together. The third voice belonged to the king's cousin, Philippe.

"Include in your article that Marie Antoinette is asking her relatives for political and military help," Philippe said. "The public's hatred for her is very strong. But for some reason they are still attached to that boob, Louis. You know, I told him that he should just give up the throne to someone better suited for the pressures of ruling, but he had neither the competence nor the courage to make even that simple decision."

"But if he stepped down, wouldn't the crown pass to one of his brothers?" the broad man asked. "The Comte de Provence or the Comte d'Artois?"

"Don't you understand, idiot?" Philippe spat. "The people are sick of this monarchy. They don't want Louis, Antoinette, Provence, Artois . . . they're all the same, a family of greedy pigs. Times are changing, the businessmen are rising up. They want their voices to be heard! They want a king who knows them intimately and who loves and respects them, but who still has the legitimacy to rule through blood. Who better fits that description than me?—What's that?"

Rowan picked himself up off the ground. He had skidded on some gravel when he shifted his position for a better view, and lost his balance on his broken heel. Now Philippe was looking right at him.

"So, what have we here? A spy?" Before Rowan could answer, Philippe drew his sword, pointing it at Rowan's throat.

"No," Rowan croaked. "I'm just looking for a way out . . ." He backed away, slowly.

The two henchmen flanked Philippe, who crept closer.

"Wait. I know you." Philippe's eyes narrowed. "Yes. The clumsy oaf on the dance floor. And now I see you are a spy for Marie Antoinette . . ."

"I'm not a spy!" Rowan protested.

"Don't deny it!" Philippe barked. "My own spies saw you eating dinner with her just this evening! What did she tell you to do? Keep an eye on me? That she needs proof of treason? You won't be able to tell her much with your tongue cut out! Grab him!"

The henchmen leaped at Rowan, who threw himself to the ground. They collided with each other, and as they disentangled themselves Rowan rolled under the bench, leaped up, and took off through the courtyard, pushing people out of his way. Philippe and his men raced after him. Rowan veered into one of the cafés, overturning tables and chairs. Outraged cardplayers joined in the pursuit, but Rowan was already rushing through the kitchen and out the door into an alley. He looked around frantically, not sure which direction to take, finally jumping into a barrel outside the kitchen door. He crouched down, making himself as small as possible. Unfortunately, the barrel contained the cook's garbage, and Rowan found himself up to his neck in rotten vegetables and severed chicken heads.

Philippe burst into the alley, followed by his henchmen and a few men from the café. "Split up!" he cried, and the group fanned out, going in both directions until the alley was clear once again.

Rowan waited for fifteen minutes and then climbed out of the barrel. In that time, the cook had dumped a bowl of fish skins on top of him as well as some potato peelings. He was covered with muck and smelled terrible. He walked along the alley, wondering how he would get through the lobby of the hotel, when he saw a figure appear several yards away. He whirled around and took off, but the figure called his name and he turned back. It was Louise.

"Rowan," she said, finally reaching him. "Don't go back to your hotel. Philippe knows where you're staying."

"What? How does he know that?"

"From the café. One of the waiters told him. I saw everything. Come with me. A friend of mine lives nearby. You can hide with him, and maybe even get a change of clothes. Come on!"

Rowan followed Louise down the alley, through a side street and into a courtyard that served several houses. She put her fingers to her lips as she walked up to one of the houses and knocked at the door. After a minute, the door opened a crack and two dark brown eyes peered out. When they recognized Louise, the door opened wider, revealing an intense young man with long, brown hair. Rowan recognized him as the speech maker at the balloon launch.

"Louise?" he murmured. "What a strange time for a visit . . ."

"I'm sorry if I woke you . . ."

"You did not wake me. I've been writing. Always writing, my dear. My wife is asleep, though, so we should not make noise. Come in." He stood aside and they entered.

The living room was small and bare, with only a few pieces of furniture. A small desk, covered with paper and books, stood on one side of the room, a chest of drawers on the opposite side. There was a wooden table in the center of the room with six chairs around it.

"Camille, this is my friend, Monsieur Rowan Popplewell, the son of the Marquis d'Orange," Louise said, gesturing to Rowan. "Rowan, this is Monsieur Camille Desmoulin."

Camille gave him a slight bow, which Rowan returned as they exchanged polite greetings.

"My friend is in trouble," Louise said to Camille. "He needs a place to hide."

"In trouble? With whom?" Camille leveled his gaze at Rowan.

"I . . . I'm afraid I've made enemies with Philippe Duc d'Orleans," Rowan stuttered nervously. "I overheard him plotting against the king. He thinks I was spying on him because he somehow knew I had dinner with the queen, and now . . . well, I'm pretty sure he wants to kill me." Rowan waited for some expression of sympathy, but there was none.

"Well? Are you a spy?" Camille asked pointedly. "You are noble, are you not? Having dinner with the queen . . . she is a friend of yours?"

"Yes . . . well, no, not really. I mean, I understand her. She's not as bad as people say she is, except for the fact that, you know, as a queen she's living an incredibly luxurious lifestyle, which can seem frivolous on the outside, but for your average queen she's not so terrible . . ." Rowan's words tumbled out of his mouth. He felt stupid.

Louise frowned, and moved away from him.

"Don't give the fellow such a hard time," a voice boomed from the other room. A great mountain of a man with a thick mane of hair leaned against the doorway.

"My God, Georges, what's the point of hiding if you're going to give yourself away!" Camille snapped.

"I tried to stop him," squeaked a slight, pale man who appeared behind the broader man. He wore a prim-looking wig with a row of tight curls that he kept adjusting. "But Monsieur Danton is so full of his own puffery he never listens to reason . . ."

"Oh, stop your whining, Max," Danton bellowed. "This young man is clearly not a danger to anyone but himself. He's confused. And if he's a friend of Louise's, then I say we should welcome him."

"Monsieur Danton, Monsieur Robespierre?" Louise murmured. "Forgive me. I have obviously interrupted a secret meeting."

"Not so secret anymore!" Robespierre sniffed.

Camille sighed, exasperated.

"Monsieur Popplewell, this is Monsieur Georges Danton. He is a lawyer, as is Monsieur Maximilien Robespierre. And this is not a secret meeting, we were merely having a discussion. Though one must be careful what one says in unfamiliar company . . ." Camille directed his last comment to Danton, who brushed by him.

"We were discussing what should be done about the king's decision to get rid of Necker," Danton said, sitting down at the table. "It is an outrage and cannot be ignored! A clear signal of oppression, in my view!"

"Careful, Monsieur!" Robespierre cried, indicating Rowan with a nod of his head. "Do shut up for once in your life!"

"I am surrounded by cowards!" Danton bellowed. "Hiding in kitchens! Whispering in dark alleys! Can we not stand up for what we believe? We are entering an age of truth, my friends, and there is no room for quibbling! Stand up and be counted! I don't fear this boy. Look at him! He's got a fish head in his pocket!"

Rowan blushed.

"Oh, stop making pretty speeches," Robespierre snipped. "Yes, truth is important. That's obvious. But I put it to you that there is no room for confusion either. If you are not for us, you are against us. There is no in-between. We must be a virtuous society if we are to avoid the mistakes of the past. That starts with a leadership of unimpeachable character . . ."

Danton threw his head back and laughed. "And I suppose that is you? With your squeaky voice and shaking finger? Liberty is protected by humans, not saints, Max. Virtue is over-rated. You should take all your passion for virtue and get your-self a girlfriend. It would be a huge improvement, I think!"

"Well, I'm going." Robespierre glared. "I didn't come here to be insulted." He swept toward the door, passing Rowan and Louise. "Good night, Louise," he said.

Camille turned to Danton, who was polishing his shoe with the cuff of his jacket.

"Why did you do that, Georges? You know how sensitive he is."

"He's annoying," Georges answered with a wave of his hand. "Too rigid. We're better off without him."

Camille gave an exasperated sigh and turned to Rowan.

"Look, I don't trust you. However, your enemy is Philippe, and I trust him even less. But at least I know where he stands; he looks out for his own interests. You . . . you are dangerous for another reason. People without convictions are as reliable as shifting sand. You say you are Louise's friend; I hope so, sir. Max is right in one respect: if you are not for us, you are against us. If I find out I have a royalist sleeping in my house, you need not worry about Philippe. I will kill you myself."

CHAPTER NINE

BASTILLE DAY

THE NEXT MORNING, ROWAN AWOKE WITH A JOLT. He'd dreamt he was being attacked by a lion. He opened his eyes and found himself staring into the broad face of Georges Danton.

"Wake up!" he commanded, his large hands gripping Rowan's shoulders. "Get dressed! It's starting!"

Danton dropped Rowan back onto the quilt that he had used as a bed and charged out of the living room. Rowan reluctantly pulled on his clothes. They had dried stiff and still smelled terrible. He finished just as Camille swept in, adjusting his jacket. Danton followed, with Louise in tow. It occurred to Rowan that she and Danton were together.

"People are on the move!" Danton bellowed, slapping Rowan on the back. "The king has mobilized his army. We are going to the Bastille to demand they release arms for the people to defend themselves!"

"Come with us!" Camille cried. It felt more like an order than an invitation. "Now is the hour! It has finally come down to this!"

"I . . . I can't," Rowan stuttered. "I've got to meet my friends . . ."

"All friends are at the Bastille," Danton said pointedly. "We must stand together."

"Yes, Rowan, you must come!" Louise urged. "This is the moment of truth!"

"But I have to look for my sister at . . ." Rowan stopped. He didn't dare mention Versailles.

"You said your sister ran away to see the excitement of Paris," Louise said. "Surely she will be at the Bastille!"

"Unless," Camille added slowly, "these are *not* your friends at the Bastille. Perhaps your friends are of a nobler sort?" He cocked his head, eyebrows raised. Through the opening of Camille's jacket, Rowan glimpsed a holster with a pistol.

"No, I'm with you," Rowan said, clearing his throat. "I wouldn't miss this for the world."

Camille nodded firmly, opened the door, and they descended down the stairwell into streets that were already buzzing with activity.

People swarmed over the cobblestones. Rowan hoped he could lose Camille and Danton in the confusion, but Danton held him firmly by the arm. They found them-selves within the courtyard of the Palais-Royal, not so far from where Rowan had overheard Philippe talking with his henchmen. Suddenly Camille jumped up onto one of the tables.

"Listen!" Camille cried, raising his arms. A crowd started to gather. "Listen to Paris and Lyon, Rouen and Bordeaux, Calais and Marseille! From one end of the country to the other the same universal cry is heard . . . everyone wants to be free!"

The crowd roared. After Camille quieted them, he detailed the crimes of the monarchy, how their extravagant appetites had brought the country to near bankruptcy, how courtiers lived off the sweat and taxes of the poor, and how they kept the people from having a voice in their government. Camille used his voice like an instrument, and much to his surprise, Rowan felt moved by it.

Camille reached into his coat and pulled out the pistol. "To arms! To arms!" he shouted. "I call my brothers to freedom! I would rather die than submit to servitude!"

As if by magic, weapons appeared in the crowd. People waved them in the air, shouting oaths of brotherhood and solidarity.

Just then Rowan saw Xavier and Xanthe. They were waving to him from across the square. Rowan started toward them, but was yanked back by Danton, who pushed him into a carriage where Camille and Louise were already seated.

"I saw my friends . . ." Rowan began.

"Good, you'll beat them there," Danton answered tersely.

It was then that Rowan realized Danton didn't trust him any more than Camille did. He was their hostage. Louise must have made a major mistake in revealing their midnight meeting to him. The only thing that protected him was Louise's friendship; without her he was like any other noble to them, and nobles were becoming increasingly unpopular. The only thing to do was pretend enthusiasm for storming the Bastille. Rowan clapped his hands together, raising a fist for brotherhood. Danton eyed him suspiciously.

The carriage veered and came to an abrupt stop. Camille and Louise jumped out and Danton pulled Rowan out with him. The crowd gathered in front of the building chanted "Death to tyrants!" At a moment when Danton turned his head, Rowan finally slipped out of his grasp, but the walls of people pressing forward forced him toward the medieval fortress that was the focus of the public's rage.

The Bastille had eight round towers, seventy feet high, dotted with only a few tiny windows. Some very large cannons pointed at the crowd through the ramparts, and from the activity on the roof it looked as though the guards were mobilizing for battle.

"Give us the Bastille!" the crowd cried. "Give us the guns!"

Suddenly the drawbridge fell, its chains cut by someone in the crowd. It happened so suddenly that it struck a man, pinning him beneath it. The besiegers took no notice, pouring over him into the prison courtyard. Rowan found himself swept along with the roiling mass.

"Back!" the guards screamed. "Get back or we'll shoot!"

Somebody fired—it was unclear who—which started a volley from both sides. People stampeded. Rowan was shoved to the ground. He tried to rise but was knocked down again by the people rushing for cover. He started to panic. *I'm going to die here*, he thought. *I'm going to be trampled or shot . . .*

Rowan staggered over to a hay cart that had been set on fire and crawled behind it, making himself as small as possible. The smoke stung his nostrils and throat, and the heat was unbearable. Still, he couldn't move; he was terrified. He started whimpering. It felt good to hear his own voice; it was proof that he was still alive. Then he stopped and concentrated on the rhythm of his breathing, which was shallow and fast. As he started to see bright flashes and felt his head nod, he realized he needed fresh air. The last thing he saw before he passed out was a group of people rolling in two heavy cannons.

He awoke when a hand pushed a goatskin canteen filled with water into his mouth. It didn't taste very good, but he was thankful for it and drank.

"This is why we shouldn't split up anymore," a familiar voice said softly.

Rowan opened his eyes. Xanthe smiled down at him.

"C'mon, let's get out of here," Xavier said, running up. "Hey! You're okay!" He gave Rowan's back a firm slap.

"What's going on?" Rowan asked dully. He could see that the second drawbridge, leading from the courtyard into the prison itself, had fallen, and the crowd was now pushing its way inside. They had prevailed.

"We were going to ask you the same thing!" Xanthe answered. "We've been up all night searching for you! The next thing we know we see you getting pulled into a carriage by some big guy, heading toward the Bastille! I thought we all agreed not to split up again. How could you . . . oh Rowan, I'm just so glad you're safe!"

"I thought I was going to die," Rowan said, sniffling. "I would've been killed if you guys hadn't found me." His shoulders shook as he held back his sobs.

"It's okay, Rowan. Don't . . ." Xanthe put her arms around him. "You just inhaled a lot of smoke, that's all." Xanthe started to cry, too.

"You guys, can we save the crying for later?" Xavier urged. "This isn't over yet!"

Xavier and Xanthe helped Rowan to his feet just as the newly released prisoners of the Bastille emerged to cheers and applause. Rowan expected a parade of triumphant criminals, but there were only seven men. They stumbled out looking confused but happy. The crowd celebrated as though they had liberated a thousand.

In fact the mob was growing unruly. They seemed not to know what to do with themselves. Somehow the victory was not enough; they wanted more. They dragged a man out. From the shouts of the people around him, Rowan guessed that he was the Marquis de Launay, caretaker of the Bastille.

"String him up to the lamp post!" a voice screeched.

"Drag him in the street!" cried another.

"Cut out his heart, the heartless scoundrel!" and so on.

Rowan watched, horrified but fascinated. As they bound Launay, he lashed out, kicking and shouting. The mob fell upon him, weapons raised.

"Rowan! Come on!" It was Xanthe's voice, buzzing behind him. But he couldn't move. He was transfixed. Xanthe pulled him away from crowd. "Come *on!*" she screamed.

Xavier was running toward a group of horses tethered to a tree. Rowan finally shook off his trance and followed him. Xavier boosted him onto one of the beasts, and after Xanthe mounted another, the three of them took off, away from the smoke and the noise.

Rowan glanced back over his shoulder as he rode away. An impromptu parade had formed, led by a man holding a long pike with an oblong ball bobbing at the top of it. Rowan squinted, then turned away, shocked. Everything in his stomach flew to his throat. He grabbed the horse's mane to keep from sliding off as he retched. The ball hoisted on the pike was Launay's head.

MASQUERADE

The murky river rippled over Rowan's body, washing away the ash from the burning cart. But nothing could wash away the horrible image of Launay's disembodied head, dangling from the top of a stick, his anguished expression forever frozen on his face. Rowan had wept bitterly as they rode away from the scene, not so much from his fear of the violence and destruction, but because of his inexplicable desire to be part of it.

After they stopped by the Seine, Xavier had gone off to find clothes for Rowan. Rowan sat in the water and filled Xanthe in on the events of the past evening, leading up to when she and her brother had found him. He told her about overhearing Philippe, the chase through the Palais-Royal, being saved by Louise, and staying the night with her friend Camille Desmoulin.

"That explains who busted down your door at one o'clock in the morning, Philippe's men," Xanthe had said. "Madame

Vontighem tried to stop them, but they slipped by her. I could tell from the noise something was wrong, and when they opened your door and found your room empty, I really knew something was wrong! And that's when we started looking for you. I recognized that guy, Camille Desmoulin, from the balloon festival, and then we saw you next to him. I gotta tell you, after what happened at Notre Dame, the last place we expected to find you was storming the Bastille . . ."

Xavier rode up and vaulted off the horse. Rowan thought he heard Xanthe murmur "show-off" and it cheered him to hear their familiar bickering. Xavier held up some dark breeches, a wool vest, and a white shirt.

"Sorry," he said. "No coat. It's not exactly a nobleman's outfit, but I think you can pass."

"It's great," Rowan said, hoping Xavier had lost any animosity he had from their argument the previous evening. He seemed to have moved on. "We should get going," Rowan said, starting to get out of the water. "Uh . . . Xanthe?"

"What?"

"Could you? . . ." Rowan gestured for her to turn around.

"Oh, yeah! Sorry." Xanthe walked over to the horses and turned her back. Rowan climbed onto the bank of the Seine and got dressed, remembering to transfer the money, watch, locket, and alleviator key into the various pockets of his new outfit. As he put his wig back on, he told Xavier the same story he'd told Xanthe.

In the second telling, Rowan realized he hadn't related the whole story. He'd described his movements, but how could he explain to anyone what he hardly understood himself? Yes, he had been afraid. He hated the violence and the chaos. And yet there were moments when he had felt like he was part of the mob. Something had risen in his blood that he'd been fighting for ages. Lying naked in the river he'd felt he had lost track of everything; who he really was, who he was supposed to be, what he was doing. He really was lost.

By the time they arrived at Versailles for the recital, the music parlor was crammed with people. There seemed to be no concern at all about the events happening in Paris. The audience sat motionless, basking in the sweetness that poured from the piano at the front of the room. There, manipulating the keys in a way no other human could, was Wolfgang Amadeus Mozart.

Rowan quickly scanned the crowd for his sister. Unfortunately, he couldn't see beyond the forest of high hairdos. Some of the wigs reached as much as three feet above the heads of their owners, others were fashioned into bizarre designs: a clipper ship, a heart, a hot-air balloon. Mixed in with these fancy coiffures were equally fancy hats and headpieces. The ladies' skirts were so wide they looked like cars with their doors open. There was little chance of fitting inside the room, so they waited outside.

With the last, thundering chord, the audience burst into applause. They rose to their feet as Mozart took his bows, and clustered around him, though this required a good deal of maneuvering by the women in the wider gowns. As Mozart pushed his way to the exit, they followed slowly, pressed together in a bizarre sort of cattle drive. Nina did not appear to be among them. Rowan searched desperately. The chaos at the Bastille had frightened him, and he wanted to find her before things got any worse.

"I don't see her," he murmured to Xavier and Xanthe.

"Me either," Xavier said.

Xanthe put a sympathetic hand on Rowan's shoulder. "Don't give up yet, Rowan," she said. "As long as Mozart is in the building, she may still try to get close to him. There was a guest list, remember? She probably wasn't on it."

"This is her only chance to ever see him in person. I half expected to find her sitting at the piano with him, playing a duet."

"She's got to be here somewhere," Xanthe assured him. "I know! Maybe she got a job in the kitchen so that she could be a server at the banquet!"

Rowan rubbed his chin thoughtfully. "That would make sense," he said. "We should be looking at the servants more than the guests."

Just then Queen Marie Antoinette swished by in a dazzling white gown that stood out so stiffly and spread open so far that she looked like she was stuffed into the center of a dining room table. She was surrounded by her circle of friends, whom Rowan recognized from dinner. One of them held two children by the hand, a fair-haired girl and a younger boy, both with sweet, angelic faces. Rowan could tell they were the prince and princess by their proximity to Antoinette. He thought of what was coming for these children in the near future and shivered. Within the next several years, those two young royals would be imprisoned and orphaned.

"Rowan!" Antoinette broke from one of her ladies and greeted Rowan warmly, kissing him on both cheeks as Xanthe and Xavier gaped.

"Your Majesty," Rowan stammered, "I wanted to apologize for our last meeting . . . I hope you are not distressed at my presence . . . ." The queen waved him off cheerfully. She murmured something to the lady holding her children, who nodded and led them out a different door. Antoinette turned back to Rowan, her eyes sparkling.

Rowan sensed a difference in her behavior. The relaxed atmosphere of the Hamlet was gone. Instead, Antoinette was giddy and self-conscious, as though she was performing. Her hair was styled so high Rowan wondered what feats of engineering made it possible, and her dress was frankly ridiculous. He looked away from her face, embarrassed for her.

Rowan introduced Xanthe and Xavier, and Antoinette immediately began fussing over them. "Oh, no," she trilled, appraising Xanthe's gown. "This won't do at all. It's a ball, my dear! A masked ball! You need something more . . . more fanciful! Exotic! Mysterious!"

"I'm sorry, I didn't come with a costume . . ." Xanthe said politely.

"Your Majesty, we are very pleased to have been invited to your party, but are you aware of what's going on in Paris right now?" Xavier said.

Rowan glared at him.

Antoinette's expression darkened, but then quickly regained its cheeriness.

"Yes," she said softly. "But that is outside. And we are inside. There's nothing to be done at the moment, and we will concern ourselves with it in due time." She grabbed Xanthe's arm intimately. "Come to my parlor. My ladies and I are going to transform ourselves. I'm sure I can find you a costume more fitting for the occasion, perhaps something Oriental in nature!"

Xanthe looked to Rowan pleadingly, but he had no idea how to discourage a queen with a mission.

"We'll look for you at the ball," Rowan called after her. "And if we miss you, we'll see you at ten, at the banquet!" Xanthe nodded and gave him a thumbs-up as Antoinette pulled her down the corridor.

Rowan was about to suggest to Xavier that they find the kitchen, when Xavier whispered, "Rowan, is that the guy who chased you in the café? Philippe?"

Philippe had emerged from the music parlor escorting a woman who wore a wig shaped like a harp. His eyes were riveted on Rowan, who gulped and nodded.

"I am a little surprised to see you here, spy," Philippe growled under his breath, resting one hand delicately on the handle of his sword. "I thought our last encounter would have soured you on court life. If you think the Austrian harlot can protect you here, you are sadly mistaken." His eyes darted in the direction of the queen.

Rowan and Xavier stepped back, but were blocked by the broad man who had been with Philippe at the Palais-Royal.

"Sir, I have no quarrel with you, I am only here as a music lover," Rowan squeaked.

Xavier nodded, for once speechless.

"Now, why don't I believe that?" Philippe said, cocking his head.

"You must believe me," Rowan pleaded. "It's all a big misunderstanding. I'm only here to find my sister, who's run away from home . . . I couldn't care less about your political aspirations. Really. If you want to be king, fine with me. Go for it. I just want to find my sister."

Philippe stared at Rowan. "My, my. You're either very brave or an idiot," he said finally. "But it really makes no difference. I'm done with you. Now, there's no need to make a scene. Why don't you come quietly and we can settle this like gentlemen?"

"You don't mean . . . a duel, do you?" Rowan sputtered.

"Well, in your case it will be more like an execution," Philippe said matter-of-factly. He drew his sword.

Rowan looked around. The corridor was now empty. Everyone had gone into the Hall of Mirrors.

"Wait . . . I don't have a sword!" Rowan cried.

"How unfortunate for you," Philippe said, advancing.

Suddenly Xavier plowed his fist into Philippe's henchman's stomach. "Rowan, RUN!" he yelled, grabbing him and pulling him into the Hall of Mirrors.

The broad man doubled over onto the floor but Philippe raced after them.

Inside the crowded room, they saw a table holding a collection of elaborate masks, capes, and hats.

"Grab something!" Xavier said.

Rowan quickly pulled a helmet-style mask over his head and wrapped a blue cape around his shoulders. Xavier had grabbed a mask that looked like a big glittering sun and a shimmering orange cape to match.

"Spread out, we'll look less conspicuous," Xavier said, easing himself along the wall.

"Keep an eye out for Xanthe," Rowan reminded him. "And look for Nina, she's got to be here somewhere."

"How can we tell who she is if she's wearing a mask?"

"I don't know," sighed Rowan. "Just try to figure it out."

Xavier gave him the OK sign and continued down the hall.

The Hall of Mirrors was possibly the most spectacular room in the entire palace of Versailles. Floor-to-ceiling mirrors lined one side of the room, while windows lined the other. Gilded fleur-de-lis decorated the supporting walls and a line of blazing, crystal chandeliers hung from the ceiling. The mirrors made the room look twice as large as it was, and they reflected everything outside the windows. During the day, this probably gave the room a warm, naturalistic look, but at this late hour it surrounded the revelers in darkness.

Rowan saw himself in a mirror and realized to his dismay that he had chosen a mouse mask. As he stared at himself, he noticed two figures come up behind him. The broad one wore the head of a snarling bear, the tall one wore a harlequin costume with a pàpier mâché clown mask, the mouth pulled up in a disconcerting leer. They scanned the crowd. Rowan ducked behind some dancers, heading toward the other side of the hall.

As he crossed the back of the room, he noticed Mozart, who was disguised as a monkey. The crowd, which had attached itself to him, followed his every word and gesture, falling over themselves to prove who was the most entertained by his jokes. Rowan knew Nina was too respectful of music for that sort of fawning, so as he tried to hide himself he looked for a small figure, for someone perhaps standing to the side and worshiping from afar.

And for a moment, he saw someone. A little slip of a person with wild, black hair, wearing shimmering, rainbow-colored butterfly wings, and a silvery mask that covered half her face. Rowan tore off his own disguise and waved to her from across the room, but she was so focused on Mozart that she didn't notice him. Rowan started toward her, but got caught up in the swirl of dancers between them. The next time he looked in the corner she was gone. In her place stood a large figure in a hooded black cape and the face of a hawk, looking directly at him.

Suddenly the hawk moved toward him, swooping through the dancers. Rowan quickly pulled his mask back on and looked for an escape route, but the orchestra blocked the closest exit, the other door seemed whole football fields away, and he could barely move through the maze of whirling skirts. Rowan pushed past the dancers, but the hawk was gaining on him. And then, to his great shock, the hawk was in front of him! Impossible, and yet . . . but no, it was just a trick of the mirrors.

Rowan dropped to his knees and crawled along the floor, between the legs and skirts of the dancers. Though kicked several times, he made a path diagonally across the room and crouched beneath a marble table. After a minute he poked his head up and saw that the bear and harlequin were blocking the exit. He could see Xavier had positioned himself behind Mozart, a good place, Rowan thought, if the butterfly came back. He hoped Xavier could recognize her.

Suddenly a black boot came down hard on Rowan's finger. He almost yelled, but shoved his cape in his mouth to stifle it. He waited for the owner of the boot to move on, but he just stood there. The pain was excruciating. Then he noticed the silver jeweled scabbard that hung under the man's black cloak and a prickly feeling crept up his spine. It was the hawk, and the hawk was definitely Philippe. His cloak brushed Rowan's cheek. Rowan tried not to move, or even breathe, but he was cross-eyed with pain.

Finally Philippe shifted his weight. Rowan fell back, shoving his crushed finger into his mouth and sucking on it to keep from crying. As he pressed himself against the wall under the table, he felt the wall give a little bit. He ran his fingers along the molding near the parquet floors. He felt a groove in it. On closer inspection the groove seemed to extend up the wall and disappear behind a large painting of Louis XIV. Rowan pressed the crack and felt it move. It was a door! A hidden door on an unmirrored panel! He carefully leaned against it. As the door opened, he quickly rolled through and closed it quietly behind him.

Rowan found himself in some sort of study or library, but unlike the other well-trodden rooms of the palace, this room was distinctly private. A subtle untidiness, a warmth, a stillness, and a slight smell of pipe tobacco betrayed the fact that someone actually lived here.

He started toward the carved door that looked like it might be an exit, but he happened to glance at a beautiful, cherrywood, rolltop desk with ivory and marble inlay. On it were a variety of locks that had been taken apart, a set of tools and keys, and a small book, held open to a page by a china plate upon which sat a half-eaten apricot custard tart. It reminded Rowan of his own bedroom, where he had often holed himself away with a book and snack when his parents had their dinner parties.

Rowan crossed to the table to take a quick look at the book. It was about locks. He touched the pages, but stopped when he heard a small cough.

"You may have the rest of that tart," said a slightly nervous voice, "but perhaps you would prefer some cheese."

Rowan turned to see a stout man in his forties standing in the doorway. His brown hair was pulled back with a black ribbon, and he wore a silk robe and velvet slippers. His face was soft, like a marshmallow, with a hammock of fat that connected his chin to his neck. His hands, however, looked strong and capable. There was no doubt who this was.

"Your Majesty . . ." Rowan stuttered. "Forgive me for intruding . . . I'm quite lost."

"Evidently," Louis said, maintaining his position at the

door to what seemed to be the bedroom. "I'm not sure whether to call the guards or set a trap."

Rowan remembered his mask and realized that this was a joke. He removed his mouse face.

The king smiled.

Rowan gave him his deepest bow, flourishing the mask behind him as though it were his hat.

"I am Rowan Popplewell, the son of the Marquis d'Orange, at your service, your highness." This bit of honest respect seemed to please the king immensely. Rowan suspected that he was unaccustomed to it.

"Are you interested in locks?" asked the king, shuffling by Rowan to his desk.

"In a way," Rowan answered. "I'm pretty good at opening things."

The king tossed him a lock. "See what you can do with this."

Rowan picked it up. It was large, with a unique design. He settled himself at the desk, found a thin, metal rod among the tools, bent it, and inserted it into the keyhole.

"I was admiring your library," said Rowan, to fill the silence in the room.

"Oh?" the king answered. Rowan glanced up to see Louis's expression. The king watched him eagerly, tapping his fingertips together. Rowan realized that he may have finally met a worse conversationalist than himself.

"Yes, I . . . I read quite a bit. Fiction, mainly." Rowan tried to think of a book that Louis might have read. "Shakespeare. I like Shakespeare. Do you? . . ."

"The histories," interrupted Louis. "I do enjoy the histories. Not the comedies though. I don't really see the point of them. And the tragedies, well . . ." the king shrugged.

"I've seen a few of his plays performed."

"Hm. Don't really care for plays," Louis sniffed. "That's the queen's realm. She loves all of that spectacle and make-believe. I can't stand it."

"Yes, I couldn't help but notice that you're not participating in the masked ball."

"No. Definitely not. What's the point? Dressing up in silly costumes. Clopping about until your feet hurt. A huge annoyance is all it is. And the noise keeps me from concentrating."

"Concentrating on what?" Rowan asked. He hoped he hadn't sounded too flippant. Obviously during this volatile period the king grappled daily with serious affairs of state. But small talk was not Rowan's best skill, as he seemed to prove over and over again.

But the king didn't seem offended. He merely opened the top drawer to his desk and pulled out several bound volumes. "Let me show you my writings," he said. "These are my private journals. In them I record significant events and my thoughts surrounding them."

Rowan put down the lock and took the first volume from the king. He opened the book and started reading, mumbling the words aloud:

May 14, 1789
Took black horse out early. Overcast, but no rain. Two male pheasants, three rabbits, no deer.

May 15, 1789
Took out dapple gray, late afternoon. Raining. Four wild geese.
Where have the deer gone?

May 17, 1789
Was sick on the 16th. Took out dapple gray again. Warm and
balmy. Two rabbits. Buck sighted, but no kill.

The volume continued with pages upon pages of hunting
excerpts. Rowan flipped ahead to that morning's entry,
expecting to find some mention of the Bastille. Instead he
found:

July 14, 1789
Nothing.

Nothing? On the day the Bastille had been taken over?
Rowan closed the book quietly, wondering at first if the king
didn't know what had happened that day. But Louis's eyes
were dark and sad, and a palpable gloom filled the room. He
knew all right. And his response was . . . nothing.

Rowan felt sorry for him. Just looking at him, cocooned in
this room of books, locks, desserts, and hunting journals,
Rowan could tell the king was lonely, condescended to, and
ignored. He remembered from his research in the Owatannauk library that Louis's older brother had died as a boy, and
that the unprepared Louis suddenly became first in line for

the crown. It was a responsibility he neither wanted nor felt equipped to handle. His weak rulership turned out to be disastrous. Subsequently, he became less sure of himself, eventually becoming a recluse. Rowan looked at the king and saw . . . himself. And he didn't like it.

"Your Majesty," he said, returning the journal and choosing a different wire with which to explore the lock. "I think there's something you should know. The Bastille has been taken over and its prisoners have been released by a huge mob."

"Yes, I know. I've been informed of the revolt," the king said, resigned.

"No, Your Majesty. Not just a revolt. A revolution," Rowan replied. He looked for a reaction. The king seemed to sag even more. He turned his back on Rowan and moved to the other side of the room, pretending to look at his books.

"There has been a lot of fighting, and I believe they're coming here, to Versailles, to demand to speak with you."

"Hrmmph," the king responded, and no more.

"Perhaps there is something you could say to them," Rowan pressed further. "To put them at ease?"

Louis was silent for a few moments, then turned slowly. "I supposed it would come to this," he said. "I'll have to alert the guards to keep them out."

"If you don't mind, Your Highness," Rowan started again, "perhaps you should go out to them. Listen to what they have to say. Let them know that you care. They think you've been trying to attack them."

"That's preposterous."

"Maybe, but that's what they think. All they know is what they read in the pamphlets."

"All lies. Not a bit of truth printed in any of them . . ."

"So set the record straight. Let them know your side of the story."

Louis shook his head sadly. "I'm not much of a public speaker," he muttered. "I'll just call the guard."

"Your Majesty," Rowan persisted, "you keep yourself secluded here. You can move, you know. You don't have to stay in one place. This palace is becoming your prison."

All of this sounded vaguely familiar to Rowan, but it was good advice, even if it wasn't his own.

Louis mulled it over, but then his whole pudgy body seemed to sag under the weight of the inevitable future. "I'm very tired," he said. "Perhaps you'd better go."

Rowan handed him the lock. "I'm sorry," Rowan said. "I wasn't able to unlock it."

"Don't feel bad," Louis replied with a little smile. "I can't either. And I made it."

With that, Rowan bowed deeply and exited through the door by which the king had entered. As he ran through the adjoining drawing room and the corridor beyond it, he suddenly realized that if Louis had taken his advice, Rowan might've been responsible for unintentionally changing the course of history. He'd have been unable to return to the future that he knew. It made him shiver to think how close he'd come.

But had he really come that close? Changing the king's behavior was like trying to derail a train. Louis XVI was on a track leading to certain doom, and it would take more than a nudge to get him off. It occurred to Rowan that the course of history is not just accidental events, but a culmination of many things; changing one small element probably had little effect on the big picture.

He checked his watch. It was nearly ten o'clock. He hoped Xavier had found Xanthe, and worried about whether he could get to the hallway without running into Philippe or his men.

As Rowan turned the corner, he nearly ran into someone who was racing down the hallway. Glittering wings, silver mask . . . it was the butterfly! Without thinking, Rowan reached out and grabbed her arm. She whirled around with a shriek. With his other hand Rowan ripped off his mask.

"Nina!" he cried joyously. "I've finally found you!"

But something was wrong. The large blue eyes that stared back at him from behind the butterfly face had no idea who he was. He slowly lifted the mask, but he already knew what the problem was. Nina didn't have blue eyes. This girl was not Nina.

She did have a familiar face though, and after she recovered from the shock of being grabbed, she squinted at Rowan, trying to place him.

"Who are you?" Rowan asked. He wondered if he'd seen her at the Palais-Royal, or if she was staying at the Hôtel Genève.

"My name is Marguerite," she said haltingly. Then her eyes widened. "Oh my God!" she squealed. "You were at the restaurant! With your aunts! I'm Margaret, Hilda's daughter! What a wild, crazy coincidence!"

Rowan had been thinking the same thing, but then in almost the same instant he knew it wasn't a coincidence at all.

"So you were the one who took the alleviator here on July 12?" he groaned, his heart sinking.

"Yeah, that was me . . . oh wait, you called me 'Nina.' You thought I was your sister, didn't you?"

"Yes, I thought I had followed *her* here." Rowan closed his eyes. He felt the panic in his chest. He'd followed the wrong person. This was all for nothing. It was an error of cataclysmic proportions. He felt like throwing up. Instead, he told Margaret his story.

"Gee, that's awful. I'm really sorry," Margaret said. "I came here to work on my senior thesis for college. It's funny you should think I look like your sister, though I guess I am on the short side. People always say I look young for my age."

Now looking at her, Rowan realized that perhaps much of the resemblance had come from wishful thinking. Margaret's hair was similar to Nina's, but it was more wavy than curly, and it was a shade lighter. Her posture was different, her hips were wider. He should've noticed these things. His mind was playing tricks on his heart.

"I'm sorry," Rowan said, "but I've got to find my friends and get out of here. My sister could still be in trouble . . ."

"You don't think she can find her way back from wherever she went?" Margaret asked.

"No. I don't. I think she's lost." Rowan recalled that someone had said the same thing about him. Obviously, they were right.

He wanted to get away from Margaret and run headfirst into a wall. How could he make such a mistake? Where had he gone wrong? Just then the hulking bear and the tall harlequin rounded the corner. Philippe's men! The harlequin pointed, shouted something, and broke into a run. Rowan took off in the other direction, racing down the stairs with the harlequin in pursuit.

The bear stopped in front of Margaret, tearing off the mask. "Margaret!" Agatha wheezed, winded from the short sprint down the hallway.

"Hi, Ms. Drake. Great costume," Margaret said, confused. "Are you here on business?"

"I'm afraid so, dear," Agatha answered. "Did Rowan tell you where he was going?"

"I think he was running away from you," Margaret answered. "He said he wanted to find his friends and go back . . . I was just about to go meet my mom at the Apollo fountain. She thought she'd get some more pie recipes from the chef and help me with my paper. She's worried about me being here alone. I don't know why, I am twenty years old after all . . ."

"Wait dear," Agatha interrupted. "Did you say that Hilda was coming?"

"She's already here. She came at the last golden hour."

"Oh my. Oh my, that won't do at all. I thought I felt something strange in the air."

Gertrude returned, her harlequin mask tucked under her arm. "He's fast! I lost him out in the gardens . . ."

"Gertrude, we've got to find him! There's an instability!"

"What are you talking about?" Gertrude lowered her head to Agatha's eye level.

"Hilda's here. It's too many people. Rowan, Xavier, Xanthe, me, you, Margaret, and now Hilda. That's too many."

"I thought I felt something," Gertrude said. "We must find him before he disappears. Xanthe and Xavier as well. Come on!"

Gertrude dashed down the corridor.

Agatha turned to Margaret. "Go find your mother," she said. "You'll want to be with someone if you start skipping through time."

Margaret nodded. Agatha took a few deep breaths then jogged down the hall, the echo from her feet slapping the marble tile getting fainter until she disappeared down the stairwell.

Rowan stopped to catch his breath. He'd dashed through the gardens, darting in and out of groves and doubling back several times in hopes of losing his pursuers. He seemed to have succeeded, but now he found himself utterly confused in the darkness. There were no lights in the garden tonight. Everyone was supposed to be at the ball and the banquet. Rowan sat on a stone bench, chin in hand, and tried to figure out what to do next.

He couldn't believe what a mess he'd made of things. He was responsible for his sister running away and everything he'd done to fix it only seemed to make things worse. Xavier had tried to help him, had even gotten injured in the process, and what was Rowan's response? He'd offended him. This, of course, after offending the queen of France. And how about Emile, the noble who befriended him? How did Rowan repay his kindness? By helping his daughter escape to Paris. And how did he repay Louise for her protection? He offended her and her two patriot friends. In fact, Rowan mused, he seemed to offend almost everybody he met. And now all of that was for nothing. If he thought he was a loser in the twenty-first century, he was the king of the losers in the eighteenth century. Him and Louis, together.

He looked at his broken finger. It was purple and throbbing. He stuck it in his mouth, then he noticed he was sitting in front of the fountain of Enceladus, the beaten Titan, covered in rubble. This was where he had watched Louise sketching. *If she wanted to draw a tragic figure, she should've drawn me*, he thought.

The sounds of the gardens at night were wild and strange, the trees whispering secrets in their tree language. Rowan heard animal sounds: a chorus of frogs, the hum of insects, an owl. A lion roared in the distance and he remembered Emile telling him that there was a menagerie of animals, a sort of small zoo at the far end of the property. He heard monkeys screeching, and a bird squawk—perhaps a parrot. Then Rowan heard a human cry. Off in the distance he heard talking and muffled noises, and footfalls scattering dirt.

He crept toward the voices. As he got closer he recognized

Philippe's voice, as well as his henchmen's. The last voice he heard was soft and earnest. It was Xanthe.

"We don't even know who you're talking about," she said. Rowan could hear in her voice that she was trying to be brave, but her fortitude was failing her.

"Liar!" Philippe snapped. Rowan heard a slap. He ran faster, but was careful to step lightly. "I saw you both with him at the recital, just before you left with your friend, the queen."

"She's not my friend, I'd only just met her . . ." Again a slap. A gasp, a sniffle.

"Stop it," Xavier cried. "Okay, we know him! We don't know where he is. There's nothing we can tell you."

"I'll be the judge of that," Philippe hissed. "Believe me, I've found very interesting ways to make people talk."

Rowan peeked through a tall hedge. He saw the broad man holding Xavier's arms behind his back. Xavier was a mess, his clothes torn, his nose bloody. Rowan shifted his weight to get a look at Xanthe. The tall man was holding her. She was dressed in an Oriental costume; black billowy pants and a long gold and red silk robe decorated with dragons and Chinese lions.

"You're holding back on me," Philippe accused. "I am not going to let that rat friend of yours destroy everything I've built. He thinks he can get the king to have me thrown in prison? Have me executed for treason?"

"He doesn't think that at all!" Xanthe sputtered. "He doesn't care about politics! There's nothing he can do that would stop the course of events . . ."

"Shut up!" Philippe pulled his sword from its sheath. "Only a minute ago you said you didn't even know him!" He held the sword to her throat. "Somebody is going to tell me where he is. If I don't get a satisfactory answer, I am going to cut something. I'll keep cutting until I either get my answer or you are completely drained. Now. Where is he?"

Xanthe gulped.

"Leave her alone! Start with me!" Xavier yelled. He was silenced by a knee to his stomach. He fell over, gasping. "He . . . he's hiding at the Hamlet!" Xavier gurgled.

Philippe's eyes narrowed.

"You're willing to gamble her life on that answer?" Philippe asked. There was a pause. "You're lying." Philippe laughed. "That's going to cost her a finger."

Rowan saw red. He'd had enough.

#2. I hate everything.

Suddenly it was all so clear to him. For a whole year he had been fighting it, covering it up with dutifulness and responsibility. But it hadn't disappeared, it was always there, under the surface, ugly and festering. He was filled with hate, and it catapulted him into the clearing.

Rowan knocked Philippe down, kicking the sword from his hand. He picked it up as Philippe scrambled to his feet, holding it, weighing it for a moment, tempted to slash at Philippe's horrified face . . . Instead he launched it into the night sky.

"Fool!" Philippe cackled. He motioned to his men. "Kill him!"

Rowan fought Philippe now with one thing in mind, Xanthe stalwartly defending him. She was the best person he knew, and Philippe was going to torture her, and then take her life. For no good reason, somebody Rowan loved would be ruined and then gone. Just like his mother.

The surprise attack had given Xanthe just enough time to wrestle free and give the tall man a sharp karate kick that sent him into the hedge. Then she ran. Xavier managed to raise himself to his knees and trip his captor. He climbed on top of him, trapping him in a wrestling hold.

Rowan rained punches upon Philippe. Each blow was an assault against injustice. That one was for his rotten school! That one for all the bullies in the world! That one was for the crummy cot in his crummy apartment! Here were more for his needy sister and his father, who wasn't there for them! He hated them all. He hated how unfair life was, he hated his own cowardice, but most of all he hated his mother. He hated her for dying and he hated God for taking her from him. He heard a voice screaming. It was his own.

Philippe clawed at Rowan's face. Rowan clutched on to him like a pit bull and sank his teeth into Philippe's hand. Out of the corner of his eye, he saw one of Philippe's men running toward him with the sword. He felt a wave of dizziness. As he blinked his eyes he thought he saw a hallucination, Xanthe returning to the grove with the Sisters, Agatha and Gertrude, dressed in odd costumes. Behind them were Margaret and

Hilda ... Now Xanthe and Xavier tried to pull him away, but too late. The silver blade entered his shoulder, tearing through his flesh, the tip pushing through his shirt, now stained with his blood ...

The world undulated, like a blanket being flicked. Rowan felt himself thrown back as the scenery rippled around him. The Sisters, Hilda, and Margaret rippled in other directions ... then all went black.

CHAPTER ELEVEN

PRISON

When Rowan awoke, he thought he was in hell. At first he couldn't tell whether his eyes were open or shut, all he could see was blackness. The air was hot and thick, like a swamp. His chest hurt; with every breath a searing pain stabbed his shoulder blades and flashed down his back. Beyond his own staggered breathing he heard low moans, cries, and muffled talking. His nose twitched from the sharp, acrid smell of urine and blood.

"Rowan?"

Rowan tried to answer but could not. He took a breath to say something, but the pain knocked the wind out of him and he groaned instead. The voice was Xanthe's, and it relaxed him. Just hearing it made him feel a little better.

"I think I saw his eye twitch," Xanthe said quietly.

"How can you tell? It's so swollen," Xavier responded. They spoke in hushed tones, as though viewing a body at the morgue.

"Yes, but look, there it goes again."

"Yes! You're right! And his breathing's gotten better!"

Rowan wondered how long he had been out. He tried to flutter his eyelids again. They hurt, but they did open, and he could see that he was in a room, not as dark as he thought. There were three slitlike windows that allowed sheets of sunlight to pierce the stone walls, illuminating the cell with a brownish haze. He lay on a cot pressed up against the wall. The moaning that at first seemed so far away came from just outside the door.

Xanthe's and Xavier's concerned faces filled his vision.

"Yes!" cried Xavier, "he's awake! Rowan! It's me, Xavier. Xanthe's here, too. Do you recognize us?"

Rowan willed his head to nod, which he supposed it did, because a bolt of pain streaked down his neck to the base of his spine. He managed a labored grunt.

"Don't try to talk, Rowan," Xanthe said, putting a cold cloth on his face. It felt wonderful against his skin. It was such a small, simple act of kindness, but at that moment it meant everything to Rowan. He felt the sting of tears welling up.

"Oh, don't, don't . . ." Xanthe said soothingly. "You're going to be okay, Rowan. You're going to be okay."

Rowan wondered about that. He hadn't been "okay" for a long time.

"I want to thank you, you know," Xanthe said, smiling a little. "The way you rushed in and went after Philippe. It was so . . . crazy! And brave. I didn't know you had it in you."

Rowan felt his face flush. If she only knew that it wasn't bravery but anger that had compelled him to attack Philippe. But he did have to admit he had not been afraid. In fact, even now his fear was gone.

"Xanthe came into the Hall of Mirrors with the queen about ten minutes after I left you," Xavier said. "We must've spent a half hour looking at everybody who could even remotely be Nina, and turned up empty. We saw Philippe looking for you, but we couldn't see you. We figured that maybe you'd slipped out somehow and that we would try to meet you in the hall."

"Unfortunately, when we tried to slip by Philippe he recognized us. We totally forgot how much we stood out." Xanthe rubbed her cheek and smiled wryly. "Philippe's thugs grabbed us and carried us out to the garden. Xavier tried to fight and got beat up . . ."

"I wouldn't say that," Xavier protested. "Sure, they got in a couple of lucky punches . . ."

"Xave, your face looked like a pizza."

"Yeah, well, it looked a lot worse than it was. And that big guy's got two fewer rotten teeth he has to worry about thanks to my right uppercut."

"Oh brother. You are no boxer, believe me. Forget being a heavyweight or a flyweight. You're just a paperweight."

Xavier laughed, despite himself. Once again Rowan was glad to hear their familiar bickering. It relaxed him and he chuckled. The twins mistook it for a coughing fit.

"Okay, okay," said Xavier. "Just listen, don't talk. After you flew out of the trees and jumped on Philippe, something really weird happened. There was a funny . . . I don't know how to describe it . . . like a wave in the air. Kind of like the feeling you have when you're on a really big roller coaster, your stomach goes up and down, up and down . . ."

"Yeah, and then four people showed up," Xanthe added. "One of them was Hilda from the Owatannuk coffee shop. I didn't know the other three, but I think two of them were your aunts? . . ."

It took some effort, but Rowan nodded. "Yes," he finally croaked, clearing his throat. "I saw them, too."

"Well, after they showed up, I felt dizzy . . . Xanthe, too . . . and we felt that wave again, and I could hear them yelling at us to hold on to each other. So I grabbed for you and Xanthe. Next thing I knew we were surrounded by people wearing funny red caps and red-white-and-blue ribbons."

"I think we frightened them, appearing out of nowhere in the middle of their picnic like that," Xanthe added.

"Who knows what they thought we were doing there?" Xavier said. "They clearly weren't nobles, but they saw that wig on your head and Xanthe's costume, noticed how scared we looked, decided we were guilty of something, and brought us here."

"Where's here?" Rowan said, turning himself over with considerable effort.

"We're in a place called 'the Conciergerie' . . . it's a kind of holding prison. There's a huge hall, just outside the door, filled with people like us who are 'enemies of the state.' You wait here until you're called for your trial, then you stand before the Revolutionary Tribunal. They decide if you're innocent or guilty. If they say you're innocent, you're released. If they vote guilty . . . well, you don't come back. And by the way, in the last three days nobody's been judged innocent, so don't hold your breath."

"I've been out for three days?" Rowan gasped.

Xavier nodded. "Yeah. That stab wound was pretty bad. If we hadn't fluxed right at that moment, you might not be here today."

"There must have been too many people from the future in one place," Xanthe reasoned. "Which sent us through that time warp, or whatever Otto called it. You can't really tell from in here, but there's been a big change outside. The patriots are all organized now. When we got here, we heard from others that the king had already been beheaded and the queen is locked up in here somewhere. I think we skipped about four years ahead, placing us right in the middle of the Reign of Terror."

Xavier put his hand on Rowan's shoulder. "I think the only reason we're still together is that we were all holding on to each other. I don't think Nina skipped the four years with us."

"We've already looked around this place, and asked about her," said Xanthe. "Sorry, Rowan, she's not here."

"I know," Rowan said, sighing. "To tell you the truth, I've got some . . . well . . . some bad news."

Xavier and Xanthe frowned.

Rowan took a deep breath. "I'm pretty sure that . . . that she was never in Paris at all. We picked the wrong alleviator."

Xavier gaped at Rowan. "What?" he finally sputtered. "You mean we came all the way out here for nothing!"

Rowan nodded. "I found out the person who used that alleviator wasn't Nina at all. It was a girl named Margaret, Hilda's daughter. She's working on a paper for college . . . it's hard to explain."

"But . . . how could that happen? And where is your sister?" Xavier gurgled. He was breathing hard, like a bull in a bullfight.

"Xave, calm down," said Xanthe. "We've got other things to worry about right now."

"I'll say we do! This whole trip has been a nightmare!" Xavier ranted. "I mean, it's not exactly how I planned on spending my summer, Xanthe. I could've gone to basketball camp! But all right, I'm up for a little adventure. I'll put myself in danger, if there's a good reason . . . but for *nothing*? I'm going to lose my head over a *mistake*? Nuh-uh, I don't *think* so!"

"I'm sorry. I guess things would've been better if you'd never met me," Rowan said, trying to sit up. His whole body resented him for it, but he forced it up anyway. "You can kick my butt for it later, but I think we should spend the time trying to find a way to escape."

"What do you think we've been doing for the last three days?" Xavier snapped. "Do you think anybody would still be here if there was a loose brick in the wall that you could squeeze through? If there was a guard you could bribe? Get real! We've been waiting for three days for you to wake up, Rowan, just so we could tell you that we're all going to die!"

"We're not going to die," Rowan said confidently. He stretched his arms, his legs, and his neck. He could hear them cracking, but they weren't broken, only covered with bruises and welts. His back and chest felt tight, but when he ran his fingers over the area he realized it had been tightly bandaged. Miraculously the sword hadn't killed him. He realized that if he could bear the pain, he could move. No matter what insanity happened around him he could still move. He slowly swung his legs off the bed and tried to stand.

"Do you think you should be doing that?" Xanthe asked.

"Why not?" Xavier muttered. "What's the point of being in the best of health when you're just going to have your head chopped off?"

"I told you, we're not going to die," Rowan said again.

"What makes you so sure?" asked Xanthe.

"Because . . . I don't know. I guess I have faith."

"Faith in God?" Xanthe ventured.

"No," Rowan answered. "Faith in myself." He stood up, wobbling a bit. Streaks of pain shot up his back, but he stood until he got used to it. Then he took his first step.

That afternoon and evening Rowan gathered information from the other prisoners. He discovered that generally they kept men and women separate; the only time they saw each other was through a grille that looked out on a courtyard, where the women would come once a day to wash their clothes and bathe themselves. At lunchtime men and women sat across from each other, separated only by a barred partition. Xavier managed to keep Xanthe from being separated with the other women by buying a better room where the three of them could stay together, using the remaining gold pieces in Rowan's pouch.

People who couldn't afford to pay for a private cell stayed in the main hall of the Conciergerie. There were no beds; inmates

slept on the straw. There were no toilets; people relieved themselves in corners of the room, though some didn't even bother to
do that. Lice were rampant. Rowan was amazed that even under
these awful conditions people kept their spirits up; they played
cards, gossiped about the new inmates, and tried to catch rats for
pets. Their amusement was always interrupted, however, by the
minister of the tribunal calling out the names of the accused, and
the sound of the wooden carts clattering over the cobblestones
outside, carrying the guilty to the guillotine.

Rowan quickly realized that nobody was allowed to leave
the Conciergerie for any reason except to appear before the
tribunal. There were many guards, and they watched the prisoners carefully. These guards were in turn watched by other
guards. No one was above suspicion. Bribery seemed to get
inmates certain favors, however. Rowan wondered how far you
could go with a good bribe. He mentally went over what he had
on him that he could use. He didn't have any money left, but he
had the pocket watch, the locket, and the alleviator key. He
snuck the key out of his pocket, cupped it in his hands, and took
a peek at it. It still gleamed and sparkled. Apparently the jump
in time had not affected its power.

The key. It was the only thing that set him and Xanthe and
Xavier apart from all the other prisoners. Slowly an idea
began to form in his head. It might be hard to convince the
twins, but it was the only thing he could think of, and they
only had one day left.

Though their keys had roughly forty-eight hours before
they would disintegrate, Nina's key would disappear twelve

hours earlier. That meant they had only thirty-six hours to figure out where she was and bring her back. Clearly the first step was to get out of revolutionary France as soon as possible.

When Rowan told Xanthe and Xavier his plan, they stared at him in stunned silence.

Finally Xanthe released a long sigh. "It sounds kind of dangerous," she said. "Isn't it possible Nina's already back? Now that we know she's not stuck here?"

"I can't take that chance," Rowan answered.

Xavier nodded. "Great plan, Rowan," he said, slapping him on the back. "I wish I had thought of it."

Rowan couldn't think of a better compliment.

At dinner there was a considerable amount of discussion about one inmate in particular who had been sentenced to be executed the next morning: Marie Antoinette. Rowan let everyone know that he wanted to see her. It was part of his plan. It didn't matter whether or not he actually got to see her, but he figured if the tribunal got wind of his request they would surely speed up his trial. He approached one of the guards with the intention of bribing his way into her cell with his pocket watch.

The guard did not appreciate the offer. He shoved Rowan in the stomach with the butt of his gun, and was about to crack him on the skull when another guard ran over, stopped him, and dragged Rowan to the opposite side of the room. Once Rowan caught his breath, the guard helped him to his feet.

"Thank you," Rowan said, rubbing his stomach. "I guess that was a mistake."

"You should be more careful," the guard answered tersely.

"I just wanted to see the queen," Rowan said. "I think . . . I think I need to talk to her."

"She is not a queen anymore," the guard said.

"Yes, yes, of course," Rowan answered. "She's just a regular person, like all of us." He brushed himself off, but his clothes were so dirty it didn't make much of a difference.

The guard peered at him for a long time, then smiled a crooked smile. "I will help you," he said.

Rowan looked at the guard, surprised. The young man's eyes looked familiar. A young man with an old man's eyes.

"Do you remember me?" the guard said. "I'm Sebastien. Four years ago you gave me your coat. I still have it."

"Yes, of course I remember you . . ."

"I wore that coat in an interview for a job. With that job I was able to eat, and rent a room, and meet some people who could give work to my friends . . ." Sebastien's eyes grew moist.

"That's great," Rowan said, genuinely pleased. "And now you're here."

"I'll help you," Sebastien said, staunchly. "Tonight, at eleven o'clock. Meet me at the gate to the women's prison."

Rowan met Sebastien five minutes early. Sebastien gave him a cloak to disguise himself. They went through a series of wicket gates before they reached Antoinette's cell, with its iron-barred windows. Sebastien whispered something to the two guards, who nodded, unlocked the door, and walked several yards away, leaving the keys with Sebastien. Rowan entered the cell with his stomach doing backflips. He felt as if he were being given a pop quiz; he had not expected to ever see her again.

"You have ten minutes," Sebastien whispered as he locked the door.

Marie Antoinette was waiting for him. She wore a plain, white dress. Her youthful looks had been aged by recent events. Her hair, now thin and white, hung in a limp bun. Her skin was drawn and gray. Rowan suddenly noticed a line of acne bumps on her forehead and his anxiety melted away. She really was human after all.

"Monsieur Popplewell," she said sadly.

"Your Majesty," Rowan began, then caught himself.

Antoinette smiled grimly. "You can lose your head for calling me that," she said. "What can I do for you, Monsieur? I have nothing, I'm afraid. I have nothing left."

"I came here to talk," Rowan said, not exactly sure where he was leading. "I just want you to know . . . that somebody cares. That I know you are being treated unfairly, and that you don't deserve this. Nobody deserves this . . ." He looked around her cell. It had a bed, a table, and two chairs. The lavishness of Versailles was a distant memory for her.

"I am to die tomorrow," Antoinette sighed. "You heard about my trial, no? How they accused me of masterminding Louis's political decisions? And of plotting the murder of Philippe Duc d'Orleans? They had no proof—all just gossip and hearsay— but I was found guilty of course. I should be used to it by now." Suddenly tears filled Antoinette's eyes and she covered her face with her hands, her shoulders lurching in huge sobs.

Rowan wasn't sure what to do.

"My God! Death is welcome!" she moaned. "Anything to relieve me from this torture!" She looked up. "My captors have destroyed me, for they have stolen and defiled my last source of happiness. Charles. My son Charles has been turned against me. At my trial they forced him to testify that I abused him in unspeakable ways. And somehow they have made him believe those lies. My son's fond memories of me have been replaced with ugliness and horror. How can he go on, when his mind is filled with such poison? Without the memories of his mother's love? Do you know what that does to a person, Monsieur?"

Rowan shuddered violently. Yes, he did know. *He did know.*

Rowan reached out slowly and placed something in Antoinette's open hand.

"I wanted you to have this back," Rowan said. He got up and went to the iron bars. Sebastien unlocked the gate.

"Thank you . . ." he heard her whisper as the gate clanked shut behind him. As he followed Sebastien down the stairs, he glanced back at her. She was looking tearfully at the picture contained in the heart-shaped locket; a miniature painting of herself with her husband and four children in happier days.

As soon as Rowan returned he woke up Xanthe and Xavier. "I know where Nina is!" he announced.

"What?" Xavier said, rubbing his eyes.

Rowan quickly revealed Nina's location to his friends.

"You're brilliant!" squealed Xanthe.

"No I'm not," said Rowan. "It was in front of me the whole time. I just didn't see it. I should've listened more to my heart."

• • •

Early the next morning Marie Antoinette was asked if she wanted anything to eat. She refused. She put on her plain, white dress to which she added a white linen cap. Soon after, Charles Sanson, the man chosen to be her executioner, hacked off her thin, white hair. Her hands were bound behind her back. She was carried to the Place du Carrousel in an open cart to the shouts of "Long live the Republic!" There, the guillotine separated her head from her body shortly after noon.

Rowan heard from the rumors of the other inmates that Marie Antoinette had gone with dignity and grace. He didn't want to think about it; he cried when she died, even though he knew history was just playing itself out. Still, he found it remarkable that she had faced death without fear. He was glad he'd been there to comfort her the night before. At least he had given her that.

But he didn't have too much time to dwell on the former queen's death. His plan had worked. While Antoinette was receiving her haircut, the minister of the tribunal had called Rowan's name, along with Xanthe, Xavier, and twelve others. The tribunal had determined Rowan and his friends to be an immediate danger, and by early afternoon the guards had arrived to take them before the court.

As they approached the courtroom, Rowan was surprised to hear the unmistakable voice of Georges Danton thundering from behind the doors. Suddenly they burst open and he strode out, followed by a flurry of people tripping over themselves trying to catch up with him.

"Outrageous!" Danton bellowed. "Everywhere I turn I am surrounded by the feebleminded!" He stopped in front of Rowan, cocked his head and furrowed his brow, obviously trying to place him.

Rowan saved him the trouble. "It is me, Monsieur Danton, Rowan Popplewell. I was friends with Louise . . ."

"Hah! Monsieur Popplewell!" Danton roared. "So finally the idiots have caught up with you, too. Have you decided which side you are on yet?"

Rowan smiled. "Which side is winning?" he asked.

"We're all losing," Danton replied. "Anyway, there are too many sides to keep track of. The only one who is winning is Charles Sanson, the executioner. As long as there is a Frenchman standing in France, he will have work."

Camille Desmoulin rushed out of the courtroom. "Georges, please, we need you inside . . ."

"What's the hurry, Camille?" Danton huffed. "So they behead only forty people today instead of fifty. What a tragedy. Say hello to Monsieur Popplewell. You remember him, don't you? Your houseguest?"

Camille jumped when he recognized Rowan. "Ah! Monsieur Popplewell. I am truly sorry to see you here. This is a one-way courtroom, you know. Justice has taken a holiday."

"Our friend, Monsieur Robespierre, is completely out of control," Danton added. "He is obsessed with the idea of Republican purity, and will not rest until he has his 'Reign of Virtue.' Unfortunately, most people fall short of his expectations. French citizens are being executed by the hundreds, based on practically nothing. He is infuriating!"

"Georges, you are not doing either one of us any good by goading him," Camille muttered. "Sometimes I regret supporting you so much. I'm sure it will cost me my head."

Rowan bit his tongue, remembering his research. Camille couldn't have been more right. Within six months Camille and Danton would both be decapitated.

As Camille and Danton turned back to the courtroom, Rowan called out, "Monsieur Danton, how is Louise?"

"Louise? You mean my wife?" Danton asked, raising an eyebrow. "She is as well as any woman could be in the middle of a bloodbath. Excuse me, sir, I must return to hitting my head against a brick wall."

Danton straightened his jacket, shook his hair, puffed out his chest, and marched back into the courtroom with Camille in tow. Moments later, the guards led Rowan, Xanthe, and Xavier into the room. Danton and Camille sat in the audience. Rowan was glad to see Louise with them. Her eyes widened as she recognized him and Rowan thought to wave, but his attention was suddenly riveted to the front of the room.

There, on a dais with several other men, stood Maximilien Robespierre. He had the same ferret face, steel-rimmed glasses, and perfectly curled, powdered wig. But now he had the aura of power, and it gave him an almost supernatural quality. He picked up the large, brass bell on the table and rang it. The room settled to a hushed silence.

"You have been brought here for crimes against the people," said Robespierre in his high-pitched voice. "At first, Monsieur Popplewell, I must admit that when you and your friends were brought here you were something of a mystery. Fortunately, we were aided by citizen Philippe Egalité, who recognized you immediately."

Philippe stood up in the audience and gave a slight bow in Rowan's direction. He no longer wore the wig or the sword, but the smirk was the same.

"He's a patriot?" Xanthe gasped.

"Of course not," Rowan whispered back. "He's just looking out for himself. As always."

Robespierre continued. "I, too, recall a short conversation with you many years ago. You were quite morally conflicted at the time." He turned to the prosecutor. "Proceed."

The prosecutor then stepped forward and started to list their crimes: attempted murder of Philippe Egalité, formerly known as the Duc d'Orleans, conspiring with enemies of France—Louis Capet and his wife, Marie Antoinette—to undo the social and political progress of the people, sympathizing with the royalist cause, and being of titled aristocracy, an automatic criminal offense in the eyes of this virtuous body of men and women.

As the prosecutor concluded the charges, the virtuous body whistled and howled, waving the weapons they'd brought with them into the courtroom. Robespierre rang the bell again, and the spirited group reluctantly calmed themselves.

"You've heard the charges," Robespierre snapped. "How do you answer?"

Before Rowan could say anything the crowd started shouting.

"Give him a taste of the hot hand!" somebody cried out, referring to the guillotine.

"Let's see what his neck may spit into the basket!"

"He needs a shave with the national razor!"

"Lighten the heavy load on his shoulders!"

Robespierre again rang the bell. "Speak man! What say you?"

Rowan held up his hands for silence as hundreds of greedy eyes fixed upon him. He'd had enough of lies. It was time to tell the truth.

"Citizens," he began. "My name is Rowan Popplewell. I am not, as you believe, the son of the Marquis d'Orange. There is no such person. He is a lie. There is nothing remarkable about me, I'm afraid. I don't have a gift for speech making, like Monsieur Georges Danton, nor do I express myself with the eloquence of Monsieur Camille Desmoulin. I am a very ordinary, common person, except for one thing. I am from the future, and I come with a warning."

There was an audible squeaking of chairs as everyone in the courtroom leaned forward. Xanthe and Xavier looked at each other with raised eyebrows. Rowan had already told them what he was going to say, but they were wary of the unpredictable nature of the mob.

"I came here to find someone," Rowan continued, "and I did, but it wasn't the person I thought I'd find. It took a lot of time, too. The person I found was hard to recognize.

He was angry at life and didn't know what to do about it. That anger held him hostage. I look at you and think perhaps many of you know what I'm talking about. You may not see it, but your anger has twisted you into something monstrous. For your own sakes I hope you can find who you once were. If you don't, many more innocent people will be murdered, including people in this room, Monsieur Maximilien Robespierre among them."

Rowan sat down to silence. After a few moments the crowd started murmuring, then erupted into shouts of disagreement. Robespierre's voice rose above the din.

"The prisoner has very deftly avoided answering the charges, and is attempting to frighten us with a veiled threat. I submit to you that he is guilty, and hopes to save his neck by appealing to . . . what? He asks us to set aside our righteous anger and extend to him our mercy? Mercy is a weakness, my friends. Just as a doctor cuts off a gangrenous limb so that it won't infect the rest of a healthy body, so we must amputate those individuals who would threaten the health of our virtuous society. We have not lost ourselves, citizens, in our anger we have discovered our true selves; people who no longer tolerate oppression and greed!"

The crowd burst into applause and shouts once again. The judges took a vote, were unanimous in Rowan's guilt, and he and the twins were condemned to death that evening by guillotine.

CHAPTER TWELVE

THE ELEMENT OF SURPRISE

Rowan, Xanthe, and Xavier spent their final hours in a small, dark room at the Conciergerie reserved for the condemned. Xavier paced the floor.

"Xavier, stop it. You're making me dizzy," Xanthe said.

"Are you sure this is going to work?" Xavier asked, stopping in front of Rowan. "I mean, it really takes things up to the last minute. We can't afford to make a mistake, there won't be any second chances."

"I know, I know," Rowan said, sounding more confident than he actually was. "But we've already gone over this a million times, Xave. We have less than twenty-four hours before our keys disintegrate. We can't escape as long as we're in prison. Our only chance to get away is when we're outside, and the only time they are going to let us out is when they take us to the guillotine. That's when we have to use the element of surprise."

Xavier didn't look convinced. Xanthe stood up.

"Rowan's right, Xave. It makes perfect sense. Just because everybody else goes to the guillotine without a fight doesn't mean we have to. They'll never expect us to try to escape, so their guard will be down."

"Maybe they don't expect it because only the dumbest idiots in the world would try to do it," Xavier said.

"We would be the dumbest idiots if we didn't have someplace to escape *to*," Rowan explained. "Remember, we're not escaping to the woods, we're escaping to the twenty-first century. The alleviator is waiting for us in that field. We're just going to disappear—poof!—like magic. Do you guys still have your keys?"

Xanthe and Xavier both checked their pockets, holding up the large golden keys that still shimmered, even in the shadowy room. Rowan held his up as well.

"Maybe they still work, but maybe they don't," Xanthe murmured. "What if we run to the field and we find out that our little time jump skipped us four years past our time limit, so that the alleviator isn't there?"

Rowan shrugged. "I guess then you should keep running."

"I suppose you've got a point," Xavier admitted. "But do you really think we're going to make it to that field when we're surrounded on all sides? It's got to be at least three miles away, if not more, and we're going to have our hands tied behind our backs."

"Well," Xanthe said slowly, "even if we don't all make it, it will still be worth it if just *one* of us makes it."

The three of them looked at one another with an awful

realization as Xanthe's words sank in. It probably would be impossible for all three of them to run several miles to the field without being caught, but if two of them provided a strong distraction, the third person could slip into the crowd, and perhaps walk away unnoticed. Of course, the two who provided the distraction would be killed, but Xanthe was right. The sacrifice was worth it if even one of them could get away.

Xavier reached down and solemnly picked up three pieces of straw. He held them up.

"Who wants to go first?" he said.

Rowan shook his head. "I'm not picking," he said. "After that scene in the courtroom, I'm the face the crowd will recognize. I can't possibly escape unnoticed. Besides, it's not fair for your family to lose both of you. You guys pick. I'm out of it."

"But you're the one who's got to get Nina," Xavier said. "She's not going to listen to either of us the way she'll listen to you."

"We don't know that. Look, I'm the one who got us all into this. I don't want you guys paying for my mistakes."

Xavier turned to Xanthe. "You go, Xanthe. Women and children first, right? That's you on both counts."

"Thanks for the sexist thought, Xave, but you have the best chance of actually making it. You lie better than anybody, and if you do have to run, you're faster and stronger . . ."

"Man, I've never heard you give me so many compliments," Xavier said. "We should get into life-and-death situations more often."

"Then it's settled," she said.

"Nope," Xavier retorted. "You're right, we should pick whoever would be the most likely to succeed in escaping. And maybe I am stronger, but my strength is going to be a lot more useful as the distraction. Rowan and I can get into a fight and really haul away at each other."

"But Xave . . ."

Xavier put his hands on his sister's shoulders. "Shut up, Xanthe," he said gently. "Let me be the hero, all right? To tell you the truth, I couldn't live with myself knowing I'd let you sacrifice your life for me when I had the chance to do the same for you."

"But I couldn't either . . ." Xanthe started.

Rowan laughed. "Can't you two agree on anything?" he said.

"It would make me feel better if we did eeny meeny miney mo," Xanthe whispered.

"I agree with Xave on this," Rowan said. "I want you to be the one that lives. Maybe it is a macho thing, but I just want it to be you."

Xanthe opened her mouth a few times, but nothing came out. She grabbed the two boys in a hug. They stayed there until their names were called to make the journey to the Place du Carrousel, where they would be made to pay for their crimes.

As the little open carts, the tumbrels, rumbled over the road, they stopped several times to keep from hitting people who jeered and threw stones. The crowd lined the streets, watching what seemed to Rowan like an endless death parade, a feeling enhanced by the incredibly tall, hooded figure driving their cart, his legs folded up like a praying mantis, his black cloak draped so closely around him that all you could see were his bony fingers wrapped around the leather reins.

Rowan waited for the moment when he and Xavier could start their fight. The field lay beyond the square where the guillotine sat, so it behooved them to wait until the last minute, but he felt certain that they should do it while the cart was still moving. Once it stopped, the guards would surround them and the opportunity would be lost.

CRACK! A stone hit Rowan's head and a trickle of blood ran down from his temple. Rowan actually wished the crowd would throw bigger rocks. At least he could see them coming and dodge them. Besides, he was secretly collecting them into a pile with his feet, preparing to launch a few back when the time was right. Xavier was doing the same thing, and kept glancing at Rowan for a signal. Rowan shook his head. *Not yet. Not yet.*

The plan was simple. Though their hands were tied behind their backs, they could easily slip their bodies through the circle of their arms and end up with their hands in front of them. Additionally, the knots were not impossible to untie, and Xavier had already loosened Xanthe's to the point at which she could slip her hands out when she needed to. When Rowan gave the signal, he and Xavier would start a loud fight, hurling stones at one another, pushing Xanthe out of the wagon. She would then try to slip away while they were being subdued. Rowan hoped to take their scuffle to the front of the wagon where he could get a good shot at the driver. If he could topple him off, then he might be able to get the horse to rear up and kick a few people, causing more havoc.

As they turned the corner, the scent of blood tinged the air. There, maybe a hundred feet away, stood the guillotine, stationed on a large, wooden platform, the blade glowing in the golden light of the descending sun. Hundreds of people had come out for the event, as they had no doubt come out for many such events. They knew the routine, and Rowan smiled grimly to himself, knowing that they were about to get the show of their lives.

He was startled to feel Xanthe squeeze his hand. The warmth of her expression struck him, and suddenly he knew that he had something with her that was special. He squeezed her hand back in response.

"Good-bye," he whispered.

"Good-bye," she whispered.

Rowan raised his eyes to Xavier, who had been watching them. Rowan nodded. Xavier nodded back, stuck his tongue out at his sister, and gave her a tight smile. She gave a wobbly smile and stuck her tongue out, too. Then Xavier and Rowan wiggled their bodies through their arms.

Xanthe positioned herself at the back corner of the cart as Rowan and Xavier picked up the largest stones from the wagon bed. As Rowan made his way to the driver, images of his life flashed through his mind. He saw among the crowd faces from his past: his best friend from second grade, bullies from the new school, his nursery school teacher with her bag of marshmallows, his father, depressed and lonely. He remembered the smells of his father's bakery, always filled with extraordinary cakes and doughnuts and muffins, and he felt a yearning for his childhood that was so strong he nearly swooned. But now he was back in revolutionary France, and he smelled only blood and the medicinal scent of horehound drops.

Horehound drops? Rowan sat up and looked around. Was it possible? . . .

"Aunt Gertrude?" he whispered to the driver.

"Yes," she grunted. "Sit still. Don't draw attention to yourselves. Wait until they execute the prisoners in the fourth cart, then hold on tight."

It was all Rowan could do to keep from cheering. Xavier looked at him questioningly. Rowan eased himself back over to his friends and relayed the news as quickly and quietly as he could.

The first tumbrel stopped and the doomed passengers were led to the blade. Rowan, Xanthe, and Xavier averted their eyes. CLUNK! *Thud.* CLUNK! *Thud.* CLUNK! *Thud.* The first tumbrel moved on and the second pulled up. CLUNK! *Thud.* CLUNK! *Thud.* CLUNK! *Thud.* And the second tumbrel had concluded its business. With the third and fourth it was the same.

They were in the fifth tumbrel. As Rowan counted the twelfth CLUNK! he carefully wrapped his sweaty hands around the side of the cart as it pulled forward, up to the blood-soaked platform. But then new sounds pierced the air; the crack of a whip, the alarmed whinny of horses, and the gleeful shout of Gertrude as she urged them forward.

The people in the crowd rushed about like ants in a rainstorm. Once they registered what was happening, they charged after the tumbrel, which clattered wildly down the road. Gertrude's cloak had unfolded in the wind and now flapped around her shoulders. Her sharp features poked out from under the hood like a Halloween witch's.

Guards on horseback galloped up on either side of them, swords raised. Gertrude produced a long staff from under her seat. She twirled it over her head, swiftly brought it down on the neck of one, then immediately thrust it into the chest of the other, knocking them off their horses in a matter of seconds.

Rowan could see the field just ahead. Grass spread out like a large green carpet before them. The sun rested lazily on the treetops, turning the landscape into a mixture of shadow and light . . . the golden hour. Sure enough, there in the field, a glimmer vibrating in the distance, easily overlooked at first, but becoming more distinct by the second, stood the alleviator.

The cart collided with a boulder hidden in the tall grass. One of the wheels snapped off, and the cart spun around.

"Rowan!" Xanthe cried. "I'm slipping!"

Rowan tried to reach her with his hands but couldn't, so he thrust his leg toward her. Xanthe clutched on to it, pulling herself back into the wagon. The shifting weight strained the wood.

One of the horses staggered and fell, pulling down the other, and they dragged down the splintering wagon with Rowan, Xanthe, and Xavier, clutching for a firm handhold on anything they could find. The wagon slammed into another boulder, the other wheel came off, Gertrude was thrown from her seat, and the three passengers rolled onto the grass, the world whirling about them.

Xavier jumped up and pulled Xanthe to her feet.

"There it is!" he cried, pointing. "Come on!"

Rowan's eyes stung from a clump of dirt that had flown into them. He rubbed them as he ran, conscious of the stampede behind him. Some people fired at them. Fortunately, guns did not seem to be accurate in the eighteenth century, but it terrified Rowan nevertheless.

He finally cleared his eyes enough to see Xavier and Xanthe rushing off several yards ahead of him. Where was Aunt Gertrude? And where was the alleviator? The twins seemed to know where it was, but he couldn't see it. It used to be there, plain as day . . . And then an awful thought occurred to him. He thrust his hand into his pocket. His key was gone.

He checked his other pockets. All empty. And then he remembered the small sound, *ting!* when he'd hit the ground rolling. He'd thought nothing of it at the moment, but there had definitely been a *ting!* It must have been his key falling from his pocket. He turned around and looked at the field, which seemed much wider than it had before. The key could be anywhere. Well, maybe not anywhere. He could try to retrace his steps. But the crowd had already overtaken the broken cart. There was no way he could run back, find the key, and get to the alleviator without getting killed. Absolutely no way.

He turned back just in time to see Xanthe and Xavier disappear into thin air. There they were, running, then suddenly gone. Just as suddenly, Xavier's head appeared. He was obviously sticking it out from behind the alleviator door because it was all you could see, this strange disembodied head floating about five feet off the ground.

"Come on, Rowan! What are you waiting for?" Xavier shouted.

"I lost my key," Rowan said helplessly. Then he noticed that the crowd had stopped and grown silent, as though they had seen a ghost. It dawned on Rowan that as far as they knew, they *were* seeing a ghost. A vision, horrible and strange, of a fallen head coming back to life.

"Xave," Rowan said, as quietly as he could. "They can only see your head. They think you're a ghost! Buy me some time!"

It only took Xavier a second to realize what Rowan meant. A trace of grin curled his lips, then he threw his head back in agony and let out a blood-curdling moan.

"OOOOOAAAHHH!" he cried, rolling his eyes back in their sockets. "Ohhhh, woe to those who murder and muti- late the innocent! Ohhh, I will not rest until I find the man or woman who separated me from my body. Who was it? Who was it? Was it you? Step forward now, so that I know who to follow for the rest of their miserable days on earth!"

What a ham, Rowan thought as he quietly crept behind the crowd and searched the grass around the broken tumbrel. He found that he could easily follow the path the tumbrel had taken for it had plowed two furrows in the earth. He figured out where they had fallen as well. It was marked by a piece of his shirt that had ripped off in Xanthe's hand when they'd hit the ground.

He got on his hands and knees and pawed through the dirt. He could hear that the ghastly performance now included the disembodied head of Xanthe, also moaning plaintively and threatening an eternity of hellfire for the culprits.

Suddenly a dark figure appeared above him. He was startled for a moment, then saw it was Gertrude.

"Hurry, Rowan," she whispered. "The hour is almost over. After that, there's nothing I can do." She started to help him look. It took about five minutes before Rowan saw a glint of gold covered by mud. He grabbed for it, and held up the key. Gertrude scooped him up in her arms, and, holding him like a football, flew through the crowd, toward the alleviator. The sun was well below the trees and the sky had taken on a pink-and-purple hue. The glimmer of the gold on the key was strobing, going back and forth between its magical state and ordinary state like a weakening pulse.

But Gertrude moved swiftly, her feet barely skimming the ground. She dove past Xavier and Xanthe, who quickly concluded their performance with a melodramatic "Beware!"

Once inside the alleviator, the key gleamed with full force. The machine trembled, vibrated, and shook, then in a flash disappeared from France.

By the time they arrived back in the twenty-first century, the hotel had already reverted to its dilapidated state. The sun was well beyond the horizon and the purple-and-gray sky was festooned with the brightest stars.

"Aunt Gertrude ... *Nina a des ennuis* ... *Je dois la ramener* ..." Rowan tried to go back to the alleviators, which were now a dull and dusty gray.

"It's too late to bring her back tonight," Gertrude said gently. "You'll have to go at the silver hour. Come now. You need to rest. And you can take out your translator."

Rowan unhooked the translator from his tooth and climbed into the truck. He was vaguely aware of Xavier climbing into the front and Xanthe joining him in the back. By the time Gertrude had started the engine, Rowan was fast asleep.

"Rowan? Rowan?"

Rowan heard the anxious voice as though it were coming from the other end of a long tunnel. He opened his eyes and blinked as they adjusted to the light. Aunt Agatha stood by his bed with a lamp.

"Aunt Agatha!" Rowan cried. "Oh, Aunt Agatha, I'm sorry I broke my promise and went to the hotel. I'm sorry I used the alleviators ... I should never have done any of it without telling you first ..."

"Oh, don't worry about it," Agatha said kindly. "I *wanted* you to go. I knew you were too timid at first, so I ramped up your curiosity. Who do you think made your reservations in the first place?"

"What? You mean ... it was you?"

"More or less. All petitions for use of the alleviators go through the town council, first, of course. They decide on who truly has a need and the reservations are made and passed along to the Official Time Travel Operator . . . that's Otto, for short. Gertrude and I made the petition and it was accepted."

Gertrude entered with a cup of tea, which she handed to Rowan. "We take a lot of care in who we allow through that portal. You can just imagine how such a vehicle could be exploited by the wrong people."

Rowan sat up. "You mean . . . you're behind all of this? Did you make Nina's reservation, too?"

"Yes . . ." Gertrude answered hesitantly.

"I don't get it. Why didn't you make them together? Why send her off first, and make us wait? What are you up to?" He was starting to feel manipulated.

"Hold on, one question at a time," Gertrude said. "Now listen, Rowan. Agatha and I brought you and Nina up here because we felt you could both benefit from our little tourist attraction, but not necessarily the same trip. You are two different people with different needs."

"What I 'need' to do is take care of my sister."

"No, dear, you were using her as a crutch," Agatha said seriously. "You two needed to be separated, even if only for a short period of time."

"Are you telling me I 'needed' to almost have my head cut off?" Rowan snapped.

"Is that all you got out of the experience?" Gertrude returned.

Rowan thought for a moment. There was something going on here that he wasn't quite getting, but one thing he knew was that he felt better now than when he had left. He felt . . . whole.

"What about Xanthe and Xave? Did they have the same need I had?"

"Not exactly," Gertrude answered, "but we were afraid you wouldn't go without them, and besides, we prefer for people to travel in pairs, in case something happens. Then one person can come back and get help. You were lucky I found you at all."

"Oh, don't be modest, Sister," Agatha clucked. She turned to Rowan. "I didn't doubt she could find you for one second. She's so good at what she does."

"What *does* she do?" asked Rowan.

"She's a detective," said Agatha. "Gertrude's a Time Detective. That's her other job."

"After you disappeared," continued Gertrude, "we all figured you'd finally gotten the courage to take an alleviator for a spin. I asked the librarian what books you had consulted, and was astonished when she told me the French Revolution. It's almost impossible to find anybody during that time . . . it's so confusing. I was able to locate you, however, and watched your progress from here, on the globe, until you started getting mixed up with the Duc d'Orleans . . ."

"I hate that man," Agatha snipped. "Such a toad. I knew you were getting in over your head so Gertrude and I went down to bring you back. Unfortunately, Hilda was also planning a trip to the same place. With all of us there at the same time it sent us into that time skip. Of course, that is probably what kept you alive. Just when Philippe's henchman stabbed you, you disappeared. You'll be happy to know that Philippe was executed by the guillotine about four months after you left."

"It took me a little while to find you again," Gertrude continued. "Agatha and I had been bounced all the way to Napoleon's era. When I finally located you in the Conciergerie, I knew I couldn't break in to rescue you, the security is too tight. I had to retrieve you after you left the building. I had to wait for your execution. I was at your trial, you know, and I was very pleased with how you handled it. I knew you were trying to get outside the building as quickly as possible. I would've let you try to escape without my help, except that I didn't want you hitting me over the head with a rock."

"Oh, you knew about that?" Rowan murmured sheepishly.

"I wouldn't have put it past you." Gertrude suddenly became serious again. "Rowan, we need to talk about Nina. We're not exactly sure where she is. She gave no indication of where she was going . . . she didn't tell anybody, she didn't visit the library . . . we were hoping that you figured it out and followed her, but when Margaret told us about that mistaken-identity business, well, we knew we had a problem."

"The power of her key is about to run out. If we can't find her and retrieve her before this next silver hour is over, she will be stuck wherever she is forever. Rowan, you're really our only hope," Agatha said.

"I know where she is," he said, standing. "I'm ready to go."

"You realize the alleviators have all been used several times since she left," Gertrude said. "You can't find her by using the 'quick return' function . . ."

"It doesn't matter," said Rowan, grinning. "I know exactly where she is. Does anybody mind if I take a shower? I feel like I haven't had one in four years."

Rowan and Gertrude stood outside the hotel in the gray morning mist, waiting for the transformation to take place. Once the resort burst into its Victorian splendor, they checked in with Otto, who gave Rowan a new key.

"Aren't you coming with me?" Rowan asked.

"No, I don't think it would do any good," Gertrude answered. "Besides, I doubt Nina is in any physical danger. I think something else is keeping her from returning."

"I just hope she still has her key," Rowan said.

"I'm sure she does," Gertrude said. "I think she just never planned on coming back."

"No, I suppose she didn't," Rowan said.

"Well, you'd better hurry," Gertrude said. "The actual time travel takes about ten minutes. That only leaves you forty-five minutes to find her and convince her to return if you don't want to cut it too close."

Rowan nodded, stepped into the alleviator, pressed the appropriate buttons, then held on as the whirling vertigo took over his senses. In this trip he wasn't frightened, but resolute. He was going to a place filled with beauty, where people had good manners, and there was a constant celebration of the arts. He was going home.

CHAPTER THIRTEEN

TRUTH

The cars were different, of course. A shoe-repair shop stood in the location of the Laundromat that would take its place in the future. The brand names on the trash collecting in the gutter were different, too. But this was unmistakably eighteen twenty-four Danforth Street, Brooklyn, New York. Rowan stood outside the Popplewell Bakery, in the year nineteen ninety, petrified.

The shop was closed, but the lights in the back were on. He could see somebody moving around in the kitchen. The night sky was turning from black to gray, the first signs of dawn. Sunrise would begin within the hour. Still, Rowan couldn't get his feet to move. He was afraid. Afraid of what he might say, what he might do, how he might feel when he saw . . . her. His conversation with Marie Antoinette during the Reign of Terror had clarified his feelings from a mass of misery to one single thought. The number one reason his life stunk.

#1. I miss my mother.

He missed her so much, it made his heart hurt. Nina must have felt the same way. Of course. How could he not have seen it? And now he was here. And Nina was here. And his mother. He held his breath and leaned forward until he had to either take a step or fall on his face. His foot stamped forward, and that started him down the alley, where he knew the door to the kitchen would be open and all the wonderful smells would be drifting onto the morning breeze.

As Rowan approached the open door, his father's rich baritone boomed from the kitchen—a selection from the opera I *Pagliacci.* He'd forgotten how much his father loved opera; it had been ages since he had played any music at all. Now his voice brought back memories of when their house was filled with music, often pieces Nina was trying to memorize for one of her many recitals, but also lots and lots of opera.

Gabriella loved music, too, but she preferred lively music. She would often grab his father and start dancing on a moment's notice. Maurice would pretend to be embarrassed at first, but in no time he'd be strutting along with her, twirling her, swinging her around his body until they both collapsed in a fit of laughter.

While Rowan listened to his father singing, he noticed how shiny the screen door was. He was so used to it being covered with dust and bugs that it looked funny and strange. It even had the price tag still on it. *It must be brand new,* thought Rowan, and then he realized that it wasn't just the door. The whole shop was new. Nineteen ninety was the year his mother and father moved to Brooklyn and opened the bakery. Before that they had lived somewhere in Queens . . . but Nina wouldn't have known that address. She must've picked nineteen ninety because she couldn't have found them any earlier. Rowan smiled to himself, pleased with his powers of deduction, then suddenly realized his father had finished the aria. He lifted his hand, took a deep breath, and rapped on the screen door.

And then, just like that, she was there. His mother. Solid. Flesh and blood. And she was beautiful. Rowan's legs wobbled. He wanted to feel her arms around him, hear her say his name . . . snuggle in her lap. He felt an uncontrollable urge to bury his nose in her neck so he could smell the sandalwood soap she always used. But through this irresistible attraction he felt a wall between them. She was a ghost, after all. She was not his mother . . . could not be his mother. He lived in the year two thousand four, and in that year, Gabriella Popplewell was already buried in the Brooklyn Cemetery.

Rowan felt his heart thumping against the walls of his rib cage. She seemed distant, aloof . . . suspicious. She didn't recognize him. Of course she wouldn't; he hadn't even been born yet. Still, he was reminded of her vacant expression in the hospital. Tears welled up, and he caught a sob before it escaped, managing to pull himself together long enough to stammer something.

"Excuse me?" she said. Gabriella's voice was the same, but something was different. She was fat. Really fat. Huge, even. Then Rowan remembered that in July, nineteen ninety, she was eight months pregnant with him. He stared at her round belly, considering the possibility that in some way he was snuggling in her lap twenty-four hours a day.

"Can I help you?" she said again. "Are you lost?" She looked wary of him, probably because they didn't usually get teenagers knocking on their door before daylight.

"I . . . uh . . . Have you seen a little girl hanging around here?" Rowan asked. "Kind of small, black hair, about eleven years old?"

"Do you mean Tina?" Gabriella asked.

Rowan nodded eagerly. "That's her!" he said. "Do you know where she's staying? I'm her brother, Row . . . Roland."

"That's strange, she told us she was an orphan and all alone."

"I don't know what she told you, ma'am, but she's got a family. We're from . . . Queens. We've been looking for her for days. It's not the first time she's run off. She's kind of . . . independent."

"That she is." Gabriella laughed.

"So you've seen her?" Rowan asked again.

"Oh, yes. She works here. We gave her a summer job," Gabriella answered.

Maurice walked over, his hands covered with flour.

"Who have we here?" he asked, raising his eyebrow.

"This is Roland from Queens," Gabriella said. "He's Tina's brother." She turned back to Rowan. "I'll go get her, she's just filling napkin dispensers." Gabriella waddled out of the room.

"Would you like a fresh bun?" Maurice asked, hands on his hips. "I just took out the first batch."

Rowan nodded. "Yes, please," he said. "Do you have any of the lemon-filled doughnuts?"

Maurice smiled. "All the way in Queens they've heard about my lemon-filled doughnuts!" he shouted to the heavens. He went to the cooling rack and plucked a doughnut, putting it on a white porcelain plate.

"You know, you look very familiar to me," Maurice said as he placed the delectable in front of Rowan. "Have I seen you before? Do I know your family?"

Look in the mirror, thought Rowan. But he shook his head, licking the lemon cream from his fingers.

Gabriella returned with Nina, and Rowan's heart jumped. She was alive, healthy, and *there*. She was not happy to see him, though. She looked downright hostile.

"Tina!" he cried, remembering her alias even in his excitement. "I've been looking all over for you!" He turned to Gabriella and Maurice before Nina could say anything. "Would you excuse us for a moment?"

"Of course," Gabriella said.

Rowan led Nina out into the alley to a stack of crates a short distance from the door. He could hear the birds starting to sing, and he knew he didn't have much time.

"It's time to go home, Nina," Rowan said.

"I am home," Nina replied stubbornly.

"You know what I mean," he said. "You don't belong here. You have a life in the twenty-first century. If you don't go back right now, you'll never be able to go back. Is that what you really want?"

Nothing.

Rowan gave her a shove. "Come on, Nina! I'll miss you!

This last week is the worst thing I've ever gone through in my whole life!"

Nina sighed. "I guess I knew you'd come looking for me," she said glumly.

"Well, yeah! I mean, what did you think I would do? Just say 'oh well' and go home without you? What would I tell Dad? Jeez, Nina I'm your *brother*. You're my *sister*. That used to mean something to you." He shook his head. "I just don't get it. You act like I'm a stranger or something."

Nina stared down the alley. A truck rumbled by. Traffic was starting to appear; all the people whose jobs began at five-thirty were on the road, looking forward to the first cup of coffee that signaled the start of their day.

"I'm a bad person, Rowan," Nina said. "You don't want me back. Not if you knew . . . I've hurt enough people."

"Listen, Nina, don't blame yourself for my misery. I spent a lot of time feeling sorry for myself, and I let that keep me from doing anything. Actually, I was mad. Really mad. But it's okay to be mad sometimes. I think once you're honest about how you feel, then you can deal with it. Does that make any sense?"

Nina didn't say anything. Rowan wondered whether she was even listening to him.

"You shut down for a year. You've come out of that. That's a lot of progress! You can go even further. We were all hurt by Mom's death," Rowan said gently. "I know how it makes you feel sick all the time. But we're alive, Nina. We've got to move on. I think I can do it now, and I know you can do it. Because I'll help you. We'll help each other."

Nina closed her eyes. "I killed her," she whispered.

Rowan blinked. "What?"

"I killed her. It's my fault."

Rowan stared at her. She chewed her lip, and looked away.

"I . . . You know that last night before the uh . . . the accident . . . Mom and I . . . we had a big fight, you know," Nina said, her voice hoarse.

"Yes, I remember there was some yelling over the phone."

"Well, I wanted to go to boarding school at the Boston Conservatory, and Mom didn't want me to because it was so far away. She said she didn't think I was mature enough. So I screamed at her . . . said some things that were pretty mean . . . and uh . . . I told her I hated her, that I never wanted to see her again. And I told her . . . I wished she was dead. And . . . and then, that night, my wish came true. So it's my fault, and now I'm here because I don't wish she was dead, Rowan. I don't. I want her to be alive. I want her to be alive, like that, in there. I didn't really want her to die . . ."

Nina was sniffling and hiccuping, refusing to cry, but Rowan could feel the hot tears in his own eyes.

"Oh, Nina," he said, trying to hold her.

"Why did God listen to me?" she said, pushing him away. "I didn't mean it! I didn't have time to take it back!"

Rowan forced her to his chest as she started to shake. "It's not your fault," he said. "Don't Nina. It was just a horrible coincidence . . ."

"I couldn't tell . . . I couldn't talk to anybody because . . . then everybody would . . . hate me . . ."

"That's not true, that's not true . . ."

"And kick me . . . out of . . . the family . . . because I'm . . . so . . . bad . . ."

"No, Nina, we love you. We know you didn't mean it. You were just angry. God knows. He doesn't grant those kinds of wishes. He knows how you really feel."

"But Mom didn't . . ." she whimpered. "She died . . . thinking I . . . hated her . . ."

Rowan wrapped himself around her. "You're not bad, Nina. You were just angry. You're allowed to be angry. It's okay. You're forgiven."

She surrendered. She cried and cried and cried. Rowan said nothing, but held her and rocked, and cried with her, until they were both damp and exhausted.

Rowan looked at his watch. He only had ten minutes left.

"Nina," he said, finally. "We have to go."

"I want to be with Mom, Rowan," she answered. She looked at him hopefully. "Stay with me. It's great seeing Mom and Dad together. They're so happy and fun . . . and you won't have to worry about Dad missing us because we'll be right here with him."

"I can't," Rowan answered. "I'm about to be born in a month. I was such a cute baby I know I'll want to tickle myself and BOOM! Instant annihilation. No thanks."

Nina let a laugh escape, despite herself.

Rowan smiled back. "Besides, Nina, it's totally unsatisfying. That may be our mom in there, but she doesn't know that. She's not going to act like your mom, she's going to act like your *boss*." Rowan faced Nina squarely. "Nina, you know that's not really why you're here."

Nina looked down, wiping her nose on her sleeve.

"Do you know why you're here?"

She nodded. She took a deep breath, eased herself off the crates, and went back inside the kitchen. Maurice was singing something from *Rigoletto*, chopping walnuts and pecans. Gabriella dusted the honey buns with cinnamon sugar as Nina approached her.

"I'm going back with my brother," Nina said quietly. "Sorry to leave you shorthanded."

Gabriella smiled at Rowan, who was standing in the doorway. "That's all right, sweetie. I'm just glad you found your family."

Nina nodded. "Good luck with the baby," she said.

"I hope he or she turns out to be somebody just like you," Gabriella said, her eyes twinkling.

"So I guess I'm just here to say . . . good-bye. And I'm really sorry." Nina gave Gabriella a tight smile. She started to leave, then turned back. "You know," she said, "if you ever have another kid, and it's a girl, and she fights with you, and she says some really bad things to you . . . you know she won't mean it. She's probably just angry and immature. Kids are like that, you know, they say things they don't mean. But they always love you. Even if they say they don't, they do."

"I'll remember that," Gabriella said, suppressing a smile.

"Really? I mean you'll really try hard to remember?" Nina pressed.

Gabriella nodded. "Of course. And I'll always love her back . . . even if she doesn't hear me say it."

Nina smiled. It was a great big toothy smile, a smile Rowan hadn't seen for a whole year. Nina was back. This time, she really was back. Nina rushed to Gabriella and hugged her, nearly knocking her over.

"I love you," Nina said. "But I have to go."

Rowan walked up to Gabriella, a little embarrassed. "Excuse me," he said. "Do you mind . . . can I give you a hug, too?"

Gabriella opened her mouth, surprised. Before she could answer, Rowan gently wrapped his arms around her, resting his head on her chest. Instinctively she stroked his head. He closed his eyes and sent a message to her, through time and space, to the future. *Good-bye,* he said. He hoped she got it.

As the sky brightened from gray to pink, Rowan knew their time had run out. He raised his head, smiled at Gabriella, mumbled "thank you," then took Nina's hand. Together they walked out the front door, just as Maurice turned the sign from "Closed" to "Open."

"Where are you going?" shouted Maurice as the line of people poured into the bakery.

"Home!" shouted Rowan. "We'll see you later!"

Rowan and Nina walked toward the glimmering box on the other side of the street, with their golden keys firmly in hand. They stepped inside and it disappeared, just as the first rays of the sun peeked over the horizon, warm and radiant. The beginning of a beautiful day.

EPILOGUE

Gᴇʀᴛʀᴜᴅᴇ sᴀᴛ ᴏɴ ᴛʜᴇ ᴘᴏʀᴄʜ ᴄʟᴇᴀɴɪɴɢ ᴛʜᴇ ᴍᴜᴅ from her gardening clogs. She had just taken about twenty snails off her tomato plants and was contemplating how she could rid herself of the pests without using a chemical snail bait, when Agatha drove up in the blue truck. Agatha stepped out of the cab with a small burlap bag and a new suntan.

"Where have you been?" Gertrude asked.

"Oh, I took a trip to Brazil . . . beautiful, beautiful area. At least in nineteen twenty it was," Agatha answered, fixing her bun.

"What's in the bag?"

"A black pearl necklace. You can't find these anymore."

"No, I suppose not," answered Gertrude, knocking the clog against the step. "By the way, we got another letter from Rowan."

"Oh, how wonderful!" Agatha sat next to Gertrude. Gertrude handed her the letter, which she opened eagerly.

"Dear Aunt Agatha and Aunt Gertrude," Agatha read aloud. "I'm sorry I haven't been able to write much, but things have been pretty busy around here. I'm going to a lot of chess tournaments, and have gotten a few first-place ribbons.

"As you know, Nina got a chance to play piano with the New York Philharmonic in a special performance featuring gifted kids. I've enclosed the program. Dad was really proud, but he told her she shouldn't get a swelled head . . . she still has to clean her room and wash the dishes every night. Dad met with a financial counselor, and it looks like he won't have to go into bankruptcy, which is great, because he seemed to think of it as something to be ashamed of. Anyway, they gave him a schedule for repaying all the late fines, so he thinks that he'll get out of it without having to sell the bakery.

"By the way, Nina and I finally got him to agree to go to grief counseling! The first session we did all the talking, but he's been coming around, and has even gone to some sessions alone. I hope everything is okay with both of you. I hope to see you next summer. Love, Rowan.

"P.S. Do you think you could get Xanthe's home phone number from Nana? She gave it to me, but it accidentally got washed in the laundry."

"He seems to be doing well," Gertrude said offhandedly.

"Yes, yes. He is," Agatha said, satisfied. "Well, I'm going to put this in the jewelry case," she said, holding up the bag.

Gertrude grunted, thinking of her tomatoes. She didn't care for snails. Aphids either. And those caterpillars! Ravenous little buggers!

Agatha went into the house and over to the jewelry case, which was crammed with rare treasures collected from years and years of travel. She had gotten most of them herself, having a weakness for sparkly things. She took out a mass of keys and opened the case. Carefully she moved aside some of the other pieces that she had collected. She would put the pearl necklace right in the front, where everyone could see it. It was such a remarkable piece, it deserved that place of honor. Besides, it was much more subtle and classy than the big, gaudy necklace that was there now.

Agatha removed the riviére necklace from its former perch, consigning it, and all of its six hundred and forty-seven diamonds, to a lower shelf behind a gold medallion from Peru. It was time to display something new.

A HISTORICAL
NOTE TO THE READER

IT PROBABLY WOULD NOT SURPRISE ANYONE FOR me to say that *The Golden Hour* is a work of fiction. Rockridge and Owatannauk, Maine, are both fictional towns and anything that happens in these places I made up. There are some things in this novel that I didn't make up, however. I spent a great deal of time researching revolutionary France, and I tried to include accurate details about the people, the political climate, and the incidents occurring during that period. I must admit, however, that I have taken some liberties for the sake of storytelling.

First the characters. King Louis XVI; Queen Marie Antoinette; Philippe Duc d'Orleans; Georges Danton; Camille Desmoulin; and Maximilien Robespierre were all real people, but they are also characters in my story. I have tried to stay true to their personalities, but clearly any interaction they have with the main characters you may assume to be fiction. Though Danton was indeed married to a sixteen-year-old girl named

Louise at the time of his death (1704), the Louise in this story is primarily a fictional character. I have heightened Philippe Duc d'Orleans' villainous characteristics. Though he was definitely an opportunist, and most certainly had his eye on the crown, he was probably not as murderous as I have portrayed him.

Marie Antoinette did not hold a masquerade ball attended by Mozart on July 14, though she did enjoy masquerades. Mozart did stay at Versailles for two weeks during the reign of King Louis XV in December 1763, when he was only seven years old. Remarkably enough, Marie Antoinette met him during this same tour when he passed through Vienna and played for the Austrian royal family. She was also seven at the time. There is a well-known anecdote about their meeting. Apparently at some point the child prodigy slipped on the well-polished floors of the palace and Antoinette (known then as "Antonia") helped him up. He thanked her, and out of gratitude asked her to marry him! At any rate, Mozart did not come to Versailles while Marie Antoinette was queen, and in fact her favorite composer was Christoph von Gluck.

I have also changed the timing of certain events to suit my purposes. Camille Desmoulin made his famous speech at the Palais-Royal on July 12, not the 14. Louis XVI did keep journals in which he recorded his hunting exploits, and the entry on July 14 was indeed the word "nothing," however I made up the other journal entries. Marie Antoinette was beheaded on October 16, 1793, not July 18. Also, Philippe Duc d'Orleans was in prison by April 1793, so he could not possibly be in a courtroom in July. He was beheaded in November of that same year.

ACKNOWLEDGMENTS

In order to write this novel I used the aid of several resources, primarily *Citizens: A Chronicle of the French Revolution*, by Simon Schama, and *Marie Antionette: The Journey*, by Antonia Fraser. Other books I found useful include *The Memoirs of Madame Roland, A Heroine of the Revolution*, by Marie-Jeanne Philpon Roland; *A History of Everyday Things: The Birth of Consumption in France, 1600–1800*, by Daniel Roche; and *Liberty, Equality, Fraternity: Exploring the French Revolution*, by Jack R. Censer and Lynn Hunt. I would like to thank Robert H. Blackman, assistant professor of history at Hampden-Sydney College for his help in filling in the gaps and answering questions not covered in these books. I owe much gratitude also to Professor Elizabeth Losh of the University of California at Irvine for her enthusiastic support and suggestions for places to find interesting tidbits about life in revolutionary France. I am indebted to Celine Guillou, who provided the French translations in the book. And I am beholden to my sister, Robin Barnes, who patiently read early drafts, helped me wrestle the writing demons, and has always been my biggest cheerleader.

Two people from two different times in my life made this book possible. The first is Stephen Teel, who taught my ninth-grade political history class. He is a gifted teacher who knew how to make history come to life for his students. He instilled in me a lifelong love for history and a fascination for the French Revolution, and I owe him more than I could ever express here.

The second is a good friend, Kate Hudec, a photographer and filmmaker. Once, on an otherwide unremarkable visit I made to her house, she looked out the window at the sun, which was low in the sky, and said, "It's the magic hour." "What did you say?" I asked, for I had never heard of such a thing. She explained that "the magic hour" described that time of day when the sun is low and provides the best lighting for outdoor "beauty shots." It's a term familiar to people who work with film but for some reason it tickled me to think that there was one hour during the day when magic could happen. A few years later that notion took flight and, well, this book is the result. So thank you, Kate.

ABOUT THE AUTHOR

Maiya Williams was born in Corvallis, Oregon, and grew up in New Haven, Connecticut, and Berkeley, California. She attended Harvard University, where she was an editor and vice president of the *Harvard Lampoon*. She is currently a writer and producer of television shows and lives with her husband, three children, a Labrador retriever, and a variety of fish in Pacific Palisades. This is her first novel.

The text of this book is set in Kaatskill, designed in 1929 by Frederic W. Goudy. It was made specifically for use in an edition of *Rip Van Winkle* for the Limited Editions Club. The type has an added interest in the fact that it was designed, cut, and set in the immediate vicinity of Washington Irving's story—in the foothills of Rip's own Kaatskill mountains, at Marlborough-on-the-Hudson.

Display and chapter titles are set in Dalliance Roman, designed in 2000 by Frank Heine for Emigre. The inspiration for Dalliance Script comes from early nineteenth century hand lettering specimens.

Enjoy this peek at Maiya Williams's
sequel to *The Golden Hour,*
The Hour of the Cobra

CHAPTER 1
CREATURE FROM THE DEEP

THUNK. THUNK. THUNK.

"Xanthe Alexander, stop banging your head on the table!"

Xanthe looked up. Her mother stood over her, arms crossed, the wooden spoon in her hand dripping spaghetti sauce onto the floor.

"Mom, you're dripping."

"Don't change the subject! You've been brooding all day. Snap out of it!" Helen Alexander flicked the spoon, spraying sauce across the back wall and the novelty sign, purchased from a roadside restaurant, that stated THIS MESS IS A PLACE. Xanthe stared at the red spatter, knowing it would forever be part of the kitchen decor.

She wished she could snap out of it, but she could not. Wallowing, brooding, obsessing, whatever you wanted to call it, was her way of punishing herself. And whether her mother understood it or not, Xanthe needed to be punished.

She did get up, however. Her mother needed all her powers of concentration to follow a recipe. Distracting her would result in a dinner overly seasoned and undercooked, so Xanthe dragged herself from the kitchen table into the living room and slumped on the sofa.

A number of things compounded on each other had put her in this dark state. First of all, Xavier was gone. She'd sensed the difference as soon as they'd dropped him off at the airport. Without Xavier she felt unbalanced and slightly confused. It was an awful feeling.

Most of their lives Xanthe and Xavier had been inseparable. As twins they'd shared everything when they were little: clothes, bedrooms, toys, friends, teachers, even underwear if one of them ran out before laundry day, though neither one would admit it. They were so tuned into each other there were times it seemed as though they could read each other's thoughts. But even best friends need space, and by the time they were ten, Xanthe had just about had it. Getting her own room helped, but not much. Four years later, she was still tripping over her brother.

She didn't want to miss him, but she did. She'd hoped his absence would make her feel liberated, as if a dark curse had been lifted. But obviously this was not the case. She could only think this was because she'd grown lazy, and come to rely on him. He was her right arm, and now her right arm was gone. Still, it was a limb she couldn't stand having anymore. She'd heard that foxes will chew off their own legs to escape from a trap; that was how she felt. It was painful, but she was willing to sacrifice the right arm so that she could be free.

But she wasn't free. Something of Xavier had been left

behind, a reminder of the event that had set her to banging her head on the kitchen table to begin with. There, barely hidden by the towel she'd thrown over it, was a trophy. The grand prize for the Cicero oration contest.

That was the second thing that had put her in this funk. By all rights that trophy should've been hers. The contest pitted teenagers from all over Boston and its suburbs against each other, as they delivered speeches on a pre-chosen political topic. The point was to promote the art of public speaking, and if there was anything Xanthe was good at, it was speaking. Especially arguing. She could twist and turn a concept like mental origami, and come up with something extraordinary. On more than one occasion she'd been praised as being persuasive, clear, and to the point. So how Xavier, who never showed any interest in politics or public speaking, could have won, she had no idea, except that he could tell a joke or two, which always seemed to get him more credit than he really deserved.

The trophy was only part of the prize; there was also a check for seven hundred and fifty dollars and a trip to Washington, D.C. That's where Xavier's plane was heading. He had an itinerary jam-packed with sightseeing, behind-the-scenes tours, and introductions to dignitaries. Of course Xanthe was jealous, but jealousy she could handle. There was something much more troubling at stake, and this third thing is what made her feel worst of all.

Xavier had won first prize. OK, that was probably a fluke. But what about her? She hadn't come in second, she'd come in sixth. *Sixth.* That's what her bright orange ribbon said. And by the way, *orange?* Whoever heard of an orange ribbon? A blue ribbon, a red ribbon—those were respectable colors. But bright, garish orange only signified one thing: that she wasn't nearly as smart as she had been led to believe.

But Xavier . . . Xavier *was.* All this time she'd been fooling herself. She was not the one with a chewed off arm. She *was* the chewed off arm. She was being left behind. For all those reasons—for dropping the ball, losing her sense of place in the cosmos, and being utterly clueless about herself—she deserved to be smacked in the head, over and over again.

She started knocking her head against the sofa cushion, but it wasn't nearly as satisfying as the bonks on the table.

"Xanthe." Helen touched Xanthe's shoulder, startling her. Helen's irritation had softened. Her large brown eyes, set in her light brown, freckled face, looked deeply concerned. "I know how you feel. You're ambitious, and you've disappointed yourself. But you're not going to win all the time. That's just life. Don't beat yourself up for being human, all right?"

Xanthe shrugged.

"Why don't you call Kendall? Or Emma?" Kendall and Emma were Xanthe's best friends, but she suspected that both of them had been jealous of her at one time or another and probably wouldn't mind seeing her knocked down a peg.

"I don't think so."

"Then how about doing some schoolwork. It might take your mind off . . . everything."

That sounded like a good idea. Because she and Xavier were home schooled, they had a lot of freedom in what they learned and how fast they learned it. They could take weeks off if they wanted to, but usually they did much more work than what was asked of them. Algebra problems sounded like just the thing to distract her from her fall from grace. Suddenly she smelled smoke.

"Mom! The meatballs are burning!"

Helen rushed back into the kitchen.

Xanthe sat on the deck with her book and a yellow legal pad of paper, quickly solved five equations, then put her pencil down. Her gaze drifted to the pond in their backyard. Home schooling had allowed the Alexanders to live wherever they wanted, regardless of proximity to good schools, and so Andrew and Helen had bought a small house on a large private pond in a Boston suburb. Two days a week Andrew drove into the city to lecture at Boston University, then spent the rest of his time at home, in the seclusion of his study, writing about American history: the early American settlers, Western expansion, and the Civil War.

Xanthe loved the pond. It was called Tyler's Pond, but she and Xavier called it the Loch Ness Lagoon because of the odd splashes and ripples that sometimes disturbed the water's surface. Helen, who had a degree in marine biology, assured them that it was probably a largemouth bass, a walleye pike, or perhaps even a snapping turtle. But it was more fun to think it was their own personal Loch Ness monster.

Xanthe saw one of these odd ripples in the water even now,

caused by something as big as a seal, flapping and splashing. Xanthe jumped to her feet. This wasn't a fish or a turtle! It was a boy, struggling to get to shore!

She kicked off her shoes and dove into the water. As she swam she searched for an overturned boat or sailboard . . . there was nothing. She grabbed the boy's sweater, flipped him onto his back to keep his face above water, and towed him back, dragging him onto the rocky beach. There she fell next to him, breathing heavily. The boy coughed up some water, then turned to her, grinning. Xanthe gasped.

"Rowan!" she screamed. "It's you!"

He slicked his hair back off his face. "Surprised?"

"Where were you . . . how did you . . . I can't believe you're here!"

It was like her secret wish had been granted. Rowan was her special friend. She and Xavier had first met him and his younger sister, Nina, last summer on the beach in Owatannauk, Maine, the small coastal town where her grandmother and Rowan's two great aunts, Gertrude Pembroke and Agatha Drake, lived. Her first impression of him then was that he was cute but dumpy, like a sloppy puppy. Since then she'd come to see him quite differently.

They had all shared a most unusual adventure, exploring the mysterious abandoned Owatannauk Resort, built by the equally mysterious toy inventor, Archibald Weber, and his wondrous alleviator time machines. Along with Xavier, they had taken a dangerous trip to eighteenth-century France, getting caught in the French Revolution, where

Rowan had surprised everyone with his courage and perseverance. And so, despite his ordinary appearance, Xanthe knew him to be a hero. Just being around him made her want to be a better person.

After they'd gone back to their regular lives, she and Rowan had traded e-mails, but a month ago Rowan had stopped, without warning. Xanthe remembered now that she was angry with him, so she shoved him with her foot.

"Ouch!"

"That's for abandoning me. What happened? I thought you'd fallen off the planet."

"Sorry, computer problems. I thought of sending a letter snail mail, but every time I started one I got distracted."

Xanthe didn't bother asking why he hadn't used a phone. Rowan's mother had died recently and in his grief his father had neglected to pay his phone bill. Now he was having trouble getting any phone service to let him sign up. The family mainly used the phone in their bakery, but the line needed to be kept open for customers.

"Well, get your computer fixed. I miss having a penpal."

"No, I can't. I mean, the computer isn't broken, I just keep getting shocked by it."

Rowan's face had turned a deep pink color. *What does he have to be embarrassed about?* Xanthe wondered . . . then it dawned on her.

"You've been using the alleviators! You've gone back to the Owatannauk!" Xanthe remembered that when they'd first used the time machines they'd been given a list of rules and regulations which warned that frequent use of the alleviators caused sensitivity to electricity and any electrical appliances.

"Where have you gone? I'm so jealous!"

"Hold on, I haven't been anywhere back in time. I'm just . . . well, Aunt Agatha's got me in training. Nina, too." Rowan was grinning like the Cheshire Cat in *Alice in Wonderland*.

"Come on, Rowan, tell me! Training for what?"

"To be her assistants! And she wants you and Xavier to join us! That's why I'm here!" Rowan squeezed some of Tyler's Pond out of his sweater. "Do you have anything dry I can borrow? I'm freezing."

"Sure. I'll be right back. But then you have to tell me everything, from the beginning." Xanthe dashed into the house and quickly changed into a pair of jeans and a sweatshirt. She grabbed one of Xavier's old sweatsuits and raced back out.

"So let me guess," she panted. "You took the alleviator here. Like a transporter."

"Bingo. If you press the button for the present year and set the coordinates, you can be transported anywhere in the world." Rowan slipped into the sweatsuit. Xanthe noticed he wasn't quite as pudgy as he used to be. She also realized he'd grown in the last few months.

"Why did you pick the middle of Tyler's Pond?"

Rowan's face turned pink again. "Actually, I was trying to land on the deck and surprise you. Setting coordinates is harder than it looks."

They sat down on the edge of the deck and Rowan filled

Xanthe in on all that had happened since he'd stopped writing. At the end of August his father had moved his business and his family from Brooklyn to Manhattan so that Nina could be closer to her piano teacher. Nina, an eleven-year-old music prodigy, had been deeply affected by her mother's death and had given up playing piano for a full year, but after their summer adventure she'd been eager to start up again.

"Since her schedule was going to conflict with school, dad enrolled us in this cool progressive school," Rowan continued. "Nina and I got full scholarships."

"'Progressive?' What does that mean?" Xanthe interrupted.

"Well, there aren't any real grades, you just work at your own level. And they don't hand out report cards either, they use some other sort of evaluation system. But the best thing is that they don't mind if you take a week off here and there, as long as you write an essay about what you've done, and make up the work you've missed. Which means . . . "

"You've got time for time travel!"

Rowan beamed. "It all kind of works out perfectly, doesn't it?"

"OK, but how did you end up back at the Owatannauk?"

"I'm getting to that. Aunt Agatha called Dad and asked if Nina and I could come up for Labor Day weekend to help out with the curio shop. At first I thought she finally wanted to sort through all that junk—you know what I'm talking about . . . "

"That would only take you a thousand years," Xanthe chuckled.

"Yes, well, fortunately that's not what she wanted. She

doesn't want us to help her organize it, she wants us to help her *collect* it." He paused, letting it sink in. "Xanthe, we're going to be frequent fliers!"

"Frequent fliers?" A slow smile spread across Xanthe's face. "Are you saying what I think you're saying?"

"Yeah! We're going to be hopping all over time! All over the world!"

"Oh Rowan, this is fantastic! What does your dad say? Does he even know?"

"Are you kidding?" Rowan said, suddenly serious. "I haven't told anyone. First of all, I doubt anyone would believe me, and second, those alleviators are the best inventions since . . . well, *ever*. If it got out, you know somebody would try to make money off of it and ruin it. Do *your* parents know?"

Xanthe shook her head. She and Xavier were the only ones in her family who knew about the time machines, except, of course, their grandmother, who lived in Owatannauk and used them herself.

Rowan peered over the treetops at the sinking sun. "I need to get back to the alleviator, and it's out there," he said, pointing to the middle of the pond. "Do you have a canoe or a rowboat or something?"

Xanthe led him to a shed, behind which lay a small purple sailboat. "My boat," she said proudly. "I bought it myself. It's called *Whisper*."

Rowan helped her drag it to the edge of the pond. After they both climbed in, Xanthe raised the sail. It immediately caught a breeze, carrying the boat toward the center of the pond.

Rowan trailed his hand in the water as Xanthe steered. Every once in awhile he would tell her to aim more to the right or left ("starboard" or "port," she informed him, were the correct nautical terms). She couldn't see the alleviator herself because she wasn't holding one of the golden alleviator keys. But Rowan did see it, and it shimmered brightly, indicating the strength of its magical power. The power would last for seven days, after which the key would disintegrate.

She didn't want him to leave. Even though she knew she'd be seeing him soon, she hadn't realized how much she'd missed him.

"So, how am I going to explain all of this to my parents?"

"Don't worry about that. It's all taken care of." Rowan looked over the side of the boat. "OK, stop," he said. "It's right below us. I'll give you back these clothes when I see you again." He dove into the water, disappearing into the blue-green ripples. Then he popped up again.

"Wow! This water is freezing!"

"Next time get your coordinates straight."

"Yeah, right." He treaded water in a circle. "I forgot to say 'bye.' So, bye."

"Wait, Rowan!" Xanthe called out before he could duck under water. "Something doesn't make sense. The last time we used the alleviators we really screwed up. Why on earth does your Aunt Agatha trust us to go anywhere else?"

"I don't know. I'm too cold to worry about it." Rowan swam to the boat and grabbed onto the side. "You're in, aren't you?" His teeth were starting to chatter. "I don't want to do it unless . . . I mean, it won't be as fun without . . . "

Xanthe laughed. "Of course, you idiot! Yes! You don't know how much I need this right now, Rowan. It's like you read my mind and showed up just in time to cheer me up."

Rowan smiled. "Yes," he chattered. "I think I did." He took a deep breath and dived under the water. A light flickered in the murky depths of the pond and she knew he was gone.

Xanthe had just dragged the boat behind the shed when Helen came out on the porch.

"You'll never guess who just called." Helen didn't give her a chance to answer. "Nana is inviting you up to Owatannauk for a week. She said a friend of hers is looking for some helpers. And she mentioned that boy—Rowan Pumplewall—he's going to be there with his sister. I think you should go." Xanthe started to say something but Helen held up her hand.

"Xanthe, I know it's not as exciting as Washington, D.C., but at least it's something."

"Well, I guess . . . "

"You can't keep moping. It's not healthy."

"If that's what . . . "

"I don't want to argue about it. We're driving up tomorrow morning, and that's that. Now come in and set the table for dinner, your dad will be here soon. We're having scrambled eggs."

"What happened to the spaghetti and meatballs?"

"Don't ask."

Xanthe followed her mother inside and set the table, then began cleaning the bits of exploded meatball off the walls and out of the light fixture on the ceiling. It was hard work but she barely noticed, because inside she was singing.

Keep reading! If you liked this book, check out these other titles.

The Hour of the Cobra
by Maiya Williams
0-8109-5970-4 $16.95 hardcover

11,000 Years Lost
by Peni R. Griffin
0-8109-9251-5 $7.95 paperback

**The Sisters Grimm:
The Fairy-Tale Detectives**
by Michael Buckley
0-8109-5925-9 $14.95 hardcover

Visit
www.amuletbooks.com
to find out more.